Changeling Press LLC

ChangelingPress.com

Angel Falls Vol. 2

Stephanie Burke

Angel Falls Vol. 2
Stephanie Burke

ISBN: 978-1-60521-825-0

Publisher:
Changeling Press LLC
315 N. Centre St.
Martinsburg, WV 25404
ChangelingPress.com

Printed in the U.S.A.

Editor: Katriena Knights
Cover Artist: Bryan Keller

The individual stories in this anthology have been previously released in E-Book format.

Table of Contents

My Protector
Stephanie Burke

Being sheriff of a small but unusual town has lots of perks. Richard knows just about everyone in town by name. He gets free coffee at the Planet Quest café. And he gets to spend as much time as he wants with Amber Graves. The woman he desires above all others.

Amber is everything he always wanted in a mate -- she's strong, kind, the perfect mother and ferocious in a fight... but still he finds himself firmly friend-zoned, much to his and his shadow-wolf's dismay.

For Richard is not any ordinary man. He's a Shadow Walker, a born shape shifter who's spent his life on the run from hunters who want to wipe him out.

When strange phone calls bring up memories of a dark past that rocks Amber's soul and strange happenings begin in the woods, Richard might not live long enough to convince Amber to give love a try with the one man who wants to protect her above all others -- even if he can't protect himself.

Chapter 1

If you want the bitch, just go and bite her.

It doesn't work that way.

Not hard, his wolf self corrected. *Just a nibble or two on her ears.*

No.

And groom her just a little. She has nice hair, full and thick. That is a sign of good health.

"No."

Flirt a little, for the gods' sake, man! his wolf half demanded. *Throw your legs over her neck and sniff her crotch!*

"I said… Legs over her neck? Sniff her crotch?" He really hadn't meant to shout that last bit. He looked around the crowded café and was thankful that, other than a weird look or two from the postmaster and a group of kids already in full cosplay in preparation for the Friday Night Parade, not too many people paid him any notice.

Sheriff Richard Strong glared at the shadow on his wall, the representation of his spirit animal and the only tangible sign of his source of comfort and the bane of his existence. "Why would I do a thing like that?" he hissed. He could speak mentally to his wolf, but the horny beast always paid attention when he spoke out loud, one of his beast's many quirks.

I said flirt a little! His wolf self sounded exasperated. That was perfect because he felt a little exasperated too. *It's how you let a potential partner know you're interested.*

"Whatever happened to just asking her for her number or to go out on a date?"

Like that has gotten you anywhere so far? His wolf was an asshole.

"Fuck you," he muttered, then his eyes widened as he saw the shocked look on Amber's face.

Amber Graves looked perfect as ever. Her hair was in a wild Afro that gave a real seventies feel to her *Planet Quest* costume. She was in full captain's regalia today, and that meant the really short gold skirt and form-fitting, long-sleeved jacket with just enough buttons to emphasize her sizable assets. And because she was in full uniform that meant... Oh, yeah. Looking down, he saw the knee-high Go-Go boots that ended right about where a foot of toned bare leg began. Those captain's uniforms for ladies were incredibly sexist and showed way too much flesh for any commanding officer to be taken seriously. But damn if she didn't fill out those sexist bits of cotton right.

"Sorry." He tore his eyes away from Amber's legs to stare into her narrowed eyes. Her lips were pouting and her arms were crossed, her coffee pot sitting on the counter. "I was thinking about something --"

"Is it a case?" she asked, her eyes widening first before her whole face lit up with her grin. "Is it the hunters? We never found the female Bryan said was the real scary one..."

"No." He shook his head rapidly in denial. "Nothing like that. Just a case that I can't... um... seem to get a leg up on."

His bastard of a wolf began to laugh in his head, and he wanted nothing more than to jab a cotton swab into his ear to shut it up. But really, that would hurt him more than it would his stubborn shadow wolf.

"Oh." She bounced, and when she bounced her boobies... "Is there anything I can help you with? You know I am good at solving mysteries." She leaned on the counter, eyes as eager as her breasts…

Holy… His pants were getting tight in some very uncomfortable ways.

How about a blow job? his naughty wolf howled in his ear, and Richard fought to keep the wince off his face… Not that it was a bad suggestion, but this was neither the time nor the place to proposition the woman he was rapidly falling in love with.

"If there is anything you can do --" he managed to choke out in a not-too-strained voice.

Hand jobs work too, the wolf interjected.

"-- I will let you know," he finished in a rush, trying not to imagine those dainty hands of hers wrapped around his swollen dick.

"Okay." Amber grinned at him. "But don't let it get you all worked up. You get this wrinkle" -- she reached out and gently began to rub at his left temple --"right here."

His dick lurched, his wolf screamed, and Richard actually felt a few gray hairs develop. His muscles bunched as he fought the urge to just leap on the woman and ravage her like… well, like a horny wolf.

"Okay," he choked out, reaching up to lightly grip her wrist.

She smiled at him and leaned closer, her golden-brown eyes glittering like the sun. Richard tried not to melt into a puddle of goo on her clean counter top and began to caress the thin skin of her wrist with his thumb. "I know you're good at puzzles --"

Like undoing your pants and delving into the mystery of deep throating, his wolf felt the need to interject. Never had Richard ever been so glad he was the only one who could hear it.

"Well…" Amber grinned. "I am one of the only regular human beings around here." She chuckled.

"It's not easy being ordinary, you know?"

"You're far from ordinary." His stupid smile fell from his face as he spoke what was in his heart. "You're one of the most extraordinary people I know."

"Who doesn't turn furry or bitey or have wings --"

"You don't give yourself enough credit," a voice chimed in from behind, and Richard bit back a very wolf-like growl to stare at the interloper.

"Oh, Bryan." Amber pulled away from Richard to rustle up a coffee mug with a series of zeros and ones dancing the tango across the sides. He had a special mug. The interfering, cock-blocking bastard had his own mug. "How sweet of you to say."

"Yeah," Richard growled. "Sweet."

"So where's your better half?" Amber interrupted the cautious look Bryan was giving Richard. Bryan turned his full smile to her.

"He's got the early shift. Winston works too hard."

"Well, health care can be a demanding field," Amber pointed out.

"Yeah, demanding." Bryan winced, and Richard knew he had to be picking up on the "you broke the men's club rules" acid look Richard was sending his way. Now hopefully he would go away --

"But Winston loves you," Amber gushed as she bustled about, filling Bryan's coffee cup and handing him a menu. "True love is such a beautiful thing." She sighed, leaning on the counter again, making Richard's heart beat in triple time. "I just wish everyone would find true love."

Richard was saved from sobbing like a baby and screaming at his love to pay attention to him by the crackling of his radio.

"Time to come in, Chief." His dispatch officer chuckled. "I want my coffee break and I want it now."

"On my way," he grumbled into the shoulder-fitted radio before rising to his feet. "I hate to cut the love-in short..." He eyeballed Bryan, who winced and snatched up his coffee. "But I got to go and relieve Betty."

After the debacle with Winston and Bryan, Richard had felt the need to hire someone to stay in the office and see to the safety of his town when he had to run errands. Betty Humperdink -- no relation to Engelbert -- was a sassy older woman who would take no guff from anyone in the town. A retired elementary school teacher, she knew almost everyone by name and had the ability to shame any miscreants he had to bring in into silence with a glare.

"And don't be so grouchy about love," Amber clucked at him as he pulled a ten out of his pocket and placed it on the counter to pay for his lunch. "One day you will meet the woman -- or man --"

"Woman," he groused, still crossing his arms and staring at her in disbelief.

"Okay, *woman* of your dreams. And when you do, nothing will keep you away from her."

Your bitch is stupid, his wolf declared and Richard wanted to scream.

He had been pursuing the woman of his dreams with a single-mindedness that scared his friends. The whole town knew he was in love with her. He brought her flowers, he took a page from Bryan's book and learned to love *Planet Quest*, he gave her daughter rides home in the rain -- he turned down a night of cold beer and cheap strippers in the next town over to unclog her stopped-up toilet. How could she not know? Even Bryan winced and tried to shoot him a sympathetic look that made him look constipated and in need of more anal from Winston to work it all out.

"Right," Richard drawled, purposefully looking her up and down. Bryan choked on his coffee, Richard's wolf was laughing at him, and Amber just looked confused.

"When you find the one you love, you will give up anything for her," Amber rallied with a smile that broke Richard's heart.

"Right." He wanted to drown himself in a lake. But his radio squawked again and he turned to leave.

"See you tomorrow," Amber called and despite the heartache it would cause him to be in the same room with the woman he loved, who didn't know he existed as a man, he would return.

"Tomorrow." He nodded and waved over his shoulder as he turned away.

Idiot, his wolf called him, and he didn't have it in him to disagree.

* * *

"Did he seem upset to you?" Amber turned to Bryan, who looked around the café, at the other patrons, anyplace but her.

"Well --"

"Just a little?" Amber held up her hand, her forefinger and her thumb about an inch apart. She had to resist the urge to peer through her fingers and pinch his head.

"Well --"

"Come on, Bryan. Something is really bothering him. He's been such a grouch lately," Amber mused as she picked up Richard's used cup. "I think he needs some friends."

"You're his friend, Amber."

"Yes, but maybe he needs some male bonding or

something. I think he spends too much time alone."

"That guy is never alone, Amber --"

"I know." She waved a hand at him. "I know all about --" She looked around before leaning in close to whisper, "-- the shadow." She leaned up and began to fiddle with the coffee pot. "But a man needs more companionship than that. Anybody would. Otherwise you would go crazy just talking to yourself all the time."

"And you think he needs male companionship?" Bryan arched an eyebrow and Amber frowned.

"Well, maybe a BFF. Everyone needs a BFF, Bryan. I've got Angel, and Angel has Klint... You have Winston..." She lifted her hands and began to tick off the names on her fingers. "Grame has Millicent and Orville, Lila has you --" She blew out a sigh and dropped her hands to her side, shaking her head. "He needs a best friend, Bryan, a confidant, someone to be in his corner."

"What about you?"

Bryan's words caused her to pause in her reasoning. To spend that amount of time on a man... a single man who kept so many secrets and owned a gun? No matter how much her heart leaned toward the idea, her common sense demanded she pull her most stupid organ back in check.

"I don't have time for that," she told him, hoping she didn't come off too snooty.

"Like you have a lot to do here," he snorted, taking a sip of his coffee.

"I have a lot going on," Amber defended her decisions. "I am running a business, if you haven't forgotten... and there's the Friday Night Parade... and Lila..."

"Because I take up so much of your time," Lila

commented as she strolled past with a dishpan filled with dishes. "You know, 'cause I have to ask Mommy Dearest for permission before I go dance out in the streets or fill out my scholarship applications --"

"You could," Amber called as her daughter passed through the swinging double doors and made her way toward the kitchen.

"I'm not about that life, Ma!" she hollered back.

"Brats." Amber snickered as Bryan nearly choked on his coffee.

"So if you don't have any more excuses…" Bryan trailed off. "Why don't you go and spend some time with the good sheriff?"

Amber felt her eyes widen as she struggled to come up with an answer. Just before she was going to open her mouth and let something stupid fall out, the office phone began to ring. "Be right back," she called as she hustled through the swinging double doors and into her office.

"Coward," she cursed herself silently as she read the caller ID. Unknown number. Probably a telemarketer. "Good gracious," she muttered, covering her face with her hands before dropping into her office chair.

Sheriff Richard Strong, she mused.

Her heart gave a tiny lurch when she thought of the man. He was beautiful, with his long, thick braid of hair and his sharp Native American features. That hawk's nose and those incredible cheekbones were a dead giveaway of his heritage. Add to that his rich red-brown skin and those piercing black eyes… The sheriff was one tasty dish. And the muscles that lurked under those tight uniform shirts -- she might not be a badge bunny, but one look at those biceps flexing in those rolled-up khaki sleeves was enough to make her want to beg to be arrested. And his ass…

She threw back her head, chuckling at her own runaway fantasies, when her eyes caught on the dented metal replica of a spaceship in the place of honor, encased in plastic right above her desk.

Her fantasies died a quick and prejudiced death.

There was one good reason why she would never trust a man to that extent again.

How could she ever be so stupid? She'd let that man nearly ruin her mind and kill her body. Never again. Never again would anyone hold that much power, that much sway over her life.

No matter how nice Richard was, no matter how protective, no matter how powerful, she knew that in an instant that power could be turned against her, that niceness was often the thin façade for the evil that lay beneath, and that protective could turn to smothering in an instant. She was never going to go through that again in her life. Never. She had too much to lose.

She closed her eyes, running her fingers over the invisible scars left by years-old bruises. Her tongue flicked over a bottom lip that had been split countless times, still feeling the phantom pain and tasting the lost traces of her own blood. In her ears she could hear his harsh breathing, him panting as his fists emphasized each breathy word, each blow punctuating his point that everything that happened was her fault.

Why do you make me do this to you?

The words were painted in her face, like a lover's silken moans, but they had nothing to do with pleasure and everything to do with her subjugation.

Amber? Why do you make me do these things? The feel of a hard fist slamming into her stomach, forcing her breath from her as the pain from her diaphragm forced vomit into her throat as her knees became weak.

I wouldn't have to correct you if you weren't so stupid. The slamming sting of his hand impacting with the side of her face, the feel of her teeth shredding the inside of her jaw... the copper taste of blood filling her mouth, choking her as she struggled to breathe. *This is the only way a stubborn woman like you is going to learn...* Lights exploded behind her eyes a moment before a pain so intense it dropped her to her knees filled her mind, stealing her thoughts and reducing her to a thing that just wanted to survive this beating... make it through this one and maybe he would stop. Maybe she would learn. Maybe... Why was she so stupid?

"Amber?"

She jerked in her seat as a hand fell on her shoulder. Eyes wide in fear, her breathing accelerated, she threw her arms before her face... *God, not my face again.* People would stop and stare and they would know...

"Amber?"

She blinked rapidly, clearing out the dark memories. Never again, she vowed as she looked up at her dented metal spaceship before turning to see Bryan standing beside her, his hand on her shoulder, his eyes filled with concern.

"Are you --"

"Fine," she cut him off. "Fine, just fine. I was just a bit distracted."

"I should say so," Bryan mused, frowning at her.

Forcing a pleasant expression on her face, Amber rose to her feet, smiling at him.

"Unpleasant memories," she muttered, shaking her head. "I watched a stupid horror flick last night and the monster has been eating away at my brain ever since." The darkest, most evil monster that not even Hollywood in all its glory could create, she thought.

"That's why I usually stick to my sci-fi. It never stays with me in a negative way."

"You know, you should be careful what you let into your mind." Bryan relaxed as he pulled his hand from her shoulder. She was grateful for that -- she didn't know how long she could hold in the shivers that were threatening to take over her gross motor functions. "What you see becomes a part of you that can never be erased."

"Don't I know it," she muttered. *"Planet Quest* reruns from here on out."

She offered him the brightest smile she could muster. "You needed something?"

"Yeah, you're getting the lunch rush, and Lila needs some help."

"On it. Captain on deck. All hands…" She looked up at the dented model one last time before turning toward the door. "Watch out."

* * *

The Master Hunter known as Mariah sat in front of the small fire she'd coaxed from the reluctant branches plucked from the dry earth away from the falls. It seemed even nature was conspiring against her ever since she had hidden when the group of walkers and their conspirators captured her fellows. She had managed to scrounge some things from visitors to the falls and a few of the inhabited cabins, but it was rough going. Not the worse she had ever experienced, but not the best, either. "Workable" was a good word for her current status.

She glared at the small flames, knowing that somehow the falls' energy was responsible and that the skinwalkers had somehow corrupted it, twisted it so that even the trees, affected by the energy the falls gave out, were against her.

But she had energy of her own. It was this personal energy she used to force the dead limbs to ignite, and it was with this energy that she slowly baked the clay pot she had created.

Made of mud from the land of her forefathers and sprinkled with sacred bone ash, the holding pot Mariah had fashioned was designed to capture the spirit of the one she sought.

There was only one skinwalker corrupting this town, and she needed him gone for the safety of those who dwelled here. With him out of the way, nature would once again control itself and the tainted one's hold on this land would diminish.

"Sheriff Richard Strong," she intoned his name as she forced the energy-infused fire to harden the pot. She had watched him take the others down. She had watched as his shadow expanded and contracted in an unnatural manner. She had watched as the shadow lusted after that poor black woman and seemed to embrace the other strange shifter. Even if no one else paid attention to the details, it was a mark of an expert hunter to notice all. "If I capture your shadow, you will be defenseless and that much easier to kill."

She chanted until sleep took her where she sat before the small fire in one of the many abandoned cabins on this side of the mountain.

She ignored the dreams filled with black, cold ash and red-hot anger. She was meting out justice, removing the tainted ones from the face of the earth. And if it stole a little bit of her soul each time she cleansed the land of the monsters she hunted, then it was a sacrifice she was willing to give.

It was her goal in life, her calling, to see each one of the two-spirited monsters put to death.

Chapter 2

You already stand shoulder to shoulder with the bitch…

"Her name is Amber."

And she has pressed her cheek to yours in many a social occasion.

Richard glared at the wall where the shadow of his other self was posturing, his hackles bristling about him, his teeth bared as his bright tongue pushed forward. Both his display of teeth and the low rumbling timbre to his voice were designed to be menacing but, in actual reality, showed confusion.

And she has licked your face.

"It was a tiny kiss," Richard snorted, rising to his feet to face his other self. "And it meant nothing to her. Humans aren't wolves."

Maybe you all should behave as wolves, his other grumbled. *Makes this existence less worrying and more stress free.*

"Yeah, and in a perfect world, no one would be trying to actively skin my ass," Richard pointed out. "We don't exist in a perfect world. We take what we can get and work with it."

And what you're working does not appear to be working, his other snapped before he changed his stance. He threw his nose up in the air, his ears forward, his tail on a level with his back, his eyes staring into Richard's.

"Oh, don't try to get all superior with me," Richard grumbled, turning his back on his wolf. "I invented that maneuver when we were still pups."

And I perfected it when we were pimply-faced, unattractive adolescents.

"So why is it that you have no difficulty in

dealing with the pimply-faced adolescent time in our lives but don't understand what it is to attract the mate you want?"

No difficulty if you proceed properly. You have to make the bitch -- Amber-- know you're interested.

"You never had any comment before about the women I managed to get with my stupid non-wolf ways."

That's because you were looking for an easy rut. How could his own voice sound so smug? *Now that we are seeking the perfect mate, it's time I add my input.*

"Right," Richard drawled as he turned and made his way to his bedroom.

You will heed my words! His shadow grew to menacing proportions, its hackles raised, his teeth bared as it rushed forward, a blurring image of black and red, peeling off the wall to snap at him, inches before his face. His teeth made an audible clicking sound in the quiet of his house, a sound that echoed through his very bones, vibrating them uncomfortably from the inside. *You will understand their meaning!*

"You might want to try that with someone who gives a damn." Richard shook his head before continuing to his lonely room.

You will listen to me!

"You will keep quiet while I masturbate," Richard called back as he stripped out of his clothing, tossing them into a hamper before he made his way into his bathroom.

This was the room that made him buy this house and settle down, and he was man enough to admit it. It held triple showerheads in the open, stone shower. There were no doors; none were needed. The room was so big as to have a separate area for the tub and a completely different room for the toilet and bidet.

The stones themselves were of a natural tan and sandstone color, his fixtures a bright beaming brass. There were two benches built into the huge square chamber, one reclining at a level where he could just hit the steam button and sauna away his troubles and another that sat close to the three shower heads where he could sit and wash away the dirt and grime when he was too done in to stand.

Only two sides of his shower chamber were actually made of stone. One wall was completely made out of tempered glass, the kind that you could look out of but not see into, and it faced the towering trees of the forests at the back of his home. The second glass wall was steam resistant and clear… and it overlooked the huge bathtub next door. He always envisioned taking a long-term lover or a mate, to be able to wash off the day's troubles while watching him or her lounge, naked and wanting, in the huge Jacuzzi bath.

It was a fantasy he held near and dear to his heart, sharing it with no one but his shadow self.

In fact, this room was so sacred in his mind that he never even took his sporadic lovers here. He always took them to one of the two guest bedrooms and showered in the comfortable but not as extravagant showers that were connected to each. No one but himself had ever rested within the walls of his personal bedroom and shower. Those were intimate -- too intimate to share with someone he just considered a good-time rut.

He started the shower, but only one head. He washed quickly, using his scentless soaps and his loofa -- a man had to take care of his skin if he wanted his woman to notice, he reasoned.

He ran his hands over his chest, the loofa providing a delicious friction that abraded his nipples, forming them into hard peaks.

Richard had fantasies about nipple play, about his mate latching on and nibbling, biting, pinching them until they were red and sore, sending flashes of pained pleasure down his chest to his dick.

It wasn't as much fun doing it yourself, but he couldn't resist plucking at his brown nipples, making them stand up.

"Looks like this is going to be a masturbation night," he chuckled to himself as he dropped the loofa and grabbed his hardening dick.

The suds were thick on his body, creating bubbly white trails that slid down his dark skin. He appreciated the contrast as his fingers trailed over his hard muscles.

He worked hard for his body, to keep it fit and in shape. Who said he wasn't supposed to enjoy the fruits of his labors? Sometimes a man just needed to spend some time with himself and his right hand -- left one too if he was ambidextrous.

He ran his fingers through the sparse hair that surrounded the base of his cock. This was one of the things he appreciated a lot about being one of The People -- the lack of coarse body hair. Oh, he didn't mind body hair on his partners, but on him? Yeah, it held the heat and gave him swamp ass. With his sensitive nose, swamp ass was a major no-no.

He fanned his fingers over his treasure trail and skipped his swelling dick altogether. He went straight for his balls.

A man's balls could tell a lot about his personality and his sex life. He once had sex with a man who defined the term low hangers. His balls were pendulous, the sac stretched and long. He was into some serious cock-and-ball torture. Richard had never had trouble giving his partner what he or she needed, but that much dedication to masochism made his own balls want to climb up into the safety of his body. That relationship didn't last long.

But then there was the beautiful trans-woman he dated for a year while living in California. She was petite and delicate, her caramel-colored skin and almond-shaped eyes telling of her Asian heritage.

She had gotten her top done, but that hadn't needed much work since she had been taking birth control pills for the estrogen since she was twelve. She would get them from her sister, who overruled their strict parents by sneaking the pills to her on the sly. Where her sister got them, she never asked, but the result was a beautifully formed body with no facial hair and no Adam's apple. It was a technique she cautioned young ones against, but Richard couldn't deny the attractiveness of the results. Her natural breasts were firm and pert and she only had a little surgery to bring them up one cup size. She was satisfied with her C cup; any more would make her form look vulgar in her opinion. She never bothered getting the bottom surgery -- she liked her dick too much, and it was a beautiful, tender mouthful.

It was a dusky rose, and thinking about how sweet she'd tasted made his dick lurch. Her balls were tiny marbles, tender and delicate, and would disappear behind her swollen cock when she was ready to climax.

Balls could tell you a lot about a man, and his own were full and round. Not too big, not too small, definitely not low hangers, but gently nestled against the base of his dick when he was hard.

He liked his balls. Women and men both liked his balls. In fact, his masturbation sessions would be a lot more fun if he could lick his own balls like he had seen his shadow do often. He felt the small laps of the rough tongue, but it was more of a phantom touch, a tease his wolf-half would engage in just to torment him.

Now women, on the other hand... women like his Amber... Oh, yes, now that was perfection.

Amber had the roundest, fullest hips he had ever seen. They flowed gently from a waist that was not as small as some of the younger things who flocked to town and flirted with everything they saw, but it was in perfect proportion to give her that hourglass shape he loved.

He remembered looking at old pinups at a garage where he and his parents had holed up for a time, and the sight of those well-rounded women had held his attention more than his favorite chocolate bar.

Amber had those curves, the full, round mounds of breasts that dipped into her waist and flowed down into rounded hips and thick thighs. The first time he had seen her in a modest, one-piece bathing suit, he wanted to rip the thing off with his teeth and just feast on her delicate skin.

Her hair was a major turn-on for him. Her Afro was always neat and soft, the whirls of curls and twists making him want to sink his fingers in and just play, they looked so soft. But he didn't dare. He had heard many black women complain about strangers touching their hair, and he decided he would wait for an invitation.

Her hands were small and yet so strong. He recalled her holding a pipe when they went to rescue Klintic from the deranged doctor who'd held him hostage. Her knuckles had been pale with the tightness of her grip, but she had stood her ground and had stormed the cabin with the others, intent on rescuing her friend's mate.

She didn't shy away from the preternatural community. Never before had he noted so many preternaturals gathered in one spot. Most women would have freaked out and run away, scared to tell anyone what she had seen for fear of being seen as crazy. Not his Amber. She just jumped right in, no questions asked, judging each person by their own merits.

He threw his head back, ignoring the wet fall of his hair as it stuck to his wet skin, and inhaled the steam deeply. He was so far gone on Amber that he didn't think he could find his way back even if he wanted to.

Her ass was divine. He could picture it jiggling as she raced across her café, unaware of the masculine eyes that followed her. The cut of her captain's jacket never left anything to the imagination. Her breasts were too big for that, but she wore her outfit with the easy, carefree way of a domme in her favorite corset or body harness.

Mmmm. Amber in a body harness.

He pictured thick straps of cream as he slowly teased the head of his dick. Cream straps that would cut across her creamy brown skin… her eyes would glisten and her full red lips would part as she…

He clamped his fist around the base of his dick. He could feel his nuts draw up and his spine sizzle with sexual energy. He didn't want to blow fast. He wanted to take his time and imagine his Amber, wet and hungry, legs parting and the shy pink lips of her labia swollen and dripping for him.

He picked up his loofa and began scrubbing. Good masturbation required a ritual to get him in the mood, and being clean was the first step.

Once his skin was exfoliated and his erection hard and pressed up against his stomach, he stepped out of the gentle spray and shut the shower off, hitting the button for the sauna.

This was his favorite place to masturbate. Here he could relax and take his time loving himself. He could let his jizz flow where he willed, scenting his territory, marking it for him and him alone until he could combine his scent with the musk of his mate.

Lying back now, he made himself comfortable while he gripped his dick with one hand, the other going to his balls. He closed his eyes, letting his moan of pleasure roll from his chest as he pictured his Amber.

She would be resting on her bed, a mound of pillows at her back. She shyly spread her legs for him.

"Richard, wanna taste?" she would whisper, her fingers dipping down between her legs, circling her clit softly. Her fingers would be slick and shiny with her hunger as her pretty little pussy wept for him.

"Mmm." She would raise one hand to her mouth, licking her fingers before dipping them into herself. Her head would go back and she would shudder, her full breasts quivering, as she arched up into her hand.

"So good for you, Richard," she would whisper, licking her full red lips as his eyes fluttered closed. "I'm being so good for you."

"And if I wanted you to be bad?" he would ask, and she would pause and whimper at the sound of his voice.

"Then I'd be very bad."

His hand pumped his dick harder, the thick length in his palm feeling hotter than the water that poured over him. His ass clenched as he arched up, pumping and fucking into his own hand. He felt his toes curl as his imagined Amber pulled her fingers free of her pussy and offered them to him.

"Taste."

God, she would be so slick on his tongue, so sweet and musky. He could picture himself moving up onto that bed, spreading her thighs wide and burying his face in her pussy. She would be hot and drenched as she began to ride his tongue. Oh, yeah, he knew how to work his tongue, pointing it and dancing it all around her swollen clit before he dipped down and lapped at her labia.

Her hands would be buried in his hair by now, tugging and pulling, directing him where to go, and he would gladly take direction. He could envision himself cupping the cheeks of her firm ass, lifting her higher and kneading the flesh as he drank her down. Those thighs would clamp around his head, holding him one place, as she bucked and squealed her pleasure.

"Richard! Oh, God, Richard, More! More! More!"

He pumped his dick faster and his other hand tugged at his balls before rolling them in his palm as his stomach tightened and electricity began to dance up and down his spine.

"Fuck," he muttered to himself as he threw his head back, his moans loud in the enclosed space. That only set his hunger higher. In his mind's eye, he could see himself sliding back, his face shiny with her slick, his tongue sore from putting it to such good use.

Her legs would slide down his back and around his waist as she tried to force him inside, hungry for the thick slide of his cock stretching her open.

"Fuck, yes," he growled, his hand pumping faster, holding himself tighter as he imagined sliding into her tight, wet pussy.

She would shudder as her tight walls wrapped around his dick. Her muscles would be firm yet giving, slick with their own juices as they bathed the head of his dick in her liquid fire.

"Damn, baby," he moaned, his hand growing tired but not enough to make him stop. He was yanking at his dick, his thighs stiffening as his back arched. In his mind, he was fucking his Amber, pounding her, relishing the sound of his balls slapping against her ass because that meant possession.

He was going to shoot his load so deep inside her that she would never be apart from him. She would crave him like she craved air, like he craved her. And her nails would carve her marks of ownership down his back.

She would scream as his hair danced across her nipples before he lowered his mouth and sucked one deep inside. God, the combination of her hard nipple and her soft breast made his dick leak faster.

The burn was traveling down his stomach, through his thighs, and up his back as he pictured her on his fat dick, head thrown back and screaming his name in her release.

"Richard! Coming!"

"Fuck, yes!" The sound of his own voice echoed around the room. His cock jerked as he began to spurt his release onto his stomach and hand.

"God, yes," he repeated, milking his dick for all it was worth, extending his climax even as his tight muscles began to relax.

Lazily, he reached for the showerhead and rinsed his skin free of his load, his eyes already closing even as he turned the water off.

"Amber," he moaned as his eyes slid shut. He was so relaxed he couldn't pinpoint the exact moment he fell asleep.

* * *

Idiot.

Richard jerked awake as his own voice admonished him. *You need liquid. You have been in the steam room for far too long.*

He blinked twice, not remembering falling asleep, but his wolf was correct.

He reached up and turned off the steam as he made his way toward his toilet room where a wide double sink waited. He flipped on the faucet and got himself a large tumbler of water, downing and refilling the glass three times before he was sated. Then he stumbled his way to his bed without bothering to towel off.

He closed his eyes and instantly was transported into a dream, a new dream, one where his perfect mate, Amber, lay on her bed, gently stroking her naked flesh.

Chapter 3

"Oh, yes," she hissed, biting her bottom lip as she threw her bead back, her eyes sliding shut.

Amber knew what she was doing was naughty, but damn she couldn't help herself. She had seen Richard on the salamander bars.

The sight of his tight, shirtless body defying gravity by lurching upwards, only a short metal rod held between his hands keeping him from plunging to the hard ground, sweat sheening his perfectly defined back… Amber was not the only one to stand in front of the gym's massive windows and stare.

She had been going for a walk, trying to clear her mind from the unsettling feeling these calls/hangups left in her gut. Walking around a town where everything was perfectly strange was always the key to calming her down. Everyone knew her here, there was safety here, her past could not find her here.

She had been enjoying the early summer heat when a crowd of people caught her attention. It was then that she saw Richard -- she would know that long, tightly woven braid anywhere -- and his feat of muscular strength as he completed his workout for the day.

Something about him made her catch her breath. It wasn't the usual hormonal thrill at seeing a well-formed male body. She had seen lots of bodies in her day, lots of well-formed muscular bodies at that, but there was something about the slim, tightly built Richard that had her drooling.

Maybe it was the way his deep voice seemed to vibrate every bone in her body. Maybe it was the way his piercing black eyes seemed to take in everything and everyone around him, assessing every environment for dangers. It definitely had to be partially because of the way he moved. His uniform pants and shirt certainly left not much to the imagination, the thin cotton sliding around the bulges of his muscular shoulders and biceps while the pants had a tendency to sink in just enough to outline those perfect globes of flesh he called an ass. Maybe it was because his full attention had been on her today.

He flirted. Flirting and Richard Strong went hand in hand. It was never offensive and he wasn't aggressive or nasty about it, but the man flirted like he was trying to get her into his bed.

And today, he had looked so lonely when they had been discussing true love. And the way he defended her, even to herself.

You're not ordinary...

He seemed almost righteous as he spoke to her, the intensity in his voice a very real, nearly solid thing.

It was this same intensity he put into getting to the top of the metal ladder by using only his upper body strength and his daring.

Of course it was this same intensity she imagined as she spread her legs, raised them until her feet were firmly planted on her mattress and slid her dildo in deep.

She bit her lip harder, trying to keep the sounds of her arousal to herself.

Lila was in her room not too far away. And though her daughter was nearly fully grown, Amber wanted to keep the aspects of her sex life -- her lack of a sex life -- to herself.

Even so, the small whimpers that escaped her control added a little extra tingle of heat to her arousal and sent a delicious shiver up her spine.

Once seven inches of purple silicone cock were

seated firmly in her slick channel, she inhaled deeply and tried to relax back on her bed. The buildup was so much more powerful when she relaxed and let her desire grow slowly.

She shifted her hips, groaning when the thick vibrator rocked up, sliding against her wet clit and making her stomach clench as pleasure began to build.

Now she pictured Richard over her, his massive shoulders blocking out the dim light cast by her bedside table. In the warm dark of her room, she could almost picture him, hear him repeating those words.

Amber, you're anything but ordinary.

God, yes, she could feel him above her, feel his heat as he moved over her body, working his hips just right, sliding his cock...

She reached down and gripped her false dick, sliding it out and very slowly pushing it back inside herself, moaning as she pictured the good sheriff sinking his dick in slowly, pulling back enough to watch himself pierce her wet pussy.

What color would his cock be?

Amber had only slept with a few men before she met -- her ex. And he was all blond and pale, his nipples a bubblegum pink while his cock was a smooth tan, a few shades darker than his skin.

The head of his penis was nearly purple, a violent red when he was aroused, surrounded by well-trimmed body hair that was, oddly enough, nearly a red-brown, totally at odds with the pale blond locks on his head.

Richard was dusky skinned, his Native American heritage clear in his slightly hooked nose, his deeply toned bass voice, and his red-tinted tan skin.

She and every able-bodied person in this town at one time or another had stopped to gawk at him doing that damn salamander bar shirtless, so she was well aware of his deep brown nipples. Still, she wondered what the rest of his body would look like.

Lazily pumping herself with her cock, her wrist flexing slowly as she slid it deliciously inside and out, she wondered what he looked like naked.

She slid the toy out fully, her thumb depressing the button, starting it vibrating slowly as it pulled free of her body. She slid it in circles around her clit, pressing it hard against her for a moment, but only for a moment. The sharp pleasure was mounting fast -- it was almost too much. She could feel her clit getting overly sensitive and backed off a bit, running the vibrator slowly up and down her labia before inserting it once again and slowly fucking herself.

Richard would be big in the dick department. She had seen how well he filled out the front of his jeans as well as the back. There was a definitely huge bulge there. She recalled watching it shift as he moved about, almost like he wasn't wearing underwear. But she knew, despite his sense of humor, he remained proper and regimented under his clothing.

His dick, though -- it would be long and thick, possibly darker than his skin and uncircumcised. He had once told her he was born on a reservation with the aid of a midwife and a *winkte* -- a two-spirited person -- so circumcision was probably out of the question.

Thinking about his possibly deep red head peeking out from its foreskin made her mouth water.

How would he taste? The sheriff didn't eat a lot of meat, was crazy over pineapple juice, and was rather healthy. His precum would be sweet with a touch of salt...

Her pussy clenched at the thought, the vibrations

of her toy pressing against her inner muscles stealing her breath for a moment. She pumped herself harder as her free hand went to her nipples, tugging and pulling at one and then the other before kneading the flesh of her breasts.

God, his mouth would be so hot here, so hot and hard and… and he would bite her, just a little. She imagined his teeth closing delicately over her nipple as he stared up at her with those dark eyes, his hair trailing like cool silken fingers over her skin, as he nipped her sharply before sucking the pain away.

An unconscious whimper left her throat as shards of heat trailed down from her stomach, through her tight muscles before her toes clenched. Her back arched and she could feel her ass bounce as she began to fuck herself harder, putting her hips into the pleasurable sensations rolling from her pussy.

Her ass -- God, yes he would love her ass. No matter how much she worked out, how many squats she did, her ass remained big and mobile. It jiggled when she moved and now it clapped lightly as she began to fuck herself good. He would love her ass. He would cup her ass and squeeze the flesh just right. He would hold her ass tightly, spreading her open as he forced his way between her legs and sucked on her clit, as he buried his face in her slick heat, as he ate her out as if it were going out of style, as if he were dying of thirst and she was his only liquid resource.

And he would do it right, too. He would suck on her clit but remember to lick her labia. He would tongue her sharply before sinking his mobile muscle deep into her, tasting her from the inside. He would groan and snuffle and take her in like she was the most perfect thing he had ever tasted. Then he would let one hand slip down and --

"Richard," she gasped, her hand leaving her breasts to slide between her ass cheeks. She was so wet she was leaking down over her tiny furled rosebud. She circled her finger there as she pressed her vibrator to her clit once more. Her hair felt like it was standing on end and electric shocks ran up and down her body.

"Fuck!" she hissed, moaning and twisting on the bed, her head rolling back and forth as she pressed the vibrator in harder.

God, she was almost there. She just needed a little more...

"Richard," she whimpered, as she slid her finger in and --

"Richard!" She screamed his name as her whole body tensed. She felt her breath constrict and her muscles tense. Her whole body stilled, her back arched high, her muscles tensed, and then all hell broke loose.

Her inner muscles spasmed, her pussy clenching hungrily around nothing. Her ass clenched around her finger; her clit burned and throbbed in rhythm to her spasming inner walls. Tears rolled down her face, and for one brief, shining moment of forever, Amber soared.

The vibrator dropped from her hand to buzz uselessly beside her, her wrist burning and her clit rapidly going numb. Her finger slid out of her ass as she slumped back to the pillows. She had to clean up and she had to put her toys away... but all she could do was giggle.

"Thank you, Richard Strong," she snickered to herself. "You have given me the best damn orgasm that you will never know about."

* * *

"The fuck --" Richard jerked upright, torn completely out of the dream he suddenly realized was not a dream at all.

"Thank you, Richard Strong, for the best orgasm that you will never know about, indeed."

His wolf -- the pervy bastard -- had decided to take a walk without him and had found his lady. As much as he wanted to bask in the images that were still flooding his mind and adding new spank-bank material for his personal love sessions, his wolf was violating a trust.

* * *

The bitch --

"Amber! Geez," Richard snarled, startling his new deputy.

After dealing with many news-making events, it was decided that Sheriff Richard Strong needed a little experienced help. With Angel Falls in the forefront of the media and the forests filling up with tourists, the governor didn't take too kindly to deputized posses running about locking up criminals. Now more than ever, with the Fae Movie being filmed and Angel Falls, the gay author and new hero for the gay rights movement living in town, the head politician in Maryland wanted to prove to the eyes of the world that even this small town held his attention.

In other words, it was an election year and the governor had his eye on the presidential nomination in about four years. That meant measures had to be taken, so Matthew Markus was quickly vetted and had been hired as the town's newest and only deputy.

"Amber, Chief?" the blond-haired, blue-eyed man asked, and Richard had to fight the urge to just smack him one good time.

Ever since he had been hired, Matthew had persisted in calling Richard "Chief." Not that it had anything to do with his obvious Native American heritage -- insert rolled eyes here -- it was a sign of respect for being the chief of police. That the police force was made up of two was no deterrent to the eager-to-please deputy. With his light hair and eyes, he was the epitome of the boy next door. Most of the ladies in town complimented him on his good looks and his "Aw, shucks" attitude that hid a degree in criminal justice. But instead of taking his degree somewhere that might need his help, like Baltimore, he'd decided to settle his boy-next-door looks right here in his town.

"Thinking about lunch?"

"Considering calling an order in," Richard decided, glaring at his shadow until it shrank down to a tiny pinprick and disappeared.

"If you do order in, can you get me a burger? I don't know what she does to them, but those things are like crack."

"Uh huh," he nodded, casually rising to his feet. "Going to make that call now. You want the special?"

"What on earth did you do to get a burger named after you?" Matthew asked, pausing in filling out reports on jaywalkers and petty thefts in the mountains. There had been a lot of that going around, and they both agreed it was because of the town's new popularity. Where tourists flocked, there tended to be an increase in petty theft.

"I'm just that good, I guess," he joked, making an effort to get along with the man he was going to be saddled with for a long time.

And it wasn't Matthew's fault Richard was in a grumpy mood. It was his damn shadow. It had taken to giving him unwanted advice almost every moment of the day. Yes, he was in love with Amber, but she had some obvious baggage he had to break through to even have a chance at her heart.

"Give it time and I'll have the Matthew Burger," Matthew called back. "Women can't resist the uniform, Chief. I will be on that menu of fame."

"Right next to the Lingo Supplemental."

"Isn't that the villain of the story?"

"Main one." Richard laughed. "And in the café, it's the liver and onion dish."

"Cold, Chief." Matthew laughed. "So very cold."

They both were still laughing when Richard closed the door to his office, shutting Deputy Markus outside to file reports all by his lonesome while Richard obsessed over Amber.

He had no more than settled down in his chair once more when he caught a blur of black out of the corner of his eye. He knew his other self was on the prowl, so he sat back to see what had caught his wolf's interest.

He concentrated on making that spot expand until the vision in his left eye was superimposed with what his wolf was watching. It had taken off pretty quick and -- what the fuck?

Amber! His perverted wolf was watching Amber again.

This time she was in her office, her shirt held in her hand as she mopped her stomach and sides with a damp cloth.

Her skin was a deep chocolate color, rich and smooth, her stomach tight with just a slight rounding near the bottom. There were faint stretch marks from her pregnancy but they only enhanced her mature beauty. This was a grown woman, not some little fashion doll who was more fun to look at than to touch.

Her breasts nearly overflowed the tight black bra she wore, the mounds of soft-looking flesh swinging as she moved to mop herself down.

"It's okay." Her voice sounded tiny, and he had to strain to understand what she was saying. "No harm done, Jamie."

He knew from experience that Jamie was her lead waitress. "A little salad dressing never hurt anybody."

She dipped the cloth into the running sink that was in the back of her office and again mopped at her stomach, leaving tiny, rainbow-hued soap bubbles across her skin, making it shimmer in the light that fell into the room.

He felt his pants tighten, his cock harden as she rinsed once more and then ran her damp hands over all that soft skin. She spun around and he could read contentment in her eyes. She licked her bottom lip, leaving the plump flesh glistening as she picked up a dry cloth and blotted herself dry.

Richard moaned the loss of that shining moisture, but seeing the give and play of her skin made him hunger to test its firmness beneath his tongue and teeth.

"And it was honey mustard. I at least like honey mustard," she laughed as she ran her hands over her skin once more before easing her arms into a fresh captain's jacket.

And it was right about then, with his thighs spread to allow space for his growing erection, his hand rubbing along his thighs, that he realized he was seconds away from grabbing his junk and beating his meat.

"Fuck." He blinked rapidly to dispel the image of his dream woman. *Voyeur! Voyeur!* he chanted, mentally admonishing his wolf.

She's better looking than reports about stupid people

doing stupid things, his wolf countered.

"Will you just... Can't you just -- I mean, what the fuck?" he railed at his wolf, slamming his hands on his desk.

There was a knock at his door and Richard looked up to see Matthew standing there, concern on his face. "You okay, Chief?" he asked, cracking open the door and leaning in.

"Spider." He shook his head, motioning to his desk blotter before jerking a tissue out of the box on his desk and feigning cleaning up the desk and his hand. "Warm weather and they just get in."

"It's bad luck to kill them, though," Matthew pointed out. "You're supposed to take them outside. If you keep killing Charlotte's children, you will be haunted by the ghost of Zuckerman's Famous Pig."

"So long as it haunts the top of my bacon burger, we're all good," Richard laughed back, tossing the tissue and picking up the phone. "Sheriff's Special, right?"

"Double the burgers." Matthew got a content look on his face. "Those things --"

"Are like crack." Richard laughed with his deputy. "I remember."

"And a bottled water, please," Matthew added. "Gotta maintain my boyish figure if I'm going to get a burger named after me."

"Deputy Delight?" Richard offered. "Bull with lots of ham."

"You wound me, Chief, surely you do," Matthew laughed, heading back to his desk. He really was an okay guy.

"I will if you don't get my reports filed," Richard called out. "And don't call me Shirley."

He began to dial numbers, but paused as his wolf

spoke softly in his ear. *Competition, maybe?*

"Shut up and stop spying," he muttered.

He ignored his wolf's laughter and relaxed in his chair. The back and forth with his deputy had managed to cool his ardor somewhat. He was just glad that his wolf was now spying around the café, sniffing at the foodstuffs and watching the citizens of Angel Falls go about their daily lives.

He had better make that call.

* * *

"Right, Richard," Amber said with a laugh. "Crack... yeah. So I'll make up two... four of them with fries. Oh, and for you a salad because I care."

"Rabbit food?"

In her best captain's voice, she told him, "You will eat that salad, mister, and you will like it." She was still laughing when she hung up the phone.

"Lila," she called to her daughter as she walked out of her office. "I need two Sheriff Specials to go."

"You still forcing green leafies on that man?" her daughter called back.

It was the lull before the lunch rush and Amber found herself slightly -- just very slightly -- disappointed that Richard would not be putting in an appearance today.

Lila stuck her head in the office and Amber had to hold her breath, her right hand resting on her chest for a moment. Her daughter looked so much like her father...

It was there in the bright caramel/golden eyes and in the shape of her chin. For a second Amber had been transported back to when she first met the man, how he complimented her so much that her low self-esteem seemed to vanish with his very presence. And the laughter... they laughed so much when they were dating, filling her heart with a lightness of being she had never felt before. For a second regret filled her and she realized that, in spite of it all, she still missed that laughter.

But that kind of lightness of being had come with a price, a price she was no longer willing to pay. She needed to be whole and hale for her daughter.

"Just keeping him fit," she called back as her daughter made her way to the kitchen, her wild tangle of hair casting odd shadows on the wall. "He can't keep us safe if he's run down with cholesterol."

"But to constantly inflict salad on the man," Lila called back, making the cook and his assistant laugh. "That's a red-blooded man, Mom. He needs some red meat to keep him running,"

"Have you ever seen him run?" one of the waitresses called out. "He jogs at five just about every morning."

"No," the cook called back. "But I have two words for you… Salamander Bar. He does that crazy wall thing at Macey's gym almost every evening. If he needs stress relief that bad, I'd be willing --"

The ringing of the phone cut off the sudden spike of jealousy Amber felt at her waitress's words. Obviously, she'd been eyeballing Richard like he was a side of beef. The man deserved more respect than that.

But, she reasoned as the phone rang again, he wasn't her man so she should not feel jealous…

The phone ringing for the third time jerked her away from those confusing thoughts as she forced a pleasant sound into her voice. "Planet Quest. How may we be of service?"

There was nothing. "Hello?" she frowned as nothing happened. Maybe it was…

An odd sound was coming through, the sound of

heavy breathing, and Amber felt anger rush over her.

"Go and find some other way to get your jollies off, 'cause I am not having this shit here." She slammed the phone down, shaking her head. "Stupid kids," she muttered and turned her attention back to her books. She had product to order and didn't have time for stupid kids' games.

She never noticed the shadow on the wall shudder in concern before it pulled back to blend in with the other shadows cast along the wall.

* * *

Brown eyes peeked out from around a low set of bushes, watching a couple scratch their heads as they searched through their belongings.

In her possession, Mariah now held several high-priced cameras and portable computer devices. She had immediately smashed the laptop computers and tablets, keeping for herself the cash and cameras she had stolen. Theft went against her sense of honor, but there was no other sure way to get what she wanted. If enough people complained, the sheriff had to visit the scene, and then she would have the skinwalker.

This was the tenth campsite she had denuded of its valuables. She knew it would take a bit more to bring her quarry to ground. The added advantage of the petty thefts was that she retrieved some of the things necessary for her plan to become a success.

There were foodstuffs -- perishable and non-perishable -- and warmer clothing. Though it was summer now, it remained bitterly cold by the falls. She had to stay near them, to try to decipher what the walkers had done to the natural pool of energy.

Every night she was torn from her sleep by the most horrific dreams of drowning, of choking, of being torn asunder by the nature she sought to protect. It left her irritable and tired, a bit slower to differentiate the world around her from her dreams -- a puzzle she usually would have deciphered in seconds.

She closed her eyes now, ignoring the soreness of the dark rings under her eyes and how her breathing felt more labored. She knew she would have to rid this area of evil soon before it took a greater toll on her health.

Now, she watched as the couple angrily began to pack while the woman punched numbers into her cell phone.

She and this woman were roughly the same size, and Mariah welcomed the clean clothing she'd lifted from the tent. She had taken some of the man's clothing as well, just to keep the police guessing at the perpetrators. She hoped they'd assume there was a small gang of teens wreaking havoc and burgling small quantities of valuables.

This was sure to bring the sheriff.

Above all, it was crucial that the sheriff come alone. She couldn't expose herself or the other hunters to anyone, and this town in the past year or so seemed to have become a mecca for the unusual, so much so that the media was keeping its global eye on the small town.

But for now, she sank back through the bushes and made her way to the winterized cabin she had claimed as her own. The new food and warmer clothing would be welcome, but the woman demanding that someone come out and investigate warmed Mariah more than the hottest fire.

Soon, she could put her plan into action and the threat of this walker, like many before him, would come to an end.

Chapter 4

"You don't look so good."

Richard tried his best to rustle up a smile for Amber as he took his usual seat at the counter at Planet Quest. After his latest tiff with his other, he'd found it all but impossible to go back to sleep.

Looking into Amber's big brown eyes made him feel guilty.

Twice now, his wolf had invaded her privacy and showed her at her most vulnerable. That wasn't fair to her at all. But every time he opened his mouth to explain what was going on, his fear made him hold back.

"Got a lot on my mind," he responded, his stomach churning as he stared into the perfection of her face. "Hard to sleep." He reached out to touch her face, just lightly under her eyes where he noticed dark rings showing through her makeup. "Are you --"

"Not getting a lot of sleep." She sighed. "Some idiot keeps calling and hanging up."

"Can you get the number off your Caller ID?"

"Nope." She reached out to pull down a mug for him as well as her captain's mug. "Unlisted." She turned toward the coffee maker and retrieved a pot of high octane for them both.

After they both began to inhale the caffeinated gold, a little more life came into her eyes. "So what's keeping young Richard Strong up at night? Is it a girl?" she teased.

"In a way," he mumbled into his mug. "But she doesn't know I exist."

"Then she's a fool," Amber decided, slamming her hand down on the table.

"No, she's exceptionally bright," he defended

Amber, even if she didn't know she was speaking of herself.

"Not if she can't see what a handsome, caring man you are, Richard."

He was stumped. He just stared at her, his eyes narrowing before he opened his mouth to spill the truth. "Amber --"

"Damn it," she snapped, turning away to answer the phone at the end of the counter.

"Damn it," he repeated softly, ignoring the maniacal laughter of his wolf in his head.

He turned as someone took a seat beside him.

"Sheriff." Bryan nodded as he leaned on the counter. "Looking… I wouldn't say bad. Flummoxed is a good word."

"Not now, Bryan," Richard muttered, glaring as he felt a headache developing. The man looked entirely too relaxed. A quick sniff told him that besides a hot shower and a good night's sleep, the man had engaged in at least two bouts of happy-good-time-love-you morning sex. "Your afterglow is blinding me."

"Does it show?" Bryan gave him a wicked grin. "It's one of the perks of being in love."

"Fuck you!"

Richard had opened his mouth to say it, but the words had not come from him. He turned to see Amber slam the phone down, her eyes glittering with something that looked like fear before she masked it with pure anger.

"Amber?"

"It's my fucking stalker again!"

"Stalker!" Richard sat up at that, his eyes narrowing. "You never said you had a stalker." His wolf began to growl in the back of his mind.

"It has to be, Richard. The bastard called my

phone last night and he keeps calling me here."

"I thought you said it was kids --"

"I thought so too. We get so many tourists around now." She shook her head looking frustrated and frightened. "But this is the third time today. I've been getting calls here but last night they started at my house. How did they get my house number? I pay extra to keep it unlisted."

"Could use a tracer program," Bryan interjected. "If they have any computer knowledge, it doesn't take much. There are companies that will report on a number or give the number to an address for a small fee, usually ninety-nine cents per number."

Richard and Amber both turned to stare at him.

"What? The info is out there. You don't even need an ANITA to figure out how to do it."

"Can you trace them back?" Richard asked, his mind whirling with the thoughts of what he would do to the person responsible for causing Amber to be afraid.

"What?"

"Can you trace them back?"

"Sure... if I can attach a line to your number, Amber. That way when they call, I can isolate the towers used and send up a ping that will bounce back to the caller. Technology is so advanced now that I can trace the towers and isolate the caller within a fifty-foot radius... especially since we are up here in the mountains."

"Do it." Richard turned to see anger replacing the fear in Amber's eyes. "Do it, Bryan. I want to pay my merry little caller a visit."

"Not exactly legal --"

"You have my permission," Richard interrupted. "You're now deputized. This is a case of escalating harassment and menacing. You find the bastard and I'll go and pay him a visit."

"And you have my permission to tap my line or do whatever it is you have to do to find them," Amber added. "I want this to stop."

There was desperation in her voice, and Richard wanted so much to cross over the counter and pull her into his arms.

Do it, his wolf urged. *Protect Amber.*

For once he and his wolf were in perfect agreement. He leapt over the counter and pulled Amber into his arms.

Perfection, his wolf howled as Richard pulled her closer. He felt her smaller softer form resist for a moment before she gave in and sank against him. He pulled her closer as her body began to shudder. He rocked her from side to side, muttering nonsense words of comfort.

He closed his eyes, buried his face in her hair, and took in the scents of lemon, verbena, musk, and melted butter that seemed to be the core scent of Amber Graves.

She felt like… In his arms, she made him feel like a man, like he finally had a purpose. With her in his arms, he could move mountains, he could triumph over any evil, he could… make her laugh?

Her shoulders were shaking harder now, and he realized it wasn't fear that was making her tremble. He pulled back, looked into her watery brown eyes, and heard the full blast of her laughter.

"Oh, my God," she choked, her whole body shaking as she began laughing harder. "Did you seriously just leap dramatically over the counter?"

"Uh --" What could he say? He had indeed heroically leapt over a counter.

"Richard!" She pulled away, covering her mouth with her hands as she nearly bent double in her mirth. "Seriously? You actually leapt over my counter!"

He frowned. She laughed harder. Bryan was snickering.

"I hope the camera's got that!" she roared. "Oh, my God, your hair -- it was flying behind you like a cape!"

So? It was just a day when he'd pulled his hair back into a tail. Sometimes he liked the feel of the waist-length hair hanging down his back.

Idiot. His wolf, he realized, was not howling in triumph. It was laughing at him too.

"Richard, you have just made my day," Amber choked, leaning on the counter as laughter echoed through the blessedly empty café. "Only you could leap to my defense, my knight in starched uniform."

"Right," he drawled as he stepped back. His pride was taking a beating, but it also insisted that he didn't turn and run away.

"My hero!"

His radio cackling to life saved him from having to come up with a valid reason for leaping to her defense. He pulled it out of its holster, giving both the still-giggling Amber and the chuckling Bryan the stink-eye.

"Sheriff," he snapped, depressing the talk button.

"I know you're on call now," Betty informed him, her familiar amused tones easing some of his embarrassment. "But we just got another one."

"Damn. Where?"

"Out near Camp Jolly Times." Betty's voice lost some of its amusement. "This time someone swore they saw a female running away."

"Great," he grumbled. "Where is Matthew?"

"Matty is out near the Mulligan place. There were some disturbances during the night, maybe wild dogs, Sheriff. He's out on a go-see."

He gave Amber and Bryan the side-eye, watching as they spoke softly together. Probably thinking of ways to turn his heroic leap into fifteen minutes of comedy gold, he thought, rolling his eyes at the pair of them.

"So are they coming in?" he asked Betty.

"Yeah, I told them to come on in and make a report, but they would surely love it if you would go out there and have a look-see of your own. Put those tracking skills to good use. If they really saw someone, maybe you can find at least one of the perps."

"You watch too many cop shows, Betty." He relaxed as the familiar back and forth with her flowed easily, freeing him of some of his embarrassment.

"Nothing else to do in this town when the sun goes down... unless you got someone to cuddle up to. And my cats aren't the kind that always cuddle back." Of course not. Betty rehabilitated sick and injured cougars in her spare time. No one in this town was normal, he thought, shaking his head.

"Okay, Betty. I'm on it. Out."

He turned to make his way to the counter break, but paused as he saw Amber with an anxious look on her face.

"Take me with you."

* * *

"You know he really cares for you."

The words cut off Amber's laughter and she turned to face Bryan, concerned by his suddenly serious tone.

Amber had been grateful for the bit of misplaced gallantry. It had stopped her from descending into another nightmare glimpse of the past.

It was like being with Todd again. He used to call her from work, just wanting to know how she was feeling, always there to rush to her rescue when things got bad.

Once, she nearly had a heart attack when he suddenly popped up to stop some idiot from screaming at her. They were on the campus at the University of Baltimore East during a protest about whatever hot-button issue had gotten the students riled up. She believed it had something to do about becoming vegan, the new catch phrase of the week, and the man shouting at her as she bit into a hotdog.

She recalled that it had been sunny, the leaves just getting a hint of the golden color that told the story of the burgeoning fall. She was running late, as usual, and instead of stopping for lunch at the campus cantina, she had grabbed a hotdog from a nearby vendor. She had just bitten into the beefy goodness when this college kid of indeterminate race and age slapped it from her hand.

"Hot dogs are murder!" he had shouted in her face.

"So are the fucking leather shoes on your feet, asshole!" she shouted in retaliation. "And you're going to buy me another one."

"Fuck you, bitch!" he shouted, and Amber was ready to read him the riot act, chapter and verse, when a tall shadow swooped between the two of them.

"I think you owe the lady another sausage," he growled and Amber had to admit, she fell a little in love right then.

Todd Ritter was everything her geeky little heart ever desired. He was tall, athletic, his hair a mid-length golden fall that just brushed his shoulders, and his voice… it was so deep it was like black velvet over gravel.

"That ain't no lady! She's a murderer," the protestor shouted, a few of his friends gathering around in support.

"And you just assaulted her." He offered a shark's grin as he pulled a badge from his pocket. "Officer Ritter, and you're under arrest for assault, menacing, and intent to do bodily harm."

As he spoke, a few more uniformed officers moved into view, making the protest group break up rather quickly.

"Hey, man --" The protester backed up. "I didn't mean anything by it. I -- I just --"

"You were observed assaulting this young woman." He spoke slowly, as if the protester had the IQ of a chimp… and thinking back on it, he probably had. "When asked to back off, you refused. You went so far as to attempt to menace me." He turned to Amber, and she fell for the deepest golden brown eyes she had ever seen. "Is that what you say, Miss…"

"Amber. Amber Graves." She felt herself flush with embarrassment mingled with a growing desire as she watched the officer come to her rescue. When the silence went on, she realized she had never answered his question. "Oh," she flushed deeper. "Oh, yeah. That's right, Officer. That's what happened. He was trying his best to be menacing."

The protestor took a step back and before Todd could say anything, he took off running as fast as his twiggy legs could carry him.

"God, what a joke!" The officer laughed, his guffaws echoed by the four men in uniform.

"Um…"

"Sorry about that, Amber," he laughed. "But

look at him run."

"Uh…" What the hell was going on?

"Todd," he introduced himself again. "Not an officer of the law, but on my way to play rehearsal. We are doing a modern retelling of Romeo and Juliet and the Montagues are cops. Say hello to Benvolio."

After that, even Amber had to chuckle. "Hello, Benvolio… my hero."

"Even my name means good will." He winked at her. "And now that I have come to the aid of the damsel in distress --"

"Not that much distress." She pouted, knowing she could take care of herself, that she had been doing so for a long time, but finding it delicious that a stranger found her attractive enough to come to her rescue.

"So, I can see that you're independent. I like that," he purred and Amber again felt her cheeks redden, this time in delight.

"We're going to be late," one of the pseudo-cops called out, and Amber realized she was going to be late herself.

"Damn," she gasped. "Professor Hickman --"

"Accounting, right?" he smiled.

"And I'm going to be late." She checked her watch and suddenly was torn between getting to her Ethics of Accounting class and staying here to try to flirt with the hot guy who'd come to her defense.

"I'll walk you over. The theater is that way -- that is, if you don't mind the company."

His eyes were so compelling, his attention so gratifying that she nodded numbly.

Returning to the present, she blinked again as she realized she was reacting half to the past and half to the sudden bolt of electricity she felt. She had only felt that one time before, and the man responsible was long gone and good riddance.

Her laughter was a relief, relief that she was not still that naive little thing and that she could feel joy in another's touch.

The *It's Complicated* tag was created with her in mind, she mused.

And then... there was Richard's face. He'd actually thought she was going to crumble into tears because some jackass was hounding her.

She had been hounded by the best and this little freak calling, while it had frightened her that he had her house number, it was more fear for her daughter than herself.

Now that steps had been discussed, she could push that fear back and let her anger take over. She was about to demand vengeance, to get a pint of the jackass stalker's blood when Richard had leapt to the conclusion that she needed help.

At first, she was angered, but then as she realized what was going on, the humor of the situation got to be too much.

Richard was a protector -- it was bred into him. She knew something about him was otherworldly -- in fact, with all the otherworldliness surrounding her, she would have been amazed if he was totally human. But even at his most pressured, Richard had never taken his frustrations out on anyone. He never stopped her from riding to the rescue. He never shoved her behind him to be saved by the big bad warrior, even when she was out of her league. Richard just was a good guy.

If truth were told, he was a very good-looking guy. But with his hair flying about him, he had leapt the counter like something out of a comic book, and his attempts to comfort her were laughably predictable, like something he'd read in a romance novel.

Of course she'd laughed.

But then… otherworldly he might be, but Richard could not read minds. The hurt look that settled on his face killed all the humor for her.

She was no better than her ex, stomping on his honest attempts to help when he thought she needed a boost.

Then she realized that even when he was holding her, he never offered to protect her, to shield her. He just wanted to be there.

And Bryan's disapproving look made it all too clear she was being an ass. She was getting ready to apologize when Betty contacted him.

She listened in and realized he was going out into the forest again. It would be a perfect place to apologize to him and hopefully not lose his friendship. She didn't want him to pull away. She had gotten used to having him around.

Yeah, she told herself. She was just used to having him around. That she'd masturbated to her mental image of him just the night before was of no consequence… really it wasn't.

"Take me with you."

The words just kind of escaped, but she stood by them. She wanted to go with him, to be the friend he needed.

And to think that he had started off the day confiding to her about his heart being broken and she had ended his morning by laughing at him. That was truly a bitch move.

So she would go with him, apologize, be the friend he needed, and then find the cunt who was breaking his heart and have a few words with her.

Richard was a beautiful, special man, and he

deserved to have someone protect his heart, even if it was someone who had never been good at dealing with conditions of the heart.

* * *

"You know you didn't have to come with me." Richard took his eyes off the road for a moment to stare at Amber. "You could have stayed back."

They were traveling at a good clip along the drive trail that lead to the camping area where the latest thefts had occurred and a possible criminal had been allegedly sighted.

He had pushed off his embarrassment in the face of Amber honestly asking to travel with him. He wondered why. Maybe she wanted to make a few more jokes and maybe have a laugh that would put him squarely in the friend zone.

After he had been ready to admit everything, to actually bare his heart to her.

And damn it, he still wanted to.

"Lila can run the place for the day." She offered him a shy smile.

Wait, that was more flirtatious than he'd expected. Or was he just imagining things?

"Yeah…"

"She's leaving in a few days to check out the Peabody in Baltimore. She and two other students in her dance class have an audition."

Richard instantly perked at that. "That's amazing. She's a wonderful young woman, Amber. You should be proud of her."

"Oh, I am." Amber grinned. "I am so proud of what she accomplished. She set out after her dreams, you know. And she's letting nothing stand in her way."

"She gets that from her mother," He offered

tentatively, just to see what she would say.

"Well, I had to learn a few hard lessons," she muttered, her eyes flooding with shadows again.

There was pain there -- deep pain -- and he had to force his eyes back to the road so they wouldn't run into a tree while he was trying to figure it out.

"You wear them well," he felt compelled to add. Anything to make her smile again.

"I -- I really had to learn to stand up for myself, you know?" She spoke softly. "And it wasn't for my dreams or anything as noble as that, Richard. I did it for Lila."

They were nearing the furthest limits of the rough road and Richard gratefully pulled to the side and braked.

He turned to examine his... his Amber. She had changed out of the sensible flat black shoes she wore in the café and was now wearing a pair of black hiking boots. Although she'd kept her captain's jacket on -- she knew she would be returning to the café after this little excursion -- she had changed into a pair of hiking shorts that showed off miles and miles of soft dark skin.

He brought his eyes up to her face and found her biting her lip as she contemplated what to say next. He left that ball in her court.

"I was married once, you know," she began, closing her eyes before she turned to face him.

"I knew that." He nodded, silently urging her to continue.

"And well... He liked to make fun of my hobbies, of the things I loved... of me. And I didn't mean to do that to you, Richard."

"It's fine --"

"No, it's not." She took a deep breath and

mustered up a smile. "It's not fine, and it's not something a friend would do."

He winced at the word "friend," and his wolf growled in the back of his head. "Amber --"

"You tried to support me when you thought I was low. You didn't promise to make everything better or that you would fix things, you were just there. You have no idea how important that is to me."

"You can handle things on your own just fine, Amber. I know that."

"Yes, I know. And that's why I should not have made fun of your honestly just being there for me, Richard. That was a bitch move, one I would have slapped someone for. I commend you on your restraint."

"Amber, I know you wouldn't hurt me --"...*on purpose*. The words were there, unspoken, but hanging between the two of them.

"But I did. And you were opening up to me too. I have a feeling that's not something you do with too many people."

"Well, you know I am different," he agreed. "There are a lot of secrets I can't give away, a lot of secrets that aren't mine to give." He tried to explain. "But -- but if it's about me, then to the right person, I am an open book."

There. That should give her a clue about what he was feeling.

Just kiss her! his wolf growled. *You're being too human. She's not acting human now.*

Richard took a good hard look at Amber. She was stiff in her seat, like she expected him to verbally bash her or throw her apology back in her face. One hand was on her chest as if she was bracing herself for a blow and the other was on the door handle, like she was preparing for a quick getaway whether the car was moving or not. She looked... well, not scared but leery.

"And you were going to tell me about that open book before I went and laughed at you." She shook her head in recrimination. "I didn't mean to hurt your feelings, and it only had a little to do with you leaping to my rescue."

"My hair flowing, like a cape?"

"Well, that was cute." She snickered, looking away for a moment and then back up at him. "But mostly it was my own baggage."

"So... I remind you of something from your past."

"No!" She damn near shouted the word, she was so adamant. She reached out to him and gripped his arm with both hands, her eyes imploring him to believe. "You never have and you never will remind me of my past, Richard. You don't have it in you to be evil."

Then, as if she realized she had spoken too much, reacted too harshly, she pulled back a little.

"Evil --"

"So if anything, you remind me of the good things in my past, Richard. Only the good. And this woman who doesn't seem to know that you exist is a fool."

Do it! his wolf demanded. Richard felt his palms sweating, his heart pounding... He turned to face Amber and then just blurted out what he was thinking.

"It's you, Amber. You're the one who doesn't know I exist."

His next thought was *Oh, shit, what have I done*?

Chapter 5

Amber fled the truck.

She didn't know how she managed it, but she was out of the truck and walking along the path before Richard could call her name again.

Her? He was in love with her?

But -- but --

How could he love her? He didn't even know her!

She walked along the torn path created by so many others that passed before her and she didn't know how to feel.

Her? But --

Part of her, some part of Amber Graves was cutting cartwheels. Apparently she was still vital enough to pull a man like Richard.

God knows she tried her hardest not to notice him like that, not to notice his wide shoulders, his large hands, and that broad chest of his. Even when her fantasies were filled with his kind eyes and his kind touch, she always kept her little crush solidly in the realm of fantasy. He was a dream that was unobtainable. And really, it had nothing to do with her sex appeal or lack of it. It all had to do with her own trust issues.

As she walked, some small part of her began to notice things about her environment, like the gentle humidity that seemed to fill the area about a mile around Angel Falls. The dampness did a lot to cool her temper. But... but she really wasn't angry either. How could she be angry when Richard Strong professed his strong desire to get to know her better? That was amazing in itself -- so... maybe it was fear.

She was afraid. She paused as the thoughts ran

over her mind, stealing every other thought for a moment.

Yes, Amber Graves was a coward and she was admitting she was afraid. No, there was no fear that he would harm her like… like Todd. No, it was more of… it was… She was afraid of herself.

What would happen if she turned into the creature she was before? It had seemed like a dream to have Todd decide things for her, to handle the small issues that sometimes made daily life an annoyance. It seemed like an extension of his love for him to check up on her so much. It didn't seem controlling until her friends started to disappear and her neighbors began to shy away. And the thing that hurt her most was the fact that she allowed it to happen. She had smiled while Todd separated her from her remaining family and friends. He took away everyone who could help her and she let him, loving him all the more for his protective nature.

She was not afraid that Richard would do the same to her -- no, he didn't have an evil bone in his body. What Amber Graves was afraid of was turning into that simpering coward who needed her man to take care of everything for her. Or even worse -- becoming a man-hating bitch who would take her problems from her previous relationship out on the innocent man who just wanted to be with her.

Either way, it was a fucked-up situation and she didn't know what to do.

So she started walking, her mind trying to find a tether to hold her still through the raging storm in her mind.

"Amber!"

She blinked as she looked around her, not really knowing where she was.

Of course she was close to the falls -- everything after a certain point seemed to draw you in to the falls -- but she was sure they had stopped the truck near a path that led to some open campgrounds that were the farthest away from the falls.

"Amber!"

She slowly turned as her name was called again.

Richard.

No… she couldn't be around him now. She had to… she had to think things through.

She turned and took off running. Fear and instinct were driving her now, her fight-or-flight reaction well and truly tuned to flight. She darted off the path and into the woods, her thighs burning as she put as much distance between them as she could manage. Deeper into the dense woods she raced, ducking under branches and leaping over fallen logs. She had to get away… she had to…

She was a mess. Could she invite Richard -- or any man -- into this madness that was her life? How could she saddle him with the knowledge of her shitty past?

After being on her own for so long, she had come to realize that the fault lay with Todd and his abusive ways, but the fact remained that she was guilty of letting her situation get that far.

Him hitting her had been all him. She had done nothing to earn that disrespect, that anger. It was all on him. But she was the one who was stupid enough -- no -- badly deceived enough to let it happen and loved him all the more until his fists started flying.

What kind of a man hit a pregnant woman? What kind of a man felt the need to correct an adult as if she were a child? What kind of man let his own insecurity and lack of self-esteem matter so much that he took his anger and frustrations about his shortcomings out on the one person who loved him the most? And what kind of woman let that go for years before getting herself out of it?

So she needed to think. She was not that woman anymore, was incapable of being that naive ever again. But did that mean she was incapable of love as well?

She needed to think, to get away. So, like she had all those years ago, Amber Graves ran.

* * *

"Fuck!" Richard snapped as he leapt out of the truck and began to give chase to Amber.

Wait! his wolf called, his shadow suddenly looming before him, growing until it was a snarling wolf about the size of a large horse. *Leave her be.*

"No," he growled. "I need to get to her -- to explain --"

She needs to be alone, the wolf insisted, stepping into his path. But unlike any other shadow, this wolf had shape, form, and mass. Richard could not push past himself. *Give her time to run.*

"I need to explain --"

You need to let her process. Amber knows how to protect herself. She must accustom herself to this mating.

"She's scared."

She's strong, our human mate. The wolf circled him, the tufts of shadowed fur rippling as he brushed against his human's body. *She needs to run alone and think free for a time. This is a good thing.*

"She could get hurt," he snarled before he called out, "Amber!"

She will not.

He glared at his shadow before calling for her again. "She might. There are people out in these woods. They're only stealing now, but when there is a vulnerable female --"

She's a worthy bitch. She will defend herself if that happens.

"But you don't know what could happen, do you? The thieves could be turning violent. They're acting less fearful and more boldly. They could do anything to her. You know what has happened in these woods in the past. You -- why do I even listen to you?"

Me? his wolf yelped, the shadow standing up on two legs and looming over Richard. *You dare blame me for this?*

"You told me to tell her."

You should have told her seasons ago. With his arms akimbo, the wolf grew into a distorted twisted shape, the kind of monster only seen with the best special effects. Its lack of color and hints of its true dimensions were scarier than anything horror masters in Hollywood could ever hope to dream up. *Instead you sniff around like an untried cub, always on the fringes but never stepping up to take an alpha's place.*

His fur bristling, his wolf's mouth grew until it was a twisted parody of a muzzle filled with long sharp fangs and a long tongue that lashed out at the air with his every movement. His eyes were glowing red slits as his shoulders hunched forward, intimidating, and his tail shot straight out behind him.

"I should have waited --"

Waiting is what gets us into trouble! his wolf roared. *An adult plans for what he wants using knowledge and instinct. I've given us knowledge. You ignore our instincts. An adult invites the bitch in and if she refuses, he walks away to find another conquest. It's our way. It has always been our way. She's not one of us. She needs to know what we are. Heed me well, my other half. We are not human. We will never be human. We need to stop pretending to be!*

"But she is."

And she knows we're not.

"She doesn't know everything," he snapped, circling his wolf as it snarled in return. Richard's hair was starting to rise on the back of his neck. His muscles bunched, doubling his own mass as he paced around his shadow, stiff-legged, his fingers curled into claws.

Whose fault is that? Which one of us has caused us to lose our way? his wolf screeched before diving over him.

What would have passed through most others struck Richard like a flying fist from a pissed-off heavyweight boxer. The impact of his shadow's blow spun him around, knocking him on his ass as his wolf shot past. Pain exploded through Richard's face as his teeth snapped down on his tongue, tearing it and allowing blood to spill freely over his chin. His eyes widened as he fought for balance, lost it, and landed on his ass. The shadow loomed over him, dark and menacing, bending low to snarl in his face.

"The fuck?" Richard's voice had dropped into a gravelly tone that silenced the air around them. The birds stopped chirping, the insects stopped humming -- even the wind seemed to still as he slowly climbed to his feet.

Faster than the eyes could follow, Richard's fist lashed out backhanded, striking his shadow across the muzzle and sending the large wolf reeling. Before the dark shape of his wolf's dark body could impact the ground, Richard's foot lashed out, catching it in the center of its chest, sending it flying, skidding along the dirt of the path. It fell in a heap of flying dirt and torn leaves and branches.

Richard winced, feeling all the blows -- the one

his shadow had landed and the ones he'd returned in his fury -- but he didn't care. In essence he was kicking his own ass, but his anger and frustration overrode common sense. He ignored the bruises he could feel rising on his own chest from where his foot had connected with his shadow and advanced again, panting as he ignored his pain, wanting only to make his position known to his wolf.

"Don't you ever --"

Coward! his wolf roared as it leapt to his four paws and rushed Richard again.

"If I had waited --" Richard roared back. "If I had waited until --"

Until her stalker was caught? The sarcasm in his wolf's tones was as obvious as it was nasty. *Until she was no longer caring for her own heart with thoughts of you in her head? Until you grow a set of testicles and start acting like the wolf you could be --*

"I am a man!"

You're a wolf! You're a wolf in the guise of a human, but there is only the basest part of humanity within you. You're a wolf! You're a skinwalker! You're part of an ancient and honored pact that existed long before the murderers invaded our land and forced our people to merge with the native populations to survive. Our kind existed long before those who betrayed us out of jealousy and a lust for power. You're a creature of light and magic, a warrior who is supposed to stand for justice and stand in the way of those who would maim and destroy out of ignorance and fear. You're a being made of instinct and raw nature... and you seem to have forgotten that in your attempt to woo and fuck a human bitch. And until you can remember who you are and what you really stand for, you'd better forget about me as well.

Richard opened his mouth to respond, but with a

silent roar that shook his mind and stole his voice, his shadow leaped at him, this time passing through his stiff body.

Richard felt the impact, felt the tearing pain as his wolf rebelled, felt his wolf, his shadow, separating itself from him.

He grasped his chest in pain, falling to his knees as his shadow passed through him and disappeared, taking off down the same trail Amber had taken.

His heart... He had never felt such tearing pain. His breath was ripped from his body as he dropped to his knees, folding over until his forehead rested on the cool earth.

His body started shaking and his teeth clenched as pain enveloped him fully, so intense he could only see white lights flashing behind his tightly clenched eyes.

It only lasted seconds before the pain began to fade, but when he was able to take a deep shuddering breath, open his eyes, and lick his dry lips, he realized something was missing. His shadow, his wolf, his beast -- it had torn itself away.

As he sat there in the middle of the path, for the first time in his life he truly felt cold. His heart... his heart was... a huge chunk of it was missing and what was worse, his soul felt as if it had been rent asunder.

His body began to tremble as Richard Strong realized his wolf had abandoned him -- and for the first time in his life, he was truly alone.

* * *

Amber ran until her chest ached, until her legs burned and her mind went numb. There was such a blissful peace in thoughtlessness.

So she ran. She ignored the branches that reached out for her, never noticing how one snagged the gold

Planet Quest communications pin off her command jacket. She disregarded the slender twigs that tangled in her hair and lashed at her face. She just ran.

But finally her body had had enough. With a painful stitch in her side and her body uncomfortably warm, she came to a stop, leaning against a tree. As she bent over at the waist, panting for breath, she slowly began to realize she had no idea where she was.

Her body shaking with her ragged breathing, she lifted her head to look around and… Damn, she was at the falls. It appeared that all roads led to the damn Angel Falls.

Snorting at her own stupidity, she pushed away from the tree and made her way to the banks of the crystal-clear lake that was fed by the foamy, falling water of the falls. She knew it was safe to drink, the rocks acting as a natural filter, so she leaned over to cup a handful and wet her painfully try throat.

"What the fuck," she cursed at herself. "Amber… what were you thinking?"

Quick answer was that she was not. She had panicked and run away, something she was awesomely good at. But now that it seemed she had outrun some of her insecurities, she was left with the realization she had created an even bigger problem by running from Richard. Richard Strong was a handsome man, a solid one, and one that deserved more than her.

"Look at you," she snipped at herself, "making decisions for the man's own good. Are you channeling Todd Ritter?"

Saying that out loud so frightened her that she dragged her aching body to a boulder near the water and took a seat to regain her scattered thoughts. Sitting led to lying and before she knew it, she was drifting off on a sun-warmed rock under the midday heat.

* * *

"You know I own you, right?"

That deep, lyrical voice had her sitting up and jerking away. "Toddy!"

"You know I don't like that name, Amber," he growled. "You know how much it irritates me to be called by a diminutive."

This had to be a dream.

Amber looked around, and yes she was still sitting on her rock by the falls... but... but the landscape was different.

There was no green foliage around, nor the sound of the falls roaring gently in the background. Instead, where Toddy stood, the earth was a twisted dry thing. The air seemed arid and dust floated around him as he moved.

"I believe I don't care," she snorted. "I am not afraid of you, Toddy."

"But you fear my legacy." He sneered, and Amber felt the blood drain out of her face.

"You don't know what you're talking about --"

"Oh, don't I?" He laughed. It was an evil, sinister sound that made the hair on the back of her neck stand on end.

With a wave of his arm, a tendril of dead earth slammed into the pool beside her. She jerked as it emerged, holding onto the struggling form of --

"Richard!"

Toddy's laughter had her turning back to him in horror, before she spun back to Richard's dangling body.

She watched as the dead earth wrapped around his neck, strangling him as his feet kicked and he ripped at the thing holding him aloft.

It did no good. In fact, the dead earthen arm

tightened its grip.

It felt so real.

Amber could smell the dry dust, smell Toddy's old cologne, feel the water splashing her face as Richard struggled.

"Stop this, Toddy!" she screamed, but he only laughed harder.

She made to stand up, to beat that thing from around Richard's neck when Toddy spoke again.

"What do you care, Amber? You can't even listen to him tell you he cares about you."

"Stop it!"

"That he's growing to love you."

"Stop it, Toddy!"

"That he would die for you!" Richard's body jerked to his side. "Look at him, Amber. Another fool who's going to be choked to death by your love."

"I -- I --"

"Your love is venomous poison," he whispered as he stepped toward her, Richard's body dangling like a macabre ornament behind him.

"Any man you will ever love will be strangled by it, by me, Amber Rose Graves. They will be crushed under the weight of your rather pitiful charms, and they will be left crushed by what I left in you. You can never escape me, Amber Rose Graves."

He was right. Amber could feel the darkness surrounding her. The perfect glade with its sun-warmed rock was just an illusion. She was a danger to any man... anyone she decided to get into a relationship with. The specter of Toddy Ritter was too strong.

"No!"

As she began to shrink back into despair, as Toddy's face began to melt, as a dark, oily miasma began to flow from him and toward her, a voice called out to her.

"Don't believe it, Amber!"

Her eyes jerked up to see Richard finally breaking free from Toddy's hold.

"Richard!" she called out, and the rotting corpse of Toddy Ritter began to shrink back.

"You know your own mind, Amber," he insisted, stepping forward, moving toward her and her nightmare. "The past does not hold you in its chains."

With each step he took, purple flowers sprouted. Grass sprang up in his shadow and the sky lightened like an aura around him.

"I'm afraid, Richard," she called out as Toddy shrank back further with every step. "I don't want to hurt you!"

"Then don't." His eyes were steady and dark, his hair flowing around his wet body.

Richard was very much alive and very much naked. This… oh, yeah, this she liked.

"You let him win every time you allow your fears to control you. You let him win every time you run away from happiness. You let him win when you run away without facing what is troubling you. The future is a big place, Amber. It's big and bright and wonderful… but it's a dry desert if you can't even trust yourself… if you're alone because of fear and poorly thought out what-if scenarios."

"Richard… I -- I am so scared I am going to treat you like trash."

"Then don't."

"But --"

"You don't know that you will, Amber. And you never will until you trust yourself."

As Richard spoke, Toddy tried to reinstate

himself, pushing himself forward, his flesh now hanging from his body in rotten-smelling, slimy trails.

"You know you can't do this, Amber. I am a part of you."

"No!"

"Then tell him to back away," Richard insisted. "Show him he has no power here. This is not the place for him. This is a place for the future. And baby, it looks bright and shiny."

"Bright and shiny," she numbly repeated.

"Just for you."

"Just for me."

And just like that, Amber began taking control of her dream.

She looked over at the shocked Toddy and offered him a smile. "Bright and shiny, all for me."

With a wave of her hand, the dry earth began to boil, to pulse as a multitude of bright purple flowers flowed over the land. The sounds of the dry wind were replaced with the babbling of the falls. The dry air was suddenly filled with the perfume of citrus, of lavender and lilacs. The scent of Toddy and his rotting corpse of fear and anguish disappeared as if it were never there.

The sun shone down on her rock, warming her skin and she closed her eyes, lifting her face to bask in its warm glow.

"That's my woman," Richard whispered and she opened her eyes to see… Where did he go?

"Richard?" she called, but the effort of re-forming her past and tweaking her inner mindscape had left her exhausted. She would lie down on her rock, just for a moment, and then she would go and find him.

She had a lot to talk about with Richard -- there were so many things he had to understand. But most of all, she was willing to tell him she was willing to try.

But first, a nap… where the sun shone warmly and a cool breeze carried her gently into sleep.

Chapter 6

"There you are."

The same smooth, deep tones pulled her from her dream. Amber pouted, whining a bit because she had been about to kiss the sheriff... but having the real thing here was better.

She opened her eyes and her welcoming smile turned into a frown as she took in Richard's appearance.

His eyes were ringed with dark circles, his hands were shaking a little, but his complexion... his dark skin was disturbingly ashen. "Richard?"

"I'm fine." He offered her a smile, but it was a weak effort at best. In fact, it made him look like he was fighting back pain.

"What the hell --"

"We need -- I have -- Amber?"

"God, I am not worth all this, Richard. What did you do? Did you hurt yourself coming after me?"

She reached up, cupping his face, growing more alarmed as she felt his cool, clammy skin.

She rose to her feet, urging him down on the rock where she had dreamed. He looked like he needed assistance. "I can run back and..." She pulled her cell phone from her pocket, cursing as the strange Angel Falls effect once again kicked in and killed her phone reception. No one could ever understand why cellular phones and electronic devices sometimes refused to work here.

"I'm fine," he insisted, reaching for her. His grip was strong and sure as he urged her to sit beside him, but he... This was the worst she had ever seen Richard look. It was bad.

"No you're not. What's hurting?" she demanded,

growing a little distressed that he was hiding his pain.

"Amber... you know... You know I am not entirely human?"

"Of course." She nodded, relaxing a bit. "No one in this town really is. Sometimes I feel outnumbered," she joked lightly, doing her best to lighten the suddenly heavy atmosphere. "You preternaturals have us normals on the run... or in relationships." She offered him a wry grin.

He didn't smile back.

"Do you know what I am?"

"You mentioned something that the hunters were after, you mentioned Indian legend but... you never really went into any details," she finished in a rush. "What does... does that --"

"What I am is called a skinwalker, Amber. Do you know what that means?"

"Only from what I've seen in the movies," she mused. "Um... they're shape shifters who wear animal skins to change..."

"Forget what you have learned." His eyes were flat and serious. "None of it's true."

He took a deep breath and sat up a little higher, tilting his head to the side. A tangle of leaves and hair flowed over his shoulders and he slowly shifted, holding his body tightly as if he was in pain.

"Skinwalkers are... we are different than the legends."

Amber moved closer, tentatively reaching out to take his hand. His skin was so cold. "If this is painful... I mean you don't have to --"

"I have to," his voice sounded weak and rough, and the thought she had done this to him was almost overwhelmingly painful. "It involves... my wolf."

Amber nodded, trying to encourage him to speak

further if he felt the need to bare his soul. She didn't think it was necessary, but she would sit here and listen while being supportive. It was the least she could do after walking out on him the way she had.

"I am a skinwalker, not a witch. The public only knows bad things, evil things about skinwalkers, so we tend to keep to ourselves to prevent us from being hunted.

"The hunters --"

"Yeah, the hunters." He shook his head, running his free hand through his hair before looking up at her and sighing softly. "And there are the rest of us."

"Your friends who helped --"

"The hunters have a network and so do we. We try to support one another, to share information, and where possible, stop the hunters from harming people in their mad quest to stop us all."

"Why are they hunting you? I mean, besides the obvious. It was scientists that took Klintic… are they a part of this too?"

"No." He pulled his hands away and fisted them both in his lap, his eyes going dull and his breathing increasing as he stared at the ground between his legs. "No, they're something new that my people are aware of… though ANITA probably set back their program for years to come."

"You mentioned before that there was more than one group out there harming people. Why are these hunters trying to harm you? What they did to Winston and Bryan -- it all smelled of black magic and terrorist plots."

"They think they're ridding the world of evil, Amber. They're justified in some ways but they're way off base with everything else."

"So there are dangerous skinwalkers out there."

"Do you know why the skinwalkers are so hated, Amber?" His eyes flashed an unnatural red for a moment, and he almost appeared angry as he turned to face her. "They're so reviled and hated because the ultimate power, the ability to take on animal form with the aid of an amulet or an animal skin is achieved only when they murder someone they love and steal their essence to combine with their own. Every unnatural skinwalker murders to achieve his goals, Amber, and it's usually a family member."

She pulled away from him, her eyes going wide as she stepped back from him.

Todd. The uncharitable thoughts popped in her head and just as quickly she pushed them right back out. But the damage had been done. Richard glared at her as she reached out for him, a look she had never seen in his eyes before.

"I said unnatural, Amber." His voice fairly growled. "Do you think that for one fucking moment -- "

"No." She cut him off, raising both hands in not a defense manner, but more of an apology. "No, that's not you, Richard. You would never do anything to hurt any one of us. You're a protector."

He still glared at her for a moment before he struggled to his feet. He was panting hard, but he pulled himself to his full height.

"I am a member of a most noble and ancient race of beings. Some know us as Star Walkers and others as Anasazi. The Navajo called us Ancient Ones… or Ancient Enemies -- depends on who you're talking to."

"You're not going to tell me that you're three hundred years old," she protested, shaking her head. "Or older…"

"I am forty-one." He rolled his eyes at her, but he

did settle down a bit and took a seat on the rock. He was not as close as before, but he was sitting again. His shoulders slumped as if their weight was too much for him to hold, and he turned his tired-looking eyes back to hers. "I am forty-one but my line goes back hundreds of years, Amber. We were here before the Pueblo, before the Maya, before the Aztec. In fact, the Aztec worshiped my people for their ability to shape shift at will."

"You can shape shift --"

"Yeah, but it - it's not like -- My shadow." He stuttered as if he didn't know how to express his thoughts.

"Your shadow?" Now some of the things she'd noticed about him were beginning to make sense. She looked around for his shadow now, but... it wasn't there. She looked up as he began to speak again.

"It's a part of me. It's alive in a way. It's my other half."

"So hunters are after you because your shadow is alive? That sounds like the greatest Peter Pan complex I have ever heard of."

"Not that easy to --" He tried to explain again. "It's... Um... Okay. My people are called Anasazi. We have been here so long even our own lore can't tell us exactly where we came from or what our original names are, but we settled in what is now known as Utah, Nevada, and New Mexico. There are other places around the world, in places like Africa and China, but most of the ruins that have been discovered are around those areas. According to my own family history, we have always been at odds with humanity."

"How?" Amber shifted a little closer and could feel some of the tension ease out of him at her actions. "I want to understand."

"We moved there from God knows where just to be alone, just to live in peace with nature. Our homes were built inside mountain ranges, hollowed out and made specifically for protection, so we could see our enemies coming from a distance and could defend ourselves. When you have a special gift, you're destined to be persecuted or envied by others."

"And your people were... That explains some things about you."

"What do you mean?" He leaned closer to her and Amber gave him a small smile as she inched toward him.

"Your escape hatch in your house that leads to the woods out back? That's taking paranoia a bit far, Richard."

"It's not paranoia if they actually are out to get you," he sniffed. "And they're always out to get us."

"But why? Your people could stop them --"

"We don't kill, Amber. We contain and we remove the threat. Those hunters we took? They will stand trial for assault and larceny and anything we can throw at them that will stick. Since part of the falls is protected by presidential decree, they're looking at federal time and will be under close scrutiny for the rest of their lives."

"Yet there are others." Amber nodded in understanding. "There are always more. Within the insanity of one lies the mob mentality of others."

"Always others," he agreed as he scrubbed his hands through his hair. He rested his elbows on his knees and turning his head to stare at her from behind his long fall of silky black hair. "We were worshiped once, not that we asked for it... not that we participated in any way. The Aztecs, they worshiped us in their art and in their carvings. They worshiped us in their dances and with their religion, but my people could not perform the miracles the Aztecs had come to expect from their gods. So they decided to force us into becoming what they needed, into becoming the gods they had created legends about."

"How can they… I mean, you can only shape shift but that doesn't really seem magical. I've seen what Klintic and Angel do, and that's powerful magic. What you're saying seems to be closer to Winston and his shifting. How can a wolf become a god or do god-like things?"

"There were other lines, Amber. I am of the Lobo line, a wolf line that was among the first to see the danger humanity offered. There were other lines that didn't heed our warnings. They were lost when human sacrifice of mortals failed to deliver what they wanted."

"Human… I know the Aztecs were great farmers and astrologers and they sacrificed bastard children and enemies --"

"And the best, most athletic among them, and strangers who wandered in who maybe looked or behaved like my people. Then there were others who were too otherworldly to be human, like the line of Dragos that they called Quetzalcoatl. Those people who sprouted feathers or could fly were taken and sacrificed when they moved against us. Anyone carrying unusual characteristics was offered up to the gods in an attempt to own what they considered magic. When they discovered we couldn't make it rain or stop diseases that sometimes ran through the villages, they decided we were being selfish withholding our power. They started the drive to sacrifice us, to release the magic we were hording by sacrificing us to the larger, more unselfish gods."

He sat up, shaking his head sadly. "Whole family lines wiped out. The Dragos, The Felis, The Xainas... Whole lines brought to ruin and extinction because we couldn't stop the sun from shining so brightly or talk the clouds into making rain. So my people ran. We left South America and mixed with the Mayans. And when the Aztec followed we fled ever northward and wound up in the Southwest where we were watched with fear and uncertainty for many generations. For a long time it was considered taboo by most to associate with us."

"But you're still here." Concentrating on his family history was enough to drive back the specter of her own sad past. She moved closer.

"Remnants of what we once were." He sat up straight and she could not resist pushing his hair back behind his shoulders to expose his face. He still looked tired and gray, but the haunted, shocked look was beginning to ease. "We interbred with the Navajo and other nearby tribes. It was safer for us to spread out a little and it stopped inbreeding that would quickly become a hazard if we kept to ourselves in our mountain. Soon, our way of life was so intertwined with The People that our past was reduced to legends as our people abandoned their stone complexes, and the truth of us was nearly lost in history."

"But some people had to know about you -- I mean, that ability had to be used for survival at least."

"You have to understand that native culture is consumed with the characteristics of certain animals being used to shape the world and their own groupings long before we came on the scene. And suddenly here we were with the ability to shift into those animals that they had learned about from their religions and their own lore. It made our people special. Those chosen to wed with us were considered blessed, especially when those who mated with us produced children with our abilities. We breed true. Our people and their progeny became healers and teachers. We held an important role until some decided we were rising above our station, that as an orphan people we should be teaching them our magic and how to call upon the animals in their lore."

"And there was no magic involved." Amber nodded in understanding. "If I am following you, what you do is as natural as breathing is to the rest of us."

He nodded as he began to speak again. "We are born with our shadows and we can act independently of them. They're a part of us, but they're like the other half of our soul." He offered a tremulous smile for a moment before it slipped away. "My soul's mate is a bossy wolf shadow who thinks he knows what's best." His eyes narrowed at those words, and he turned to stare out into the woods. "And when there is a need we can combine and I become what my shadow is. I become my wolf and we act as one body, one mind, and one unit. It's a blending that is... I can't... there is no way to explain it. We become one, and I am Richard Strong of the Lobos Clan who is also a wolf."

"When we were tracking Klintic --"

"I was running recon in the woods. That wasn't all Winston."

"And the ones who were after Bryan and Winston?"

"They were looking for me and mine." He turned to look at her again. "Bryan explained about ANITA and how they back tracked her Internet searches and found us but... It's complicated, but they were hoping they had found more of my kind."

"So all that mess of stinky water and ash..."

"Traps to capture me and my shadow. One

cannot exist without the other for long, Amber. Without my shadow I will soon wither away and die."

"They're really out to kill you."

"Are you surprised?" He gave her a side-eye that reminded her of those documentaries about wolves in the wild. It was... different, animalistic in a way. But she felt no danger from him or his revelations.

"They think it's their job, that they're protecting humanity against crazed killers who do magic and live to cause suffering and destruction. And in a way, they have done humanity a great service while at the same time taking out an ungodly number of the innocent right along with the guilty. They refuse to listen and to learn, they're so set in their mission."

"You talk like there are skinwalkers that need to be taken out."

"The unnatural ones. The ones that need to murder and kill to get the power to shift. Jealousy is a powerful emotion, Amber, and it can force you to do some... some very wrong things."

"Evil things." She shuddered, for a moment recalling Todd's eyes as he glared at her, remembering the feel of his hands as they gripped her by the arm and shook...

"Very evil." His words pulled her away from the memory and she gave him her full attention again, pushing aside the painful remembrance as if it were an annoying fly. She would deal with it later. For now she needed to pay attention to Richard.

"Some of the shaman were afraid they would lose their base of power, so they wanted my people to teach them their shifting magic so they too could fly like an eagle, swim like a fish, or spy like a coyote. There is no way to teach shifting to a person who was not born with the natural skill. You have it or you don't. It's like trying to teach someone with brown eyes to have green ones. It's impossible without the aid of science and in this case, science and magic. They devised a ritual using the bones and the remains of our ancestors. They desecrated the burial grounds of my people and they used our own genetics against us. They found a way to trap us, to take our shadows and to murder the human part. They learned to contain our shadow by trapping it within an object and to harness its shifting ability. This object is usually the natural skin of the animal the skinwalker becomes. They take this skin infused with their shadow as they murdered the human body, and they use it to change forms."

Amber felt a chill run up her spine as he spoke. There was no ounce of doubt in his words. This was the truth coming from the mouth of one who had personal experience with such trauma.

"Since my people married into families where the shaman tradition was strong, it was usually someone from within that family circle who did the trapping and the killing."

"That is disgusting." Amber wrinkled her nose at the thought of a trusted loved one turning on another with such murderous betrayal. "How did... I mean, you're still here... your family line --"

"We escaped again. We ran back to our mountains and we hid in the woods, and some of us moved east. We divided and ran but for those who wanted power, our actions only served to inconvenience them. And when we were scattered and running, a new threat came. The settlers, the land grabbers, the white men and women who wanted our land came and once again our people were called to come and help protect the native peoples."

"Your people came."

"Some of us at any rate. Family loyalty." He looked rueful as he said that. "A lot of us washed our hands of The People and moved to Canada or farther back south now that the Spanish had gone and the might of the Aztecs and Maya was broken, but some stayed and tried to help The People. Family ties are strong things, difficult to repair but almost impossible to kill. So we came and we assisted. We aided those in need and because of some of those unscrupulous ones, who were wearing stolen shadow skins and killing the settlers, we were slaughtered by those we had come to protect who feared us still, and now by those we were protecting against."

"Your people turned against you."

"You see, some still desired our power, our magic, and those made pacts with the invaders. Those unnatural skinwalkers worked with the invaders for a time and began hunting us down so they could do more dark ceremonies and steal our shadows. So many innocent people died, Amber. So many lives lost because these hunters thought they had a real natural skinwalker. Eventually the settlers began to fear them, the unnatural ones, and the hunters broke off into groups when they realized they were just murdering for the sake of the magic. Those they once aided began to turn on them too, trying to drive the white man out of their lands. The lore of how to trap us and steal our shadows was lost, except for those in long-lived hunting groups and those unnatural shadow walkers who still roam the earth."

"So you're a natural skinwalker."

He nodded.

"But I can't help but notice…" She looked down over the scrub grass and sand that surrounded this bolder they both sat on. She could see her shadow, see the legs shifting as she moved closer to him. "Richard, where is your shadow?"

"Gone."

"Is it trapped?" She lurched to her feet, watching as her shadow did the same before she turned back to him. Can we..."

"He left, Amber."

"What?"

"He got fed up with me and my humanity and he's gone."

"Why... I mean how... He's killing the both of you."

"He was angry because --"

"Richard --"

He suddenly turned toward her, his hair flying out around him like a cloak as he rose to his feet. "He left me because I was not... not wolf enough, not man enough to catch you."

Chapter 7

Richard watched as the angry, determined Amber Graves kind of sank in on herself. He hadn't meant to blurt out his problems to her, but the tear in his soul was beginning to bleed all kinds of emotional pain and he was getting tired, so damn tired.

"I -- I --"

"It's not your fault." He sighed, reaching up and gripping her hands in frustration. "None of this is your fault."

"I never -- I... Jesus, Richard. I don't have issues; I have subscriptions and enough of those to sell at news stands."

"You don't have to make things up, Amber." He snorted. "But I just wanted you to know how I really felt. And by your actions, I think I can guess where you stand." The smile he offered to her was rueful and filled with the pain that was now slowly beginning to consume him, but it was the best he could do.

He was soul sick and hurting, his wolf had turned against him, and now he was beginning to think maybe it was right. Maybe he should have immediately taken the direct approach with her, told her how he felt from the beginning. He flirted with her because he flirted with everyone he knew. It was just part of his nature to be open and friendly. But maybe he should have told her it wasn't just social niceties with her, that he was deathly serious when it came to her.

"My ex was an ass."

Her words stopped him cold. He turned to look at her, to really look at her and froze. Her hands were fisted at her sides, her body trembling.

"Amber --"

"I'm not telling you because I think we need to trade dark pasts. I'm not telling you because I want your pity." Her dark eyes met his and in them he read courage and determination. "I'm not telling you this because I want to trade who had the shittiest deal. I had enough therapy and I know who I am and what I'm capable of. I'm telling you because you need to know why I am the way I am."

"You don't have to tell me anything you don't want to." He stepped closer, reaching out to cup her shoulders in his hands. "I understand --"

"He beat me, Richard. My ex, Todd Ritter, he beat me so badly sometimes I wanted to die."

Richard froze as anger rolled over him in waves. "He beat you --"

"I met Todd when I was just a scared little girl playing at being an adult." She smiled sadly and took a step back, taking a seat on the rock once more. "He was beautiful and kind and knew just how to look for women with low self esteem. He was really good at that, reading a crowd and reading people. He knew just what to do and what to say."

Richard stepped closer to the boulder, closer to her.

"He separated me from my family, and I let him. He was white, you see, and they didn't think much of that to begin with. They thought I was going to college and getting above myself. And he read that about them and used it to drive a wedge between my mom, my sister, and me. When he had me where he wanted me, with my family all but disowning me, he asked me to marry him." She looked up at him and he saw something of the younger girl she had been. "I lapped it all up, every word he said. So I got married and I got pregnant and then I got the bright idea to help us out by dropping out of school to save money and taking small accounting jobs to bring in extra cash."

She tilted her head as if lost in memories, before she blinked twice and turned her head to look at him.

"Those were some of the happiest memories I've ever had, Richard. He treated me like his queen. Then his parents died so we moved out of town to the house they left him. I didn't even tell my family where I was going or give them my new last name so they could track me down. They didn't support me so I wanted nothing to do with them. I didn't know it was because they could see what kind of man Todd really was."

"He betrayed your trust."

"He betrayed more than that." She laughed, her wild tangle of curls bobbing around her face as a sharp wind blew through the trees, carrying the bitter sound away from them.

"The first time he hit me he apologized and I forgave him. He had graduated but there weren't many jobs for an actor in Maryland. His parents had died and left some bills that had to be paid off, so money was tight. He started working at a bar at night and was waiting tables during the day and... and I figured he snapped a little. I forgave him and he promised to never do it again. But he did and this time he told me it was my fault. I didn't have the house clean. I was six months pregnant and..." She shook her head before lying back on the rock. She looked like a cute kitty basking in the sun.

"He hit me and I believed it was my fault. I wasn't keeping the house clean and I needed to take more accounting jobs to help. Then he was drunk because his customers kept buying him drinks, and he took them because I was never there to talk to him like I used to do. And then it was because I was too busy for him. And after Lila was born, he stopped making excuses. He just wanted to hit. Everything in his life was out of control, and keeping me in control with his fists and his words made him feel more like a man."

"Amber, I would never raise a hand to you in anger."

"I know." She rubbed her arms. "It was all him and only him. You just don't have that in you. And by the time I realized I was in some very real trouble, Lila was almost one and he wasn't even making up excuses. Believe it or not, that's what got me out. He had me hemmed up in the living room when Lila began to cry. He was going for her and I realized that if I stayed there, he would he hitting her next. So I picked up my prized possession, my die cast metal figurine of the *Planet Quest*, and I bashed him over the head."

She said it so matter of factly that Richard just gaped at her.

"Then I tied him up, went to the bank and took all the money out of the account. It was a joint account, and I put most of it in there, so I had a right. Then I went to the police station and reported the assault. I also told them that I tied him up so I could get away with my daughter. I told them that I feared for my life and while they were taking photos of my face and body, I contacted a social worker and got an emergency placement. He was picked up and brought in. I identified him and got a restraining order. I jumped from homeless shelter to homeless shelter until I could swing a legal separation. After a year of hard living with Lila, he didn't show up for the divorce proceedings so it went through uncontested with special circumstances. I found my way here when Lila was about two and a half and was doing part-time work at Chloe's Diner. She let me keep Lila in a back station and the other waitress spoiled her rotten. Chloe was a wonderful old lady, was great at manning the café, but was horrible at books. So I started helping her out and saved her a lot of money when I found some major mistakes her bookkeeper was making. She admired that and said my talents were wasted on tables and put me in the office. When she found out I was staying in a homeless shelter and why I hadn't finished my degree, she gave me the apartment over the shop and insisted I finish my degree online. It was all brand new back then, and so exciting…"

She threw her hands over her head and arched her back, stretching a little, and Richard felt his mouth go dry.

"When she was ready for retirement, she let me buy the shop and I changed it into the *Planet Quest* Café."

"So… so you're not too fond of men…" Richard knew he couldn't compete with ghosts from the past.

"Oh, God, man, I love men." Amber laughed. He looked up to see amusement shining in her eyes. "I'm not a man-hating bitch, Richard. That's not why I ran."

"So you're just not attracted to me."

"Wrong again." Her laughter stopped as she sat up. "I'm not carrying around any hurt feelings or lost in my pain like a Lifetime channel special, Sheriff. I'm just glad I got out when I did. Some of the women in the shelters…" She shook her head. "It's not pretty. But the one thing that bothers me, Richard -- I don't want to --"

She inhaled sharply and rose to her feet. "I know what I am. I know what I'm capable of. I'm not afraid of men or of you… but I don't want to start treating you like… I don't want to second guess every move you make."

"What? I don't understand."

"I don't want to start a relationship and then dump all my old baggage on you."

"You think that --"

"I don't know what I'll do, Richard. You're the first man I've ever been attracted to since Todd."

She flushed a little at that comment and Richard felt his heart skip a beat. She wasn't rejecting him. She thought he was attractive.

"I mean --" she started.

"You think you can make my decisions for me now?"

"Huh?" She looked a bit confused at that.

"You think you have the right to decide for me, if I want to take the chance?"

"No..." She trailed off.

"But that's what you're doing now. You're taking away my right to even try."

"I... but... I was... protecting..."

"Who made you my protector, Amber Graves?"

* * *

His words threw her. Amber stood there, staring at one of the hottest men she'd ever run away from, and for once she didn't know what to say.

"Richard..."

"I can understand if you don't think I'm worth your time -- hell, sometimes I don't think I'm worth your time. But if you reject me, let it be because you don't want me and not out of some belief that you know what's best for me."

She blinked as she stared at him, flabbergasted.

Had she... was she deciding for him? Like Todd...

She remembered the day she left quite vividly. She remembered the warm, salty taste of her own blood filling her mouth. She recalled the flash of white and that moment of numbness before her left eye exploded in a pain so sharp it stole her breath. It had felt like he had knocked her eye back into her brain and she'd dropped to the ground in shock. She remembered the tight feel of his fingers wrapped like steel bands around her arm as he jerked her back to her feet, the sound of his hand connecting to her cheek before a bright, hot pain exploded in her face. She remembered the tears flowing from her eyes, the snot clogging her nose as she begged him -- she'd begged that bastard -- to stop. She remembered the feel of his fist as it connected with her ribs, how she felt them cave in a little before the breath was stolen from her body, how her breath raced and how her whole body shuddered in pain. Then she remembered the fear when he screamed at her, "If you don't shut that little bitch up, I'll make her be quiet." It was that declaration that had her taking arms -- well, spaceship -- against him and knocking his ass out cold.

She'd stood over him for a long moment, listening to her baby wail in the other room. She always made sure that he was away from Lila when he lost his temper even if she had to force him to chase her. It was a little eternity she stood there, fear holding her hostage as she wondered if he was alive or dead.

His groan had her leaping into action. She tied him up with nylon stockings. She threw some clothes in a bag and all the diapers for Lila she could stuff in plastic bags and ran to her car. She drove to the ATM and wiped out their meager savings on her way to the police station.

She remembered the hush of silence as she burst into the station and how a female cop had been swiftly elected to come to her aid. She must have looked a sight, her nose seeping blood, her hair torn out in patches, her crying baby on her hip.

She'd never regretted her actions, only how long it had taken her to react. And she was very comfortable with the male officers who escorted her with the female cop back to her house to retrieve more clothing and food for baby Lila.

She made sure she had therapy so she could have a normal life... but what kind of normal life was she leading if she was afraid to even date a man because of what she might do in the future?

She was being... she was being an ass.

"Richard." She shook her head. "I - I -- I'm about as crazy as a bag of cats."

"Then you fit in with the rest of the weirdoes in this town," he joked, and Amber had to return his smile. She moved over as he moved up to sit on the rock beside her.

"You ran from me, Amber. Do you know how that made me feel?"

"Bad, I assume." She hung her head for a moment before peering at him from beneath her lashes. "Angry."

"Angry." He nodded. "Just a little. But I felt sad and unworthy, Amber. I -- and there's the guilt."

"Over what? But you didn't know --"

"I was guilty over what my shadow was doing."

"He thinks for himself, yes?"

"He is the animal half of me, Amber. He thinks like an animal, an apex predator." He flushed brightly under his dusky skin and took a deep breath as if fortifying himself. "Amber, my shadow has been following you around."

"Huh?"

"My wolf. He is as enamored of you as I am. He's

taken it into his head to follow you around. Because he is a wolf, he really has no boundaries." His blush grew. "Everywhere --"

"Everywhere?"

"Everywhere. When you're in the bathroom, when you're in your office and working... and he follows you home at night."

"At night?" She knew she sounded a little sick now, but the thought of what she'd been up to at night replayed in her head like a filmstrip.

"At night." He nodded, looking a little fearful. "And what's worse, whatever he sees... I can see."

"Say what now?"

"I saw... I mean... I know..."

"You saw me... in my most private moments --"

"I didn't mean to." His shoulders shook as he turned to face her. "You have an amazing 'O' face, by the way."

"Fuck you," she shouted, unable to stop herself from balling up her fist and punching him as hard as she could on his shoulder.

"Ouch --"

"You saw me, Richard?"

"I didn't make him do it. Sometimes he just does what he wants. I can't stop him or pull him back when he is doing something. And it's not all the time, he just seems to have the knack of spying on you when you're at your most intimate. Besides," he admitted, rubbing his shoulder as he slid down further on the rock, out of punching range. "I wanted you before then. Seeing you getting off, calling out my name... It only made me want you more, made me believe I had a chance with you."

"So you're a voyeur and your wolf has been perving on me --"

"I am not," he defended, drawing himself up enough to cross his arms and glare at her. "I -- he does what he wants. I'm just... I go along for the ride until he comes back."

"So where is he now?" she growled. "I have something I want to say to him. He can understand me, right?"

"Yes." He seemed to slump as he sat there. "He can understand you just fine."

"So where is he?"

"That's the problem," He admitted. He sighed, and the sad sound seemed to come from his soul. "He's gone."

"Gone? Where?" She was growing concerned again. During show-and-tell hour at the rock, he'd seemed to be growing weaker despite unburdening his soul.

"I don't know. We fought --" He broke off and placed his right hand over his heart. "He... we never really disagreed like this before, Amber. We've never fought like that. Our fights are usually with words. This time he tried to hurt me, to force his leadership upon me, and it doesn't work that way. Man and animal have to be in harmony for us to exist and... and we're at odds. He tore himself away from me and I can't -- I don't know where he is."

"But you said you can't be apart." Her irritation fled in the face of her sudden worry. Richard was looking pretty banged up, bleeding in places, and she'd never seen him in such a depressed state. This couldn't be healthy for him.

"Well, he couldn't have gotten far. Did you try calling him?"

"Here, wolfy wolfy?" he asked, a little sarcasm settling in his tones. "It doesn't work like that."

"Then how does it work?"

"I don't know," he admitted after a moment of silence. "We've -- I mean, he's never left like this before."

"Then we'll just have to find him," Amber declared. "And then I'll give the little voyeur a piece of my mind."

She stood up, determined to set out on her path, but stopped when he grabbed her hand.

"Amber... what about..."

"Richard." She didn't want to go back to relationship-speak, but he deserved to know how she felt. "I do find you attractive."

"Enough to masturbate to," he muttered under his breath.

"I masturbate to Tom Hiddleston and Hugh Jackman too." She snorted, her embarrassment about being caught easing a little. "And LL Cool J and that gay porn star Colton Ford..."

"I get the picture," he grumbled. "But you weren't calling out their names in a fit of passion.

"You're closer." She smirked then moved in closer to him, close enough to smell his body soap and the scent of freshly churned earth that clung to him after his fight with his shadow. His dark eyes seemed to glow amber for a second and she inhaled sharply. Richard Strong wasn't human. He was something entirely different.

"Amber --"

She smiled at his woebegone look. "I... I'm not promising anything, Richard. But I think I would like..." Her words trailed off as she thought about what she was doing. This man was complicated, more complicated than she'd ever imagined. And there were people out there actively trying to kill him. Plus he came with his own living alter ego who could separate from him and exist on its own for a time. That his second half, his soul's mate as he called it, was an animal -- a wolf -- only made his situation even more complex.

"Are you saying we should date?" he asked, his eyes lighting up more. "I mean, I think we should. I think we should have been dating for a while now, but I had to get the courage to let you know. Funny how I'm not afraid of anything preternatural or human in this town. Have never been... but the thought of asking you... of baring my soul to you... it's twisting me into knots, Amber."

She stepped back and ignored his wince as her gaze traveled over his body. God, he was handsome, even with bits of twigs and leaves in his hair. His chest was broad and well padded with muscle. His thighs seemed to want to burst through the material of his uniform pants. His utility belt hung low on his slim hips and tiny waist and... who could forget the salamander ladder? His arms were corded with muscle, strong muscles that could take the abuse of him swinging himself up holding onto that metal bar and connecting with each rung as he climbed higher.

She looked him over and remembered all he had done for her, how he cheered her up when she was down, how he hadn't even tried to stop her from going on the crazy adventures that hit this town like a tsunami. Even when going after those crazy hunters, he had never shoved her behind him or insisted she stay behind. He quietly protected her while she did what she felt was best to help save their friends. He respected her strengths and never once tried to stand in her way, even when she realized her foolishness in going against supernatural beings with no protection or knowledge of how they would react.

Plus, he treated her like a lady. Always, he treated her like a lady. He respected her opinions and he flirted with her like he was declaring his intentions. Maybe he had been.

"Amber?" His head tilted to the side a little as he awaited her response. He wasn't forcing her -- just waiting for an answer.

Damn, she was an idiot.

"We should find your shadow and then go find a quiet spot to fuck."

"Amber!" His face burst into color as he stared at her, mouth open in shock.

"You've been courting me for some time, Sheriff. You've protected me while letting me go about my own way. You never harmed me or treated me like I was a weak little human. You've shown me nothing but respect and high regard. I like that." She took a step closer to him. "I find it very arousing, Richard."

She took another step, closing the gap between them as she reached up and caressed the side of his smooth face. His skin was baby soft.

"It would take so little for me to fall in love with you. It's only my own fears of the future that are holding me back. And if I don't face my fears I'll never be a complete person."

"You're a wonderful person." His hand cupped hers where she was still caressing his face, holding her to him. She could feel the roughness of his hands, a working man's hands, and wondered what they would feel like on her body. "You're beautiful, and honest, and so filled with life --"

"You're an amazing being, Richard. I know your personality. How long have we been friends? I know you a little better now. And I'm going to try to trust myself and trust you."

He moved in closer, muttering her name, "Amber," as his lips dropped to tease hers with the barest of caresses.

"Besides," she whispered just before his lips took hers. "You've seen my 'O' face. It's only fair that I get to see yours."

Then his lips were on hers, stealing her breath and making her world twist on its axis. His lips were soft and full, mobile as they caressed hers before his tongue slipped out and teased her mouth open.

She moaned, closing her eyes as she opened her mouth, inviting his tongue inside, letting it tease hers in a game of tag that soon had her tasting his mouth, breathing in the wild scent of him.

His arms wrapped around hers, pulling her close to him, right up against his hard body. She could feel his hardening cock, a thick ridge pressed up against her stomach, and her knees went a little weak. Her arms came up to wrap around his neck, to burrow in his wild fall of silken hair until she could caress the hard tendons and soft skin of his neck.

He moaned deeply, his whole body shuddering, and she found herself quaking right along with him as he lifted her off her feet.

Her legs went around his waist, trying to get her aching pussy to rub against him, to give her some friction before she passed out from this pleasure. One leg went around his waist and her world shifted…

No, her world tilted as Richard stumbled back.

He hit the boulder behind them, breaking off the kiss as his ass slammed down onto the stone. He barely managed to jerk her legs up and out of danger as he collapsed back, hard, his arms holding her safe.

She looked up into his red face as he offered her

a tentative smile.

"Sorry. I -- I'm kind of... shaky..."

His shadow was gone, she recalled as she righted herself on his lap. It must be making him weak. The man could jump his body up a metal ladder using only his upper body strength and he was nearly collapsing over her small weight. Yeah, they needed to get his shadow back and fast.

She smiled and dropped a kiss on the tip of his nose. "New plan. We find your shadow and then we go back to my place and fuck like rabbits."

"Amber." He feigned shock at her language, but she could feel his cock lurch against her at her words.

"I talk dirty," she whispered as she dropped one more kiss on his lips and pulled herself to her feet.

"I know." His voice had dropped low with a dark growl in its tones. "I've seen."

"Then you know we'd better hurry. I've got to see my kid off for the weekend and then it's you and me, buddy... and a jar of honey."

"Yes, ma'am." Richard's eyes were all but glowing as he rose to his feet, taking a moment to steady himself before he reached for her hand. "Shall we?"

"Yes. Let's," she answered as he pulled her back up the path.

She'd found the man of her dreams... the man who figured in a lot of her dreams. And she was about to make those fantasies a reality.

Chapter 8

"Stupid human," the wolf grumbled as he ran on swift silent paws through the forest. His incorporeal feet danced over the rocks and fallen trees that stood in his way and he blindly ran. "Bitch would be ours if he but remembered who he is," it grumbled.

It was angry and hurting. It had never meant to part from his human side so dramatically, but... but the anger it felt... the pain and the sense of betrayal.

"If he rejects us so much, let him see how his life is without us together."

The wolf ran blindly on until... until a scent caught his attention.

Whirling on silent paws, the shadow wolf slowed to a canter and then a walk, his nose to the ground as he began to follow the scent of Amber.

A few feet from where he first picked up the scent, he found what he was seeking. It was the small gold pin that she wore on her human clothing. It was a piece of Amber... but it wasn't on the path she'd taken.

He inhaled deeply, bending to pick the gold thing up when his legs began to tremble in fatigue.

This confused the alpha wolf, as he should be able to function many hours without being attached to his human half. He tried to step back, to use his mystical sense to find his human half when another wave of weakness swept over him.

He found himself falling, collapsing to his side, and he couldn't understand why. He whimpered, trying to call for help, to call his human half, but the sound refused to leave his throat.

The sound of footsteps made him roll his eyes upward, for he could no longer lift his head, and he froze and as and fear vied for supremacy within his mind.

"Hello, Skinwalker,"

The woman was tall with dark skin and hair... and the stink of wrong magic surrounded her. Within her hands was a small clay pot. The sight of that pot sent terror sliding down his spine yet he had no idea why.

"It's a good thing you creatures are so predictable." She smirked. "All I had to do was find the token of the one you're ensnaring with your dark powers and it led you right into my trap."

She moved closer, dropping to her knees as he tried to shift into a tiny pinprick of dark or to rise up enough to scare her. Neither tactic was working.

"What were you planning on doing with the woman?" she asked as she uncapped the jar. "Were you going to sacrifice her for more power? Were you going to just use her until you found someone else to worship you?"

The jar was slammed down beside him and she sneered once more.

"You want to be a god, to be treated as a miracle, to use and abuse the people who you trick? Well, that's not happening today, Skinwalker. With you trapped here, he'll have to follow. And when I have both of you, I'll ensure that you can never harm another human."

The shadow wolf felt, for the first time ever, terror as the mouth of the jar came closer and closer.

"Fucking piece of filth," she snarled as he pressed the jar to his face and...

There was a sucking sound, and the world began to spin nauseatingly, wildly, and the light vanished. He felt his connection to his human half weaken and all but disappear as his world became cold and dark.

"I'll set a trap for one cannot exist without the other… and when you're together, I'll make the world just a little more safe for decent human beings."

Then came a rough grating sound that made the shadow-wolf realize what had happened. He was trapped in that jar of hers somehow, and he couldn't break free. He tried to throw his head back, to warn his human, but soon all awareness disappeared.

He was alone in the dark, cold… and so afraid…

* * *

"I'm gonna miss you, Sugar Pea."

"Mom!"

"What? I have to get my teasing in somehow. You won't be here long for me to mess with and I have to get in my quota of Lila baiting."

"You're strange." Lila laughed before wrapping her arms around Amber.

"So are you," Amber reminded her, pulling back to drop a kiss on her nose.

"I get it from you." Lila chuckled, returning the gesture before pulling away.

They were standing outside the *Planet Quest* Café while Lila's friends waited impatiently in the beat-up VW bus.

"Lila!" one of the three girls called out, beeping the horn. "We're burning daylight!"

"Coming!" she called back before giving her mother one last hug. "Now," she spoke seriously to Amber, gripping both of her hands. "I already set up the work schedule for next week. Cook is requesting a day off to get some tattoos from Snake, something about protective totems or something. I already called in the delivery orders from our distributor. They should be here next Thursday to avoid the weekend delivery fees. Bryan has the house phone and the business phone wired for sound. If the creep calls back, I'm sure he can trace him within moments… at least that's what he promised me."

"Lila…" Amber groaned, rolling her eyes at her daughter's antics. "I can take care of myself."

"I know that." Lila's voice went up an octave then she smirked at her mother. "And I'm sure the good sheriff will assist in taking care --"

"Lila! Honestly." Amber fought the blush that wanted to rise. She didn't need her daughter talking about her sex life.

"I saw how you both came back from the woods. You can't keep your eyes off each other. I expected to find hickies or something."

"I'm old enough to know better than to make out in the woods, young lady." Amber tried to interject some motherly authority in her voice but knew she'd failed when her daughter continued to leer.

"Or adult enough to make out where the marks won't show."

"Lila!"

The beeping of the horn prevented her from saying anything else.

"Coming!" Lila yelled back before grinning at her mother once more. "And tonight, you can --"

"That's enough young lady." Amber couldn't fight the blush this time. "Besides, the good sheriff isn't feeling so hot."

He wasn't. They searched for hours before Richard had to call it off for the day. Amber had to return home to see her daughter off to Baltimore and the Peabody Institute, and he was growing weaker by the second. At one point, he thought he felt his wolf calling for him, but by the time they got to the spot he was sure his wolf was waiting, nothing had been there.

After that, Amber could see him visibly getting weaker.

"Why don't you go and tuck him into bed?" Lila suggested.

"Lila --"

"What, Mom? That man needs someone to look after him. He can use my room. I mean, I don't think he should be alone right now." For the first time a hint of worry entered Lila's voice. "Have you called Dr. Chase?"

"If I think it's necessary, I will." Amber had never lied to her daughter and she wasn't about to start now. "I'll keep an eye on him."

"Good." Lila picked up her backpack, the ratty old bag she used in lieu of a pocketbook, and backed away. "Student Housing has dorm rooms set up for us and I'll call as soon as we get there. I have my emergency cash and we will take turns driving if need be, though it's only a three-hour drive. We have GPS in case we get lost in the wilds of Baltimore, and the cell phones are charged."

"Good girl." Amber jerked her daughter in for one last hug before stepping back. "Be careful."

"It's how you reared me to be!" Lila shouted as she ran to the VW bus and slid in back.

Amber stood there until the rusted blue beater was out of sight then turned back to the café. When did Lila get so old? She was like a little self-contained adult now. She recalled those toothless grins and those tiny hands tugging at her skirt... There was no doubt about it. Her daughter was nearly an adult, and Amber was getting old.

She stepped into the café and saw Richard sitting at his usual spot, his head resting on crossed arms that were resting on the counter. He wasn't doing so well.

The moment they made it back to Angel Falls proper, he'd called his deputy and told him he was going to clock off early for health reasons.

Deputy Markus had been sympathetic and decided to work a double shift, putting the sheriff on an on-call status in case something came up that was too big for him to handle on his own.

Now, looking around the nearly empty café, Amber made an executive decision. "Taking off early," she called to her cook as she gripped Richard by the arm.

"About time," Cook called back, his voice amused as he peeked around the swinging kitchen door. "I'll close up tonight. You going to take the sheriff…" He paused as he got a good look at Richard's lackluster self. "… home?"

"Not feeling too good," Amber agreed. "I'm going to take him upstairs and let him camp out in Lila's room so I can keep an eye on him."

"I'll send up soup later," Cook assured her and Amber nodded as she prodded a half-comatose Richard to his feet.

"Thanks," she called out. "I'm sure he'll need it soon."

That said, she urged a quiet Richard toward the back stairs and up into her apartment.

"I can just go home," Richard said as Amber got him through her front door. "I know you didn't intend to spend this evening babysitting."

"I care about you, moron," Amber joked as she led him to her bedroom. "And I wouldn't send a dog home feeling like this, let alone the man who is going to be gracing my bed."

"Thank you." He mustered up a grin for her, but it was a pale imitation of his usual robust smile.

"You've never been parted this long from him before?"

"Not like this," he agreed as she led him into her bedroom and he paused, looking around her private domain.

Her bedroom was painted in soft, muted shades of mint green and rich chocolate brown. A nature theme was reflected in the framed petrified leaves that hung on the walls and in the massive headboard of her natural wood, king-sized bed. The bedspread was a soft, silken green that matched the walls and was trimmed in a silvery metallic thread.

Everything was neat and orderly, from the dresser tops that held a multitude of candles in holders waiting to be lit to the wooden trunk with a huge plush pillow top that was situated against a massive window that overlooked the treetops in the distance, the beginning of the woods that housed the falls.

Her room smelled of vanilla and lemon, two scents that he loved, and of Amber herself.

"Kick off your shoes and stay awhile," Amber invited as she opened a door that led to an en suite bathroom. "Bathroom's in there. I'll get you something to wear and you can rest a bit."

"You have men's clothing?" he asked, eyebrow raised in question.

"I have a lot of Angel's things around here," she offered. "He's my best friend and we've spent more time up in each other's spaces than most. We were both alone and needed someone to cling to."

"And now he has Klint." Richard nodded. "I understand. No matter how awful life got, I always had my shadow."

"I'm so sorry, Richard." Amber crossed back to him and pulled his stiff body into a hug. "I can't begin to think... I can't even imagine what you're going through."

"He'll find his way home." Richard tried to sound hopeful, but even to Amber's ears, his cheer sounded false.

"He will. You two belong together from what you've told me. You're probably both just stubborn, mule-headed males."

"Mule-headed?" That interjected some life into him, Amber thought as his arms tightened around her.

"Yes, mule-headed. Probably don't know shit stinks until you're neck deep into it."

"Not fair and not true." The smile that graced his lips now was genuine, and Amber relaxed into his hold.

"Very true. I know you, Richard Strong. You probably gave your wolf as much as he gave you. And I bet you both just need time to lick your wounds."

"Lick my wounds?" he asked, his voice dropping into a growl that had Amber's stomach tightening up as the banked need for him began to grow. "There's definitely something I want to lick."

Amber had no idea where his sudden strength had come from, but she wasn't complaining.

Richard hefted her into his arms and carried her to the bed. He hovered over her as his fingers worked on her jacket, loosening each button until the gold cloth hung to the sides of her body, exposing her breasts held teasingly within a red lace bra.

"Beautiful," he moaned as he lowered his head and buried his face between her breasts.

Automatically, Amber's hands went to the back of his head, pulling him closer and arching up into his simple caress.

The heat he gave off was amazing. She felt her

nipples harden as he turned his face to the side and gave a kiss to the flesh that mounded above her bra.

Amber had no misconceptions about her body. She was a woman in her forties who had given birth. The stretch marks on her ass and below her stomach couldn't be hidden. She never regretted a moment of those marks -- they were proof that her little Lila had been nurtured in her body and delivered safely. She had no idea how Richard would react, but she had to remind him of the reality of their situation.

"I have stretch marks," she pointed out, tugging at his hair until he lifted his head. His eyes gleamed with gold streaks as he examined her face.

"I don't care."

"I -- I mean, I'm an older woman, Richard. I've given birth. My boobs are not as firm as they once were."

"I don't care," he repeated, his grin getting wicked. "I've seen them before."

"But not up close and personal," she muttered. "I need you to… to understand that I'm proud of this body. My stomach isn't as flat as it was before I had Lila, and being a mother has wrought some uncorrectable changes."

"I like those changes," he pointed out. "If I wanted a young new thing, there are plenty of those running around this town. If I wanted an easy conquest, I could have had that a million times over. You have no idea what these tourists offer to a man who can make it to the top of the salamander ladder. I swear the owners put that damn thing by the window just to lure in passing women who are visiting Angel Falls. Hell, most days there are at least three waiting at the bottom to proposition me."

"Oh, really." Amber frowned a little.

"Badge bunnies." He rolled his eyes. "And the owners are using it to their advantage. Daily memberships have gone up and they refuse to let me change my schedule so I can do the ladder in the mornings. In fact, they came right out and told me that my usage of it was too good for their business to let me stop. I did get a free membership out of it, so I can't complain, but the point I was making is that it's easy to get laid in this town now. I'm not about easy. I'm about something that's worth the fight."

"And I'm worth the fight?" It was childish of her, she knew. But she wanted some reassurances.

"So damn worth it," he agreed, his voice dropping into that sexy, growling timbre again.

"My underwear doesn't even match," she pointed out.

"Ohh... let me see --" he demanded. He backed off enough to pull her denim shorts from her legs after swiftly untying her boots and casting them aside.

"Thongs." He closed his eyes, a look of religious fervor entering his eyes... as if he were worshiping at the feet of his most beloved idol. And yet... there was only Amber here... only Amber Graves with her stretch marks and her not-as-perky boobs in a green lace bra -- a green lace bra in a size double D was a miracle -- and her orange thong undies.

She arched one eyebrow at him, the need to cover herself disappearing as he tilted his head down, inhaled deeply, then looked up toward the sky, "Thank you, God," he breathed, "for bringing me such a fine meal."

Before she could move or even think of a reply to his very honest declaration, he was spreading her legs and pushing her thong aside, holding it away from her with his thumb. The cooler air hitting her moist flesh made her shiver, made her arousal grow as he licked his lips.

Her legs found a resting point over his shoulders and he lowered his head, his expression worshipful. "Thank you for the meal I'm about to receive."

Then just like in her dreams, his hands were cupping her ass, lifting her to his mouth and --

"Sweet mercy," Amber managed to gasp as his mouth attached itself to her. Then she could see no more as her eyes slammed shut and she collapsed back into her bed, her body a mass of shaking muscle.

He was making slurping, growling sounds as he feasted, his tongue slipping below the hood protecting her erect clit, the tip of it flicking as he worked his chin against her slick labia.

Her hands went to his head, carding though his hair as she pulled him closer. Her heels pressed into the firm muscles of his back as she bucked against his hold, doing her best to get closer to that ecstasy-delivering mouth.

"So fucking good," he murmured between laps, dipping his head down to lick the wet slick from her labia and teasing the entrance to her pussy before he again suckled on her clit. "Do you know this?" he muttered, inhaling and burrowing his face into her. "So fucking good, Amber. All for me. Say it --" he demanded, pulling away.

What the fuck? Amber's eyes popped open and her hand tightened its hold in his hair. Where was he going?

"Eat my pussy!" she demanded, her voice high pitched and breathy as she tried to figure out why he'd stopped.

"Say it," he teased, his thumb sliding over her sopping pussy, teasing her, sending shivers of pure electricity running through her groin. "Come on, say it, Amber."

"It," she replied, clamping her thighs around his head, trying to force him back where he belonged. "Now get back to work. Ding-ding, the dinner bell has rang."

"No, that's not what I want to hear." His grin was nearly lethal as he licked her shiny fluids from his lips, his thumb slipping lower to tease at her trench, barely grazing her asshole.

"Richard --"

"That's my name."

"Please?" She was dying. Heat was consuming her from the inside. She needed him back on her clit, and she needed it now.

"Better, but not what I want." He pressed against the furled muscles of her asshole, driving her need to be penetrated higher. "Say it, Amber. Say it so I can go back down on you, baby. You're so wet." His other hand went to her clit, his thumb pressing it firmly as his other hand continued to tease her ass. "You need it so bad, baby. Come on, tell me what I want to hear."

Oh, fuck, this man was lethal. Amber's whole body began to tremble with the double stimulation. His voice was so low -- so growly -- and the beautiful filth he was uttering poured unselfconsciously from his lips. In fact, he was nibbling on his bottom lip now, swollen from their earlier kisses, as his fingers played her masterfully.

"Come on, baby. Tell me what I want to hear. I want to taste you again, so badly. I want to suck your clit until you're screaming. I want to drink you down as you wet my face. I want you to come on my mouth --"

"Yours!" she all but shouted as her tugging in his

hair turned to outright jerking. She wanted that nasty little filthy mouth back on her, pleasuring her, making her come. She wanted to feel his cock slide deep inside her pussy, in her ass -- she just needed to be penetrated by him. "Yours, Richard! Please!"

"That's what I wanted to hear. I hope you aren't attached to these --"

There was a pressure against her ass and then a ripping sound and the scrape of her orange thong, which really didn't match anything she owned, but was on sale when she got it, went flying across the room. She couldn't bring herself to care because his mouth was back on her pussy and her head was floating.

He hummed -- no, he was growling, and the sensations flew along her clit, making her writhe in his grip. Her hands left his hair and flew over her head, gripping the pillows, tearing at the sheets, as he began to use the rough flat of his tongue to lap from her clit to the entrance of her pussy. He was making frequent stops to tongue her labia, before he went back to slurping at her swollen, weeping opening.

The urge to scream overcame her as he held her still, his strength holding her where he wanted her, so she jammed her fist into her mouth.

Instantly he stopped. Her eyes popped open and she looked down to see him frowning at her.

"I want to hear you," he demanded, his black eyes damn near glinting with his hunger. "Don't stop yourself."

"B-but --" she stuttered, but he cut her off.

"I want to hear you, Amber. No one is here to listen. Lila is miles away and if someone from downstairs wants to listen in, let them. Good if they are. Then they'll know you're mine. I want the whole damn world to know that you're mine!"

"Rich --" she tried again and jerked upwards, a scream leaving her mouth as he slid two fingers deep inside her pussy.

It stung and it burned and it felt so damn good. God, it had been years since anything but silicone or her own damn fingers had slid inside her and after her long drought, she was getting what she was craving.

Growing out of control, she arched her back and threw her pussy up into his face, using her heels on his back to force herself back to that mouth.

"Fuck, yeah," he breathed and lowered his head again.

Amber was spinning, her mind wheeling as she whimpered and groaned, as she screamed and cursed as he ate her out right.

His tongue was everywhere, flicking at her clit, tasting her labia as he cleverly used his thumbs to hold her open while he examined her closely.

"So pink and pretty," he moaned. "Such a pretty little pussy. And it's all mine." He lowered his head to lap at her again before resting her on the bed and slamming two fingers back inside her.

"Rich!" she bellowed, her inner walls rippling around his fingers. She was getting so close. She could feel her orgasm just beyond her reach. She was sobbing now, her fists slamming into the bed as her body stiffened and --

"Hell, yes. I can feel it. Come on my mouth, Amber. Come on my mouth."

He ordered and, just like magic, her body tipped over. She threw her head back and screamed as her orgasm washed over her.

Her inner walls squeezed around his fingers, her clit burned as he lapped at her, her whole body was a sweating, shaking mess as her spine turned to liquid and her body danced for their mutual pleasure.

She was whimpering, his lapping keeping her orgasm going, before she collapsed back on the bed, weightless... wrecked.

"Your work isn't done." His dark, laughing voice had her eyes opening as he rose above her.

She watched, sprawled out and unable to move on her bed, while he unbuttoned his shirt and carelessly cast it aside. His utility belt went next, but there he stopped for a moment. He spied her bedside table and moved over to it, removing his sidearm.

Before she could stop him, he slid the drawer open, obviously intending to store his gun there, and froze at what he saw.

"Well, well, well," he teased as he cut side-eyes at her. Amber didn't think it was possible for her to blush any harder, but her face was now burning with the heat of her embarrassment.

She opened her mouth, but he tutted at her as he placed his gun inside and began tossing things on the bed.

A pair of latex gloves, a string of condoms, and her favorite purple vibrator.

"Richard --"

"Oh, it's time to play."

Chapter 9

His pants were discarded so fast she barely saw them go. Then he approached the bed, mischief in his eyes and a huge bulge in his boxer briefs. He straddled her prone body and ran his hands down his chest, teasing at his nipples as she watched.

"I like to play games," he murmured sweetly to her as he cupped his bulge, squeezing it as he tossed his head back and closed his eyes. "I like to close my eyes and pretend it's your pretty hands on me, Amber."

He peered down at her, a smirk on his face as his thumbs went to his waistband.

"I like to imagine it's you undressing me. That the sight of me naked would leave you hot and dripping. Are you dripping for me again, Amber? Is your hungry little pussy getting itself ready for me?"

Obviously he didn't expect an answer because, with a flourish, he whipped his underwear down and his thick, uncircumcised cock dropped out.

"Fuck!" Amber knew her eyes were wide, but she was staring at one hundred percent Grade A beef.

His cock was a thing of beauty. It was thick and ringed with heavy veins. He was uncircumcised, as she'd thought; his foreskin was retracted leaving the weeping, plum-colored head exposed to the air and her sight. The shaft was a deep brown, almost visibly throbbing with his need. There was a spattering of soft-looking, neatly trimmed pubic hair above it, teasing at the thick base. His balls were round and high, telling of his extremely aroused state.

As she watched, licking her lips, it rose until it was pressed against his stomach, a hard pillar of flesh designed to bring her the ultimate in carnal pleasure.

"You wanna taste, little girl?" he asked, lazily fisting his dick.

Numbly, she nodded. Her body was reacting without her mind, because she was suddenly on her knees and his arms were wrapped around her.

"This has got to go." He -- very carefully, she noted -- unclasped the four hooks on the back of her bra and peeled it away, pulling her arms from around his body to do so. "It's a crime how much these things cost," he breathed, his eyes on her full breasts, their swollen nipples, as he spoke.

He was the one who pulled back, her fingers helplessly gripping at his shoulders as he put some distance between them. Amber pouted, but it quickly turned to whining as he began to nurse at her nipples.

"Fuck, so perfect." Her breasts weren't the firmest after getting pregnant and nursing her child, but if he thought they were perfect, who was going to complain or point out her failings? Not her. Her mama didn't rear many fools.

She leaned into him as he nibbled and licked at her nipples, his hands cupping her sides, his thumbs hoisting her boobs up for him to suck. It was arousing in a whole different way than his pulling at her swollen clit. She could feel a tugging deep inside that told of a deeper arousal. She could feel her clit coming to life once more, her pussy lubricating itself as her thighs began to shake.

"Fuck," she hissed, her head going back as he bit at one nipple -- he liked to bite, she noted -- and then lapped away around it, soothing the burn of his teeth.

"Soon," he promised, transferring his attention to her other nipple.

"Now," she demanded, her hand traveling up his shoulders to his neck, her thumbs rubbing behind his ears. She watched him shiver before her hands fisted in his hair. It was easy to shove him back and straddle his thighs as he fell backwards.

"Amber," he whined. "I wasn't done playing."

"But I am."

She slid down his body, biting hard at his nipples, listening to him hiss as he fisted his hands in her hair, teasing at the soft kinkiness of it before he pulled her closer to his chest. "Make me feel it tomorrow," he growled as she complied, gnawing and biting as he hissed, his back arching into the pain. He sighed deeply when she sucked at his nipples, making them as hard as hers, before she began to travel lower.

He had practically no body hair, and his muscles were hard and firm. She counted each muscle of his eight-pack with her tongue, before she delved into his navel and watched as he giggled a little.

Then her hands were around his dick, feeling the heat and the weight of him. His skin was soft, as soft as she'd imagined, and he smelled so good. He didn't have a normal scent of male musk though it was present. He smelled wild, like growing things and spice. She ran her cheek across his swollen head, her eyes going to his as he peered down at her before his hips thrust up a little at her.

Grinning, she opened her mouth and let her tongue travel over the head of his cock, lapping up the clear fluid that leaked from it and closing her eyes at the flavor. He was like salt and sugar, and fucking pineapple. She pulled back and stared up at him in surprise. Damn, he tasted unexpectedly fine. She was never one for blow jobs -- her enjoyment - of the act came from watching her partner come apart under her hands -- but this... him and his unexplainable flavor... Oh, yeah, she was going to enjoy this.

She lapped at the slick trails that ran down his shaft, humming happily before she sucked his tender head back into her mouth.

"Amber." He was moaning, his hips rocking from side to side, his hands fisting in her hair, but not pulling her down or forcing himself in deeper. He had better control than that. "Fuck, so good, baby. You mouth is so good, so hot and wet…"

He hissed as she sucked him hard, rolling her tongue around his head, flicking at his slit and sucking down his sweet precum.

"Fuck, baby, better than my fantasies," he moaned as her hand slid down to fist his base.

He was too big to even think about deep throating. She was no porn star, but she wanted to impress him with her oral skills. She sank down as far as she could go without gagging, and used her fist as a stopping point. She looked up at him, holding his gaze with her own before she closed her eyes and began to bob her head.

God, he was making her wet. Just the act of doing this had her pussy clenching in hunger. She squeaked in surprise when he sat up, careful not to dislodge her, and slid his fingers down her ass trench.

"In a moment," he panted, "I'm going to pull you off and finger this beautiful ass, Amber. I'm going to slide your purple vibrator deep inside you while I fuck you into next week."

His hands left off squeezing her ass, and there was the snap of latex as he donned a glove. She whimpered because she knew exactly where that hand was going. Then he pulled himself from her mouth and reversing their positions, laying her on her back and sliding between her sprawled legs.

"If you don't want to let me into his beautiful ass,

now is the time to speak up."

"I want it," she whispered, biting her lip as she imagined the past pleasure of having her fingers and her toys in her ass. "This isn't my first time at this rodeo," she informed him. She was recovering nicely and was still hungry for more of him.

"That's my baby," he threw his hair behind his head and grinned.

Then she hissed as her vibrator sank into her pussy.

"Hold this for me --" He spoke in a very conversational tone, which was ramped up her arousal as he absently flicked the vibrator on its highest setting.

"Fuck!" The thing buzzed happily within her, making her whole pussy vibrate and ache. It was turned so high she could feel the vibrations in her ass, which was probably what he wanted because he began to finger her clit with his bare hand as he reached for a lubed condom.

"If I do this right," he explained, "there will be no need for lube. You're positively drenched." He caressed her stretched labia around the vibrator before bringing his finger back to his mouth and licking it clean. Then his finger returned to her clit, brushing lightly along its side, which did more for her than direct stimulation.

Her hips arched and he chuckled low. "You feel that, baby?" he asked. "You like that feeling?"

He opened the condom and gripped the base of her toy. He very slowly pulled it out and then ran it over her slick labia, pressing very deliberately on her clit.

She made some inhuman noise as the vibrations tore into her already sensitive clit. It was like being punched in the face with need. She bucked up against him, her legs dropping open wide as he slid the vibrator back into her pussy and began to fuck her slowly with it.

"Fuck me," she was babbling, her hips arching.

He slid her vibrator out once more and she watched through tear-filled eyes as he slid the condom down over it before opening another one. She watched as he slid it down his length, stroking himself for her benefit.

His hands parted her thighs, lifting them back to his shoulders as he lowered his head once more. The vibrator slid inside as his tongue began to lap at her clit.

"Fuck, Richard!"

"Soon," he breathed against her mound before he began to lick her hard.

The vibrator slipping back into her pussy was a small relief. She grunted, pushing into the penetration and gasping as he ran it along her walls, searching for and finding her G-spot.

Then he played with it, twisting the toy so it grazed her spot softly as he opened her up.

She was groaning like an animal in pain, ripping at his hair as he licked her harder, dropping down to nose at her clit as he licked around the vibrator.

"Soon," he promised. "Soon I'm going to fill this pretty little kitty."

He sank her toy in deeply and she felt her inner walls clench with the need to come.

"Nope." He pulled it back as he continued to lap at her, running it over the mouth of her pussy before lifting it, considering the latex-covered device.

"Yes." He slid it deep and held it there with his bare hand. The gloved hand was wiping up her slick, coating his fingers, and he eyeballed her.

"Going in your ass, little girl," he promised as she spread her knees wider. The first finger just lightly circled before pressing firmly at the guardian muscles.

Her breath hitched as she pressed up into the caress, wanting something, anything to fill her up. She was so empty.

With amazing ease, his finger slid inside fully. She could feel the vibrations from the toy more intently now that his finger was sliding inside. He prepared her carefully -- there was no pain, only a feeling of fullness that she craved.

She tossed her head to the side, her mouth open and panting. She screamed as he bent his head and began to tongue her clit. Another powerful orgasm ripped though her as she pushed back against his finger. But it only made her hungrier.

"Fuck, I love it when you come on my mouth," he informed her, his voice deep and breathless. "I want to feel it."

She was lost, her head rocking back and forth, one of her hands tugging at his hair while the other ripped the sheets from the bed. She was flying so high that it wasn't until he wiggled his fingers inside her ass that she realized he had sunk another one inside her.

With the toy vibrating relentlessly and him eating at her like she was his last meal, Amber felt her body tightening once more.

She was going to come.

She didn't know she'd shouted that until the vibrator slid from her pussy, then his fingers were gone and the vibrator was sliding into her ass.

"Beautiful," he praised as she whimpered. He was moving so slowly, too slowly, and she wanted more. She bucked up against him and he chuckled as he held her in place.

"At my pace, baby," he informed her and pressed the toy deeper into her ass.

Her mind was spinning. She was beyond speech, making only strange vocalizations as she writhed beneath him.

"So pretty, getting spread open," he murmured. "Does it feel good, baby? Is it hot?"

"Hot," she managed, her breath hitching again and again. Her muscles were tightening, her pussy was burning and so empty --

She pressed down, and he allowed more to slip inside. She wailed his name, crying out as he finally slid the toy into her in one go.

"Fuck, that looks so good, baby. Is it good? You like having this tight little hole fucked?"

"Um hum," was all she could manage.

Then he was ripping the glove away before he lifted her hips, positioning his condom-coated dick at her pussy.

He filled her in one hard thrust.

"Richard!" she screamed, her body locking around the ungiving toy in her ass as well as the hard dick that filled her.

He was moving, fucking into her, grinding in deep and rolling his hips, knocking her breath from her body with each move.

It was going to be soon. She could feel herself peaking, her muscles tightening, her ass spasming as the movements from his dick made her toy dance in her ass.

"So tight, baby. Fuck, Amber. You feel so right!"

He was leaning over her now, fucking into her powerfully, his hand on her hips holding her in place. She could only whimper his name as she felt her pussy tightening around him, as her ass squeezed down on her toy.

Then she was coming, her ass, her pussy, her body wringing around his possession, milking his dick and making him gasp her name. Fire raced through her body as he bit kisses into her open mouth as she rode her final orgasm hard.

Then he was sitting up, ripping the toy from her ass as he slammed into her, going for his own release.

She was shuddering, her arms lifting to wrap around him as she whispered into his ear, his hair running along her body like a silk blanket.

"Come in me."

"Amber!" he roared as he slammed himself as deep as he could go.

She wrapped her legs around his waist as he began to climax. She could feel the tip of his condom grow warm as his seed filled it as his dick pulsed within her.

"Fuck, baby," he gasped as he collapsed on her. He rested there for a moment in her arms before he reached down to grip the condom and carefully pull out.

"Oh, God." Amber panted, trying to catch her breath. Her eyes were permanently closed and every muscle in her body ached. She couldn't catch her breath and her heart was racing. She was covered in sweat and other sticky fluids and her vibrator buzzed happily beside her, still wrapped in its condom. She'd never felt better in her life.

"We'll clean up," Richard panted from beside her, his long flowing hair still covering most of her body. "And then we'll do it all over again."

Fuck, she thought as her calming heartbeat began to triple its speed. What had she gotten herself into?

"Again?" She managed to get her eyes open and stared at his beautiful, sweaty, red face. He was panting just as hard as she was but his dark eyes still gleamed in hunger.

"And again," he promised. "And when I can't get it up anymore, I have fresh batteries for your toy."

It was going to be a long night.

* * *

There was an unfamiliar sound.

It pulled Amber from a very comfortable sleep. It wasn't the usual apartment noise; she would have just slept through that. This sound was foreign to her ears.

When she sat straight up in bed, it had the unexpected side effect of waking Richard, who reached out and wrapped large warm arms around her.

"What's wrong?"

Even buffered through sleep, his voice sounded weak.

After seeing her through countless orgasms -- well, at least seven -- he had finally drifted off, spooning around behind her and settling her sore and sated body before him. She could tell the effort had cost him big time, the loss of his shadow making him weaker by the hour. He fought to hide it from her, but the lethargy taking over his body was obvious to anyone who knew him.

"I heard something," she muttered, turning to stare at him in the purple light coming though the window. Dawn was cracking which meant it had to be about five in the morning.

"I'll go check," he said quietly while tossing back the blankets.

She shivered as the cooler air touched her skin, but watched him stumble to his feet.

"I'll go with you," she offered, reaching for his

discarded uniform shirt.

The one thing he'd done before they succumbed to sleep was to take his gun belt and secure his weapon in a bedside table. He had also folded his clothing neatly and placed them on the cedar chest by the window. She climbed out of bed and reached for his shirt, sliding it on, to his complete amusement as it damn near swallowed her up.

Richard, being the man that he was, didn't bother with clothing at all. He just waited naked and tempting by the bedroom door.

"No arguments?" she asked. "No telling me I'm hearing things?"

"You know your own home," he responded. "If there's something unusual going on here, you more than anyone else would know."

With that declaration, he opened the door and walked out into her dim apartment.

Her living room was clear, the shadows giving way as morning progressed to show her entertainment center with the two video game systems that Lila insisted upon. The light reflecting off the crystalline accents danced in prisms on the walls. The couch was a huge, dark shape that looked almost alien with its multitude of pillows and throw blankets nestling on top of it.

They made their way to the kitchen where a crock of soup waited on the stove.

Amber blushed slightly when she thought of her cook using his passkey to come in and place the soup there during some loud monkey-sex antics she and Richard had engaged in. She just hoped the soup had been brought up during one of the many sex breaks and not when she was riding Richard like a bucking bronco and screaming for more. Hell, they'd ignored two phone calls, though she broke away to answer when Lila's voice sounded on her answering machine. That had been embarrassing, answering the phone with a deep-into-sex voice and ignoring your child's laughter at the fact you were finally getting laid. That was right before Richard sat her on his face and her whole world became a haze of pleasure as he plucked at her nipples before sinking one finger deep into her ass, stroking her clit with his tongue while setting the nerves in her tight little hole on fire.

"I think I'll start breakfast," she mumbled, a blush heating up her face. "It's too late for me to go back to bed. I usually get up around this time."

"Me too." He offered her a smile as she flipped on the kitchen lights. "I jog… a lot. It's a good way to deal with frustration."

"I just bet," she mumbled as she moved the crock of soup to the refrigerator.

"I have a feeling I won't be jogging this early for a while. Something about bedroom exercises keeping me in shape."

Snickering, Amber swatted at his shoulder, noting his trembling arms in passing.

"Richard, you don't --"

"I'll be fine," he assured her before she could ask. "I've just never gone this long without him before. I'll adjust."

"How long until this becomes a more dangerous problem?" She didn't want to nag but she was really concerned. Richard had always seemed so unflappable. Even in bed, he performed to almost superhuman levels, but she was beginning to understand he was growing weaker by the moment even though he tried to hide it.

"I don't know," he answered honestly. "I never

heard of someone's shadow tearing itself away in anger, but my wolf has always been a stubborn bastard. I'll be fine for now."

"Richard --"

"I'll go and check the rest of the place," he cut her off. "I remember what most of the rooms are from the last time I helped Bryan and Lila lug parade stuff up here."

Amber nodded as she began to pull breakfast things from cabinets and pots from the cupboard.

Her apartment was rather large. It had three bedrooms in addition to an eat-in kitchen, a dining room, and the large living room. While Richard checked the rest of the place, she put a pot of water on high to get it boiling. The sound of him moving from room to room was comforting to her.

Maybe she'd been hearing things, she decided as she pulled bacon from the fridge. She marked his progress by ear as he thoroughly checked out Lila's room, the guest bathroom and finally moved on to the third bedroom she used as storage.

She heard a thump coming from the storage room as she added grits to the now-boiling water. "Are you okay?" she called. "I know some of the alien heads are just tossed in there. They won't break if they fall over, so don't worry."

She was stirring the grits, watching them get thick in the water when she heard Richard step into the kitchen behind her.

"You didn't find anything, right?" she chuckled. "Maybe it's because I'm not used to having anyone but Lila in here with me and it's made me a bit jumpy."

"With good reason." The familiar voice made the smile drop from her face as she slowly spun around to face her worst nightmare. "Todd."

Chapter 10

"Glad you remember me, wife." Todd Ritter spoke softly, but the menace in his voice was very real.

"Todd --"

"Because I remember you."

Todd looked the same, dangerously beautiful with his long, golden-blond hair pulled back in a low ponytail. His body was still athletically fit, his strength hidden in his ropy musculature. His eyes were still a startling brown, and age seemed to only make him more beautiful.

"What are you doing here?" She backed away from the stove, putting some distance between the two of them. It was an automatic maneuver that was now more of a muscle memory when someone hemmed her up in the kitchen. She remembered the first time he really went at her, she'd been standing near the stove and a hot kettle of water had splashed on her as he knocked her into the burner. After that, any time he was really angry, she ran from the kitchen, not wanting to add second-degree burns to her other aches and pains. Burns took longer to heal than bruises. "What do you want?"

"What do you think, Amber?" His voice was smooth and deep, and she was no fool to fall for this illusionary calmness.

"I --"

"What the *fuck* do you think, Amber?" He took a step closer, the heels of his polished black shoes clicking on her wooden kitchen floor and Amber, with her soft bare toes and the shirt that hit her mid thigh, had never felt so naked.

"Where's Richard?"

"Your little boy-toy?" He sneered. "One tap to

the back of the head and he went down like a bag of rocks. What's the matter, Amber? Can't find a man with staying power?"

"What did you do, you son of a bitch!"

"Nothing he won't recover from." Todd took another step. "But all that can change if you don't give me what I want."

"What do you want?" Amber screamed. "After all this time, why did you come back?" Her heart was racing a mile a minute. She was shaking uncontrollably and wanted to curl up in a corner and pretend this wasn't happening. Or better yet, she wanted to pinch herself to make sure she wasn't dreaming. She had to be asleep. This was all a dream -- a horrible, horrible dream that she would wake up from at any moment. God, let this be a dream!

"I want what you stole from me, cunt," he snarled, stepping closer. "I want what you took away from me. Can you go back in time and fix this, Amber? Can you?"

"Tell me!" Amber screamed, tears beginning to flow down her face. "Just tell me what you want and then go away! Go away!"

"I want my child, Amber. I want Lila."

"No!" Amber felt her anger sweep over her like an unstoppable wave. How dare he come and demand this?

"I want to be a father!"

"Then go get one of those bitches you fucking knocked up!" she railed, her hands fisting in her hair as her trembling muscles began to out-and-out shake. "You were so happy with them, Todd. You were fucking enough of them when we were married. And then you came home and --"

"And tried to teach you to be a good woman."

He sneered. "What was I thinking, trying to turn ghetto trash into a treasure?"

"Fuck you!" Amber roared, her anger knocking away more of her fear. "Fuck you, Todd Ritter! Fuck you up your lying ass!"

"You'd know about that, wouldn't you? Isn't that what your little long-haired chief was doing?"

Amber paled. He'd been in her apartment that long? "None of your fucking business --"

"Funny, that word fuck... You were never into it with me, were you, Saint Amber? That was half the problem right there. Maybe if you fucked me a little better, I wouldn't have had to resort to the barflies. You were such a bad lay --"

"Didn't stop you from coming back for more."

"That's because you were carrying my child, Amber. Family is all, don't you know? My fucking family meant the world to me."

"Which is why you tried to beat me to death, Toddy? Out of your sense of family obligation?"

"That was only to keep a little bitch like you in line."

Even after all this time his words managed to hurt her. "Get the fuck out." Her eyes were narrowed in anger and her feet stopped retreating. Already her eyes were drifting over the kitchen, looking for serviceable weapons.

She had to get out. She had to find Richard, had to see if he was still alive. But she had to get Todd the fuck out of her home.

"Yeah, worked out well for you." She sneered, her eyes dancing from the knife block to him -- then to the kitchen counter with its array of crocks and back to his face. She spied the dish rack with its set of clean plates and mugs she used for morning tea... then back to him. "How'd you like the concussion? The doctor said I nearly cracked your skull."

"Oh, you're gonna pay for that."

"And risk going back to jail?"

"Statute of limitations for assault is one year, Amber. I'm free and clear. The only reason I didn't kick your ass for this sooner is that I couldn't find you."

"And all my hard work went for nothing," she spat at him. Tears were still flowing, fear was still there, but as long as she kept him talking he wasn't going for her.

"Not nothing, wife --"

"I divorced you!"

"I never signed the paperwork."

"It went through uncontested with special circumstances. You lose, Toddy. You failed again, just like you failed at so many things in life."

His eyes narrowed and he took a step closer. "Give me my daughter, bitch!"

"Why? So you can try to hit her too? So you can try to be the big man and fail again?"

"Amber --"

"She knows all about you, Toddy. She asked about her daddy when she was young, and I told her he had gone away. She asked again when she started high school and I told her the truth. I showed her the pictures, the transcripts. And she hates you almost as much as I do."

"Fuck you, Amber!" he roared, visibly shaken by this turn of events. "I have the right to know my child!"

"She knows, Toddy. She knows the reason I turned on you was because you threatened her."

"You don't have the right, Amber! I would not have hurt my child!"

"But your wife was fair game? Is that how it works for you, Toddy?"

"Stop calling me that." His hands were fisted at his sides now. "Never call me that again." He looked all around the kitchen, taking his eyes away from her, and Amber moved closer to the stove. Maybe she could reach the knife block --

"I would never harm my child." His eyes snapped back to hers and she froze. "I would never harm my angel."

"Your angel doesn't even carry your last name." Amber laughed, watching as he paled and then turned bright red with fury. Toddy-baiting wasn't smart, but if she could get him off balance then she could reach the chef's knife on the magnet bar behind the stove. The knife block on the counter was too far away.

"What did you do, bitch?" He stepped closer, his hands reaching for her.

"I changed it legally the minute the paint was dry on the divorce decree."

He lunged for her and Amber easily sidestepped him, moving toward the kitchen door. When he missed, she took her eyes off of him, but only for a moment, then looked back before she started to run, but stone hands grabbed her by the arm, spinning her around again.

"Bitch --"

He raised his hands to smack her, but a noise above her made him look up.

There was a meaty *thwap* and Todd reared backwards.

Amber looked up as Todd jerked her toward him and saw Richard, his hair all but standing on end, in a towering rage.

"Let her go!" he roared, but Toddy was, if

anything, persistent.

He jerked her, dragging her closer to his body, and Amber flailed out with her free hand.

She winced as it passed the heat of the stove and then brushed the handle of the pot of…

"Fuck you, Toddy!" she roared, gripping the pot handle and flinging the hot grits directly into his face.

The noise he made was unlike anything human or preternatural Amber had ever heard. He released her, jerking away from her as both hands went to his face where he tired to wipe away the stinging hot, sticky grits, but to no avail. He wailed again, spinning around, shaking his head and shrieking in pain, moving him closer to the large window that overlooked the main street.

Righteous anger filling her, Amber wound her arm back, tightened her grip on the pot, and swung like she was trying to knock a baseball out of the park. She put all her weight behind her swing and felt nothing but satisfaction when the pot clanged against his face, sending him reeling backwards. The crash of breaking glass was an unexpected bonus as Todd fell ass over teakettle out of her kitchen window.

"Damn," Richard breathed, stepping around her and up to the window as Toddy fell.

They both watched as he bounced off the tight vinyl awning of the *Planet Quest* Café and slammed into the metal mock up of the *Planet Quest* mothership before landing face first onto the ground below.

"Um --" It was kind of anticlimactic. Amber stood there, dripping pot in hand, watching as her greatest foe, her arch enemy, the magistrate of her nightmares was laid low by a common Southern breakfast food.

She turned to Richard, but he was gone in a flash

of long hair and naked, bronzed skin.

She listened as he fled to the front door, leaving her standing there in her kitchen. She stared out at a groaning Toddy for a moment before reflexively grabbing up a kitchen towel. Thoughts of cross contamination and bio hazards ran through her mind as she stared down at the broken mess of glass -- was that a blood drop? -- and grits that littered her kitchen floor.

Then common sense prevailed and she dropped the pot to race out after Richard.

When she made it to the ground floor, he was standing there, gun pointed at Toddy while a crowd of early risers began to gather.

"You have the right to remain silent --" Richard growled, and Amber turned away as the first of the giggles started.

She looked over and saw a group of teeny-bopper joggers and some matronly older ladies staring at her man and... his goods.

"That's why she keeps him around," one sage spinster said to another, pointing to his impressive but flaccid cock.

"Oh, I agree," someone else tittered. "His buttocks are so round and firm."

"Thighs like that are good for fucking," a spry senior citizen out for a morning stroll with her pink poodle stage whispered to her friend.

"No," her friend with a matching purple poodle and hair responded. "It's the strong back, dear. It looks flexible enough to put some hump in her dumps. What a lovely stud, if I do say so myself. Makes me miss my dearly departed Mortimer. He died in the midst of it, you know... seventy-nine and still fucked like a jackhammer. He came before he went --"

"Damn it!" Amber roared, racing to Richard's side and trying to wrap the minuscule dishtowel around his waist. "Richard, you can't arrest him!" she hissed.

The growing crowd of women booed her actions.

"I got him on assault, battery, breaking and entering, menacing, assaulting a peace officer --"

"You're naked!" she hissed.

"I don't give a fuck," he returned, never once taking his eyes off the groaning man.

She was about to argue with him some more, much to the delight of the morning set, when the sirens from the patrol car split the chatter of the early morning.

Within moments, Deputy Markus was strolling up to Richard's side, his eyes taking in the scene before him. "You do know you're naked, right, Chief?"

"Fuck you, Markus." Richard gave him a mean side-eye.

"How about you let me handle it from here… while you go and find some pants?"

"I want him run in for breaking and entering, assault --"

"Kind of a conflict of interest thing, Chief." Markus calmly drew his gun and covered the now-crying man, who was rolling back and forth among pieces of broken glass and cooling grits. "I got him covered."

"Richard," Amber hissed, stepping behind him as he slowly lowered his weapon. "Pants would be good. Everyone is staring at my… uh… bits."

"*Your* bits?" he asked, his muscles relaxing as he turned his head to look at her. There was a trickle of blood running down the side of his face, and he looked wan and gray.

"He get the drop on you, Chief?" Markus asked as he bent to cuff the groaning man. "Looks like you could use some pants and a doctor."

"I'm fine." he turned away from Amber and stumbled.

"Okay, that's it," Amber declared, taking him by the arm and leading him back toward the outside entrance to her apartment. "You need a doctor, and we all need a reality check."

"Don't go leaving town," Markus called over his shoulder, amusement clear in his voice. "I need to get statements from you all."

"Fine," she snapped as she led Richard up the stairs. She had a man to see to... and a kitchen to decontaminate. She would discover the wheres and hows later. For now she wanted to make sure her lover -- wasn't that just a perfect word? -- was safe.

Chapter 11

Richard had cracked his knuckles on Toddy's face.

It was a fact that had Amber grinning like a loon. Richard had cracked his knuckles on Toddy's face and had broken his nose.

Dr. Fernando Chase had made a rare early-morning house call to check on both Toddy and Richard, and the man holding her lover's hand was quite amused.

"So, he came in behind the cook," Markus was explaining to them both as Dr. Chase, vampire extreme, hissed in laughter. "He never knew he was there. All that actor training, or maybe he's just an expert in stalking," Markus mused. "Either way, he apparently hid out in your prop room, Amber. He says he wasn't going to hurt you, that he was looking for his daughter, but any man who hides out in a room listening to his ex wife fu -- have consensual sex with her lover, before deciding to sneak around to get the drop on them, isn't a sane man."

"Lack of sanity was the least of Toddy's issues," Amber grumbled. "I would be more concerned with his lack of moral fiber."

Richard grunted.

He had a new set of fifteen stitches behind his right ear where Todd had walloped him with an animatronic alien head in an attempt to knock him out cold.

Though weakened, Richard had managed to sense him coming up behind and shifted so that the potentially debilitating blow only dazed him.

"He wants to sue you," Markus pointed out. "Assault with a hot pot of grits."

"The Lou Rawls treatment," Dr. Chase interjected. "But he wasn't naked and getting out of a bathtub --"

"As I was saying," Markus cut him off, eyeing the doctor harshly as he broke down in giggles once more. "He wants to sue you for knocking him out of the window and for the grits, but after taking your statements, it seems like a clear-cut case of self defense."

"He broke into my home and -- and contaminated it with his filth."

"What she said." Richard nodded in Amber's direction then winced at the movement.

"You're still in pain," Amber murmured, stroking his free hand.

They were sitting in the sheriff's office, giving statements all official-like while the doctor treated Richard.

"He was sick yesterday," Amber added, turning toward the doctor. "Really sick." She knew he would understand the need for discretion as to what she was alluding to, being a vampire hiding in plain sight and all.

"I see," Dr. Chase murmured. "Has something to do with your pre-existing condition?"

"You sick, Chief?" Markus now sounded concerned. "You never told me."

"Not exactly sick... a genetic condition." He glared at Amber for a moment, before just shrugging and giving her a smile. "I just needed some rest. Stress is a killer."

"And running through the woods looking for our sticky-fingered camp thief isn't helping." Markus nodded, not digging for more answers.

Amber liked that about the younger man -- he

never stuck his nose where it wasn't needed. In a town like Angel Falls, nosiness could make or break a man.

"When I got your call this morning about the intruder in Amber's apartment, I half thought you were playing a joke. But you never joke about the people you protect."

"Damn straight," Richard muttered as Dr. Chase patted the last piece of tape into place, securing the finger with the broken knuckle to the one beside it, then rising to his feet.

"You won't need external fixation, rods and pins and the like," Dr. Chase explained as he eased Richard's hand into a strange splint that held three of his fingers straight while allowing freedom of movement to his thumb and index finger. The brace also prevented him from flexing his wrist, which would pull on his broken knuckles. "You need to ice it frequently to keep down the swelling, and it should heal *normally* in about three weeks." He emphasized that one word that had Amber nodding in understanding. If Richard healed faster, they would have to keep the brace to keep up the pretense.

"Todd Ritter's injuries?" Markus asked, pulling out a note pad and pen, poised to take notes despite the tape recorder running on the table where they sat in the interrogation room, i.e. Richard's office.

"Well, second- and third-degree burns to his face. His nose is broken, and from the point of the nasal fracture, I'd say it was done by a fist instead of the pot he says Amber struck him with. The pot would account for the fractured orbital bone on his right hemisphere." He eyeballed Amber. "Good work. Have you thought about joining the softball league?"

Amber felt a zing of pride and satisfaction that had her grinning at Fernando and Richard chuckling softly despite the pain in his head.

"Doctor!" Markus protested, frowning.

"What? From what he was saying he was going to do to her when he got out, I figure he earned every inch of pain."

"Opinions are not needed unless they are medical," Markus grumbled.

"Very well." The doctor nodded. "Burns, which I've treated at the hospital. Nasal fracture repaired with a closed reduction treatment. There will be swelling and pain for several days, but nothing that an over-the-counter pain reliever won't cure. The orbital fracture won't affect his vision. There may be some residual scarring from the burns. I suggested lavender oil once the healing phase is completed. He suggested I shove it up my ass. Then I applied a topical anesthesia and with great pleasure removed seventeen fragments of glass from his back and ass -- uh, gluteus. All of this is in the report I submitted to you when I arrived to treat the good sheriff. I'll write up the sheriff's treatment sheet and hand that over to you this afternoon."

"Thank you, Doctor."

"I also will send you the write-up on Ms. Amber Graves, over here. Bruising on her left wrist, but that's about it. I took photos and will submit them with her report."

"Thanks, Doc." Richard offered him a smile. "You were very thorough."

"In my line of work, I have to be." He winked at Amber before slipping off his rubber gloves, stuffing them in a side pocket on his leather doctor's bag, and exiting the room.

"Well, ain't this one fine pile of shit?" Markus snorted as he clicked off the recorder.

"You should try it from this end," Richard grumbled. He was dressed in a pair of sweats, his hair a rat's nest of tangles, and still rather gray in the face.

"Only you, boss." He shook his head. "What did Bryan have to say?" He looked at Amber. "He was adamant about speaking with you."

"He called a few times to tell me the hang-up calls are coming from town. I'm assuming they were from Toddy?"

"He says he saw you in a news report," Markus explained. "He tracked you back here with that. It's a good thing you filed a report with the sheriff, cause that proves he was stalking you and that you were in peril. No judge in the world is going to do anything to you with that damning evidence. That he assaulted an officer of the law will just about add the final nails to his coffin."

"And until he goes before a judge?" Amber had to know. "I haven't told Lila yet, and I won't until she's done with her auditions. But I don't want him to have any contact with her. He's poison, and I don't want that for my baby."

"Oh, he'll be sitting right here. He's going nowhere unless someone posts his bail. And I doubt any of our good citizens will do that for the turd. When they bring him in tomorrow, he'll get his phone call and then we'll see what's what."

Markus rose to his feet and picked up his recorder. "You don't look so good, Chief. Maybe you need to sit the day out…"

"Maybe I'll just go for a walk in the woods," Richard agreed. "Bring a picnic lunch."

"Yeah," Markus nodded. "You both need to decompress. Of course I have to tell you not to leave town, but you knew that already. I got a few of the volunteers watching over Ritter while I get his paperwork done." He opened the door before turning back to Richard and Amber. "At least this is different from the campground theft cases."

"Don't remind me," Richard groused.

"Well, since your hand is pretty much busted for the better part of a month, looks like they are going to be tossed into your capable hands." He snickered.

"Have I ever told you I hate you?" Richard snorted and Markus's laughter followed him out into the hall, cut off abruptly as he closed the door.

"You okay?" he asked Amber, turning to where she was seated at his side.

"Me? I'm fine. I already knew my nemesis had clay feet. It's just a rush to know I'm the one who shattered them for him."

"Really." Richard smiled at her.

"I'm sure I'll have screaming fits and want to sterilize my whole apartment later in the week. Now I'm just buzzed that he's going away for a long, long time."

"Awesome." He reached for her hand. "I'm so sorry I wasn't able to protect you," he began but Amber swiftly cut him off.

"Who made you my protector, Sheriff Strong?"

"The good people of Angel Falls," he countered.

"And they all just got a good look at the gun you're packing too." She shook her head, rolling her eyes at him. "The bottom line is that you don't have to protect me. I can protect myself."

"With a pot of hot grits, no less." He snickered.

"I'm lethal in the kitchen." She smirked at him. "And I've been doing all right on my own thus far, Sheriff. I'm not going to turn into some dainty little thing who needs you to come riding to my rescue. I handled him pretty well on my own."

"I got one punch in," he reminded her, pulling her over to sit on his lap. "That felt good."

"If it felt anything like hearing him squeal when he got hit with the grits, then that's a mighty fine feeling indeed."

"Mighty fine," he agreed, placing a light kiss on her lips. She was thankful they'd taken the time to brush their teeth and dress before the morning's legal circus landed on them. "But I should have done more. If I had my shadow --"

"You both would have fucked him up, and I would've gotten the show of a lifetime. But things happened the way they did, Sheriff. I couldn't have done it without you." She reminded him, "You distracted him --"

"You would have hit him with the grits anyway." He chuckled. "Now that was gratifying to see."

"I'm a tough woman."

"I'm falling in love with a tough woman."

That earned him another kiss, this one with tongue and heavy breathing and nips to his bottom lip, which he really enjoyed.

"You like being bitten."

"It's the wolf in me." He laughed, then sobered again and looked away.

"Hey." Amber grabbed his chin and pulled his face back to hers. "We'll find him. I know we will."

"We'll find him," he agreed, closing his eyes for a moment and resting his forehead against hers. "Now," he spoke again, pulling himself tighter and leering at her. "We have to brave the people over at the *Planet Quest* to get the rest of my things."

"And to pack a picnic," Amber insisted. "We

have to go back to the woods, but we're going to really make a day of it. You'll be having so much fun that your wolf will run back out of sheer jealousy."

"My wolf really likes you too," he spoke softly, placing a kiss against her lips before urging her to her feet. "Just like I really like you."

Amber felt a pleased blush heat her cheeks. She hadn't missed his earlier comment about falling in love. She wasn't ready to respond to that just yet, but in the future...

"I really really like you too," she grinned and led him out of the office.

They had things to do and if all went according to plan, they would bag a wolf by the end of the day and wind up back in her bedroom making whoopee.

All in all, it was shaping up to be a beautiful day.

* * *

This day was shaping up to be nothing but fresh survivalist hell.

Richard stumbled through the woods that surrounded Angel Falls doing his best to keep up with his woman -- the sound of that was perfect -- when just yesterday he'd owned the forest. Now he was sweating, overheated, exhausted, and his stitches pulled. He'd never had stitches in his life and now here he was, about as human as his wolf claimed he was trying to be.

He was angry at his shadow for leaving him in the lurch, angry that he might have been partially right, and more frustrated than he could ever remember himself being.

He could almost hear his wolf laughing at him now, the bastard. He was probably chasing squirrels in the trees instead of coming back to Richard -- being obstinate just to make a point.

He wasn't cut out to be pure human. He had nothing against humanity -- the woman he was going to eventually marry was human. He just... how... how could they survive like they did? If anything, this stint into humanity had taught him to respect the dominant race even more.

"Are you okay?"

His thoughts drifted from his own pitiful state to the shapely rump that was moving nicely ahead of him.

Amber Graves had a great ass.

She had a great everything as far as he was concerned, and the fact she worried about him made his trip into humanity tolerable.

"Fine," he huffed, pausing as she grinned at him over her shoulder. He knew he was giving her the sappiest smile ever, but he couldn't help himself.

Amber had bundled him up and got him out of the sheriff's office and back to *Planet Quest* within minutes of Markus dismissing them. She pulled him through the crowd of people wanting to know what was going on, ignoring the questions they shouted, and called her cook to open the café early. That done, she all but pushed him into the shower where she carefully shampooed his hair, gently washing the blood that the good doctor hadn't gotten out of his hair. The feel of her fingers on his sore scalp was like ambrosia. He had to stop his left leg from thumping in pleasure and was sure that if he had a tail, it would have been wagging. He tried to help with her toilette but that just led to him pushing her against the wall and fucking her senseless as she wrapped her legs around his waist and demanded more. He proudly wore her scratches up and down his back and felt a smug sense of satisfaction that he could make her lose it like that.

Of course then it was back to the phone to call Bryan and let him know what was going on if the gossip hadn't reached him first.

While she was explaining and re-explaining, he had taken it upon himself to clean her kitchen. He taped cardboard over the shattered window and swept up the glass and dried bits of grits. That stuff was like glue when it set and had him on his hands and knees scrubbing with a latex brush. Of course that meant he had to bleach her whole floor because he bled all over the place -- well, a few drops but he was kind of anal about blood.

Once cleanliness had been restored, he found himself being dressed in another set of borrowed clothes -- a thin Henley, a pair of dark sweat pants, and a pair of new boxer briefs right out of the pack. He knew she'd bought the things for Angel, but the little angel's wings on the ass were cute.

She'd called down to her cook while making arrangements for a replacement window, and gave him orders for a basket lunch to take with them.

Of course that meant when they went downstairs to pick it up, there was another gauntlet of questions to be run through, though he did appreciate the condoms, lube, and extra wet naps someone -- probably one of the waitresses -- provided.

Amber, dressed in a comfortable pair of beautifully tight jeans and a baby-doll T-shirt that showed off her ample boobs to their advantage, led him out of the café, promising to fill the gossips in later.

Of course she drove, and he was glad for it. He wasn't the type of guy who had to be in control of everything. He knew he wasn't at his best, so he let the best person for the job drive. He was grateful he'd left the sheriff department's SUV at the café. It meant he didn't have to stop at home to get his own.

So now they were tramping through the woods trying to find his wolf, who obviously didn't want to be found, while he was getting weaker by the moment.

"Yeah, right, you are." There was still amusement in her voice as she made her way back to him, but it only made him feel his weakness all the more, the vulnerability he wasn't used to. "You wanna take a break?"

When she took his hand within hers, he just wanted to curl up in her lap and let her stroke his cares away.

He knew that, in nature, Alpha wolves could be soothed by the Alpha bitch, so his reaction to her was understandable. Something in him recognized his need for a little coddling by his mate, and more than anything else, he wanted nothing more than to give in to that need.

"No," he decided, pushing back the urge to whimper and let her pet him as she would. "We have to keep moving. I'm worried, Amber. He... this separation..."

"It's getting to you." She nodded. "You can't be without your other half, and I'm sure he can't be without you. Can you call to him?"

"I've been trying but there's something blocking me."

"Can it be the falls?" she asked. "We're not too far away from them, and Winston said they can sometimes interfere with magic. Well, he called it natural energies, but things do seem to be drawn there."

He thought about the falls and his strange reaction to them, and had to agree. "You're so wise."

He offered a wry grin and changed directions. "They're that way," he added, taking her hand and guiding her along a new path. "They might amplify the call. The falls were one of the major reasons I moved to this town in the first place."

"One of?" She arched her eyebrow, and he wanted to lick it back down again. Instead, he began to explain.

"Yeah, the major draw to Angel Falls for me was the fact that this town is so strange."

"It's not that strange --"

"So strange that no one even noticed my shadow taking a walk on its own from time to time."

"Most people would not notice, Richard, unless they knew to look for that."

"Okay, how about magical tattoos that no one else can duplicate? Or even better, the tattoo artist who is an exact replica of her deceased grandmother who bears the same name? Or our Post Master General who has body parts being sought after by NASA?"

"You can find that in New York," she sniffed. "And NASA is probably after more than one body part up there -- there are so many genius computer adaptations coming out of there and California."

"Parades every Friday dedicated to *Planet Quest*?"

"Hey, they may make a *Planet Quest* movie thanks to our zeal," she pointed out.

"Not knocking your favorite show." He raised his hands in surrender. "It was just never a favorite of mine growing up."

"It was the only thing that let me keep my sanity." She began to walk again, tugging on him to keep up. "It was the only thing Toddy would let me have. He didn't understand it, but he liked the fact the cast was mostly theatrical stage actors."

"Well, the theme got to me." He sighed. "These people were searching for a home, a promised land to save their own kind. It was kind of too close to home for me." He brought her hand to his mouth and brushed a kiss across her knuckles. "We grew up on the run, always trying to stay two steps ahead of the hunters. The internet makes hiding easier now, but back then we couldn't help but leave a paper trail. And the legends of the Skinwalkers were so perverted by the unnatural ones that we dared not even take shelter on reservations. The elders would have turned us in as sure as my last name is Strong."

"Where are your parents now?" she asked as she gave his hand a little squeeze. In his mind, that squeeze meant he wasn't alone, and she was going to be beside him for some time to come.

"In Canada, of all places." He chuckled. "They managed to find a group of The People who knew the true legends of the Skinwalkers. They've found a safe place to rest."

"And you didn't go with them because?"

"Because the world needs Skinwalkers who are aware, to guide the true ones back to their safe haven and to stop the hunters -- manipulate them, really -- into finding the unnatural ones."

"And that person is you."

"Me." He grinned. "But now that I've found a base of operations and someone I want to spend my time with, I think my roaming days are over."

She flushed at little at that, and he took great pleasure in pulling her to him for a quick squeeze from behind -- about all he was good for at the moment.

"And you? Why do you like the show so much, besides the obvious Toddy thing?"

"Greatest moment of my life is when I picked up that heavy figure and cracked him upside his damn fool head."

Richard couldn't stop laughing at that. "You hit him?"

"About as bad as he ever hit me. I still have that figure… it's in my office."

"The one on the display over your desk?"

"Yup. That dent in the hull is from his rock head."

Again Richard dissolved into giggles. He could imagine a wide-eyed, angry Amber, brandishing the figure like a sword.

"He never knew what hit him." She chuckled. "I don't know who was more surprised, me or him. But I took that figure with me. Later when the police took me back, I was able to get most of my memorabilia. Some of it he destroyed, but I got my VHS tapes and my figurines and my models. I still have most of them in storage and a few went into the original decorating design of the *Planet Quest* Café."

"So, it's a reminder of how tough you can be." He understood that.

"That and…" She paused and stepped away from him for a moment, lost in thought. "It's more like it represented freedom. There was the need to find a place to save everyone, but for the members of the crew, the people who were locked in a world that was destined to die, people who had to know, it got them away, gave them something to live for. No matter how desolate it was back at home, they were trying to find a way to make things right, to get help, and to ultimately save those they cared about. That's a big jump, coming from being sure you're going to die and knowing almost the exact hour to be given this chance to live, no matter how slim."

"Deep thoughts." He walked up to her and again took her in his arms. He rested his chin on top of her head, inhaling the spicy vanilla scent of her hair while wrapping his arms around her tightly. "You're a survivor, you know that, Amber Graves?"

"I know that, Richard Strong." She spun in his arms and went up on her toes to drop a kiss on his lips. "And so are you."

The rest of the walk to the falls was completed in thoughtful silence, both lost in their own memories yet taking comfort in their physical closeness.

* * *

"They are back," Mariah, the true hunter of Skinwalkers, whispered as she pounded bone and ash into a powder. "You hear that, wolf?" She kicked at the jar that held the trapped shadow. "There's no way he could resist coming back. I'm not sure how he managed to keep you without an amulet or a skin, but make no mistake, I'll still have his head."

She began to chant as she rose to her feet and began to cast a wide circle with her dry mixture.

"He's brought his human with him. How he ensnared her, I don't know, but I'll kill him and free her. None will mourn his passing."

Once the circle was complete and made whole, it was time for her to spring her trap.

Chapter 12

Richard jerked to a halt, his head twisting to the right as he froze in place. Caught between one step and the next, his full attention was now on the thin link he felt with his shadow as it snapped back into place.

But... something was wrong. It wasn't steady and strong -- it felt muted, distressed, as if something was holding his beast back.

With a snarl on his lips that would have been right at home on a rabid wolf, he twirled in the direction of the link and took off running.

"Wait!"

He barely heard his mate call, but he couldn't slow down. Something was wrong and he had to get to his shadow-half.

The world turned into a blur of color and sound but nothing could stop him from going where he was needed. Previous weakness forgotten, he jumped, ducked, lurched over the flora and fauna of the forest. Animals jerked from his path, cowering as his animal-like aura grew the closer he got to his shadow. His chest was heaving and sweat ran freely down his body as he pumped his arms and his legs. Faster! He had to get there faster.

He was running so hard, so fast, that he barely noticed the barrier he crossed until he reached the other side and bounced back roughly, landing on his ass. It felt as if he had run into a brick wall headfirst. His head exploded in pain and the weakness he felt before was nothing compared to the lethargy that struck him now.

Wiping his hands across his face, he rolled to his feet, a low growl rumbling from his chest as he looked around to see what had trapped him.

"Richard!"

He turned to warn his mate not to cross into the clearing when she came tumbling down the slope, landing on her knees near the center of... It was a circle, he realized. Someone had cast a circle, and it held him trapped.

He spun around before her, standing in a defensive crouch to protect Amber as he lifted his nose, scenting whoever had them trapped. Some of his senses were dulled without his shadow-half, but Richard Strong wasn't human. His body was designed to make him the apex hunter. His nose created to pick up scents and his eyes designed to see things in a spectrum normal humans couldn't see.

A low laugh had him twisting, pulling Amber behind him, as he faced the danger walking toward them.

"Hello, Skinwalker."

The scent was familiar even if the voice wasn't.

"Who are you?" he roared, feeling his connection to his beast strengthen as she stepped closer.

"I'm your worst nightmare." She stepped into the bright light filtering down through the trees. How strong must evil be to exist and thrive in the light?

It seemed wrong that the woman walking toward him should have the scent of death and madness emanating from her pores. She was beautiful in a dark, dangerous way. Her hair was a mass of braids, liberally decorated with beads and feathers. Her skin was a rich mocha a few shades lighter than Amber's own creamy brown skin. She wore a pair of form-fitting jeans and a cream linen tunic that hung a little on her body. It looked like she'd been living rough for some time and that made him twitchy.

In her hands she held an earthenware jar, the

kind his old shaman kept around his home, one of the objects he described as ancient and sacred.

She held it in her hands as if it were a weapon and the dark, oily feel from it made his observations seem true. He wanted to back away from the thing but was strangely drawn to it as well.

"Don't you want to know what I have in the jar, monster?"

"Just who in the fuck are you?" Amber slid from around him and glared at the woman. His first instinct was to shove her back behind him, but common sense stayed his hand.

"Enthralled." She sounded almost sad as she stared at Amber. "No worries. I shall set you free."

"Enthralled? What the fuck are you talking about?"

Richard looked down at his mate and was shocked by what he saw. If she was a wolf, her hackles would have been raised and her teeth would have snarled. This woman had no fear... or she couldn't sense what it was.

"The jar," Richard managed to growl, his voice almost inhuman. "Give me the jar." He had an overwhelming urge to smash it.

"This?" She hefted the jar and Richard reached out to grab Amber's hand. She looked like she was going to rush over and smack it from the other woman's hands. "You want this jar? Then come and get it."

Richard took a step forward but she ripped the lid off the jar and sprinkled something inside.

Fire! Burning fire danced along Richard's spine. Howling, he dropped to his knees, his hands clawing at the earth as physically and spiritually he felt himself burn.

"Richard!" He could hear Amber calling out to him, but it sounded miles away and under water.

He could feel -- hear -- his shadow screaming in terror. It was an ear-piercing sound that shook him nearly out of his own pain. He tried to force it back, push it to the back of his mind, and after some terrifying moments, he managed it.

When his eyes opened, he discovered he was rolling on the ground, writhing in agony, as Amber knelt beside him.

The tears in her eyes made him swear she would never cry like that again.

He forced himself to his knees only to look up and see the evil woman standing closer. "So how do you like my medicine, Skinwalker?"

"What did you do to him?" Amber hissed, her hands fisting in his shirt. "I dare you to do that again."

"I'm just giving him a taste of his own medicine," she mused. "But you should have felt that."

"Felt what?"

"Odd." The woman, keeping her eyes on Amber, reached into her pocket and pulled out...

Richard jumped on Amber, knocking her away from the insane woman, covering her with his body as a handful of dark ash rained down on them.

Again fire ran across his skin, but it wasn't as intense as before. He bit his lip, holding in his screams as Amber rolled him over and ran her hands over his face and body.

"Baby?" She was trembling in her fear. He could smell it. "What did she do to you?"

"Interesting," the woman mused. "It doesn't have any effect on you at all."

"What is this shit?" He could feel Amber tense and looked over to see the woman moving closer.

"It's the bones of the ancient ones, used to trap his poisonous kind."

"Bones..." Richard gasped. "Anasazi -- my ancestors..."

"The only thing that can bind the demons to the earth. Sage to purify them, wolf's bane to hold them to his chosen shape... Who did you murder to get this power?"

"He was born with it, you idiot!" Amber screeched, but Richard knew it was hopeless. Common sense disappeared when speaking with the self-righteous and deranged. When someone was so sure they were right in their beliefs and everyone else was wrong, they become fanatics, and fanatics couldn't be reasoned with.

"D-don't waste your breath," he managed as he sat up.

"He's using his trickery to fool your mind," the woman insisted. "Maybe he's using fear. I sense fear in you."

"And fear leads to the fucking dark side," Amber snapped. "What game are you playing at?"

"No games," the woman insisted. "This is real life, girl. There are more things in the shadow that come crawling out, things that would consume your soul. Me and mine stop them."

"You and -- you were with the crazies who took Winston!"

"Those hunters weren't real hunters. I'm not sure what your friends are, but because my magic does not work on them, I'm not concerned. It would be curious to study them for a time, but in the long run, innocents are not what I'm hunting."

She placed the jar down and reached for Amber. "Come, it's not too late for you."

"Fuck you!"

Amber dove for her before Richard could caution her.

Both women hit the ground, kicking up dirt and screaming. He rolled to get closer to the jar -- something was still pulling him in that direction -- when the strange woman saw what he was doing.

"I don't think so," she hissed, rolling them over until she was on top of Amber and socking her in the jaw.

But instead of curling up and crying, Amber got a fierce expression on her face and returned the blow with interest, right in the woman's left breast. The woman doubled over, clutching her chest, and Amber bucked upwards with her hips, sending her sprawling.

Somehow knowing the importance of the jar, Amber scrambled for it only to fall flat on her face when Crazy grabbed her ankle and pulled.

"I'm doing this for your own good!" she screamed, and Amber's response was to kick out at her face.

The other woman let go and Amber lurched toward the jar where Richard was trying to overcome whatever was holding him back from it.

The sound of a gun cocking made them both freeze.

"I tried to be nice, to save you. And this is what I get? Kicked in the face?"

"You got punched in the tit too," Amber pointed out. "Be lucky I learned how to take a punch a long time ago or I would have gotten all Amazon warrior on your ass."

"Just move away," the woman sighed. "I'll deal with you after I deal with the Skinwalker."

"Let her go!" Richard managed to yell and she

looked at him in surprise.

"The binding should be holding you frozen to the earth. That you can move and talk is amazing to me. Maybe you Skinwalkers are evolving."

"He's not what you think," Amber began but got quiet as the gun was waved in her face.

"What to make of you?" she asked again, dropping to her knees beside Richard. Using what was left of his strength, he kicked the jar toward Amber.

But as his foot connected, there was a flash of dark and a black shadowy... thing rolled out. As soon as it touched the ground, it surged up in a wave and began to twist and writhe.

Anger washed over Richard as he lay on the ground panting. He watched as the jar attempted to call the shape back inside, but it fought, straining and tugging until a wolf's head was recognizable. It threw its head back in a silent howl that nevertheless reverberated through Richard's bones.

Richard was speechless, but he could feel the oily tendrils of black magic as they wrapped around his wolf.

Through the link he could now feel, he tried to send it his energy, to strengthen it so it could get away. But he was too weak, had gone too long without being whole. He didn't have much energy to spare.

"Bitch," he panted and the woman laughed.

He turned his eyes to Amber, watching her face pale as she stared at the shadow struggling to get free. Then suddenly he felt the link to his shadow self connect.

"You will pay." The shadow mouthed the words but they came from Richard's throat. Something of the bond was reconnecting, but it wasn't enough to free either one of them.

The woman rose to her feet, her gun pointed at Richard. This was clearly something she wasn't expecting.

"You pervert your knowledge and take delight in the pain you cause."

"Stop it!"

The dual-toned voice speaking in unison was clearly freaking her out. She began trembling as she took another step back.

"Mariah --"

"How do you know my name?" she whispered, and for the first time real fear from her scented the air. "You can't know that."

"I know a lot, Mariah. I know of the innocence you destroy in your insane quests."

"You're in the jar! The jar is sound. As long as the jar is sound, this cannot be happening!"

"Shoving me in with the remains of my ancestors will not stop the truth, Mariah. You're a murderer. You're a killer. You're far more monstrous, far more perverse than the creatures that you profess to hunt."

"No more," she whispered, reaching into her pocket for a handful of ash. "No more of your lies and your tricks!"

She threw the ash in Richard's face.

He threw back his head and howled.

He tried to push the pain away again, but it was too great, his nerves too raw. He rolled his head toward Amber and managed to shout, "Run!"

He didn't want her to see this madwoman put a bullet in his head, for that was where she was aiming.

"Destroy the host," she hissed. "Destroy the shadow."

Richard could see his death in her eyes and was determined to stare her down right to the bitter end.

He watched her face harden and her hand tense and...

The crashing sound of the jar made them both turn toward Amber. "You said as long as the jar was intact --"

That was as far as she got before an ungodly roar filled the circle. The air seemed to hold still, time seemed to stop, as the black mass fighting the tendrils of magic suddenly broke free.

"No!" Mariah threw her hand in the air as the shadow grew and grew.

Richard startled as Amber landed on her knees behind him, whispering his name, brushing the ash from his face.

They both watched as his massive shadow took flight. It circled the closed area, spinning wildly, moving nearly faster than the eye could see, willing its anger and frustration to the world... and its need for vengeance.

Mariah tried to run, but a tendril of black caught her leg, pulling her back toward the shadow. She scrambled to her feet and tried to run again, but the shadow cut her off, knocking her back toward the center of the circle. She tried a third time, pointing her gun and firing as she ran, but the bullets easily passed through the non-corporeal being. She was sobbing now, screaming in a language Richard couldn't understand... or maybe it was the gibberish of the insane.

Finally his beast began to settle into one large mass. The spinning stopped and Mariah was lifted into the air by one long mass of black.

The wolf began to take shape again, growing until it was the size of a large horse, its shadowy teeth flashing as if they were made of dark matter made flesh.

"No mercy. No quarter. No forgiveness."

Richard watched, wide eyed, as his shadow half lifted the insane hunter to his mouth and in two quick snaps, bit her in half and swallowed her whole.

"I -- I -- I --" Richard stammered.

"You didn't tell me he could do that," Amber breathed as the massive wolf began to shrink, licking his chops as it cleaned up spilled blood and viscera, almost like it hadn't just swallowed a woman whole.

"I -- didn't know."

"Break the circle." Richard blinked as his wolf spoke out loud for the first time in years. It had shrunk down to the size of a German Shepherd and was wagging its tail at Amber.

"Who, me?" His lady was tougher than he thought, but maybe a man-eating shadow was the limit of her tolerance for strangeness.

"Are you not our bitch?"

"What did you call me?" Her fear was being replaced by anger again.

"Bitch... rather, mate?" his shadow offered, dropping his tail in submission. "If you prefer --"

"Damn straight I do. I'm not a female dog, a Skinwalker, or a ghetto girl to take that name as a compliment."

"Forgive?" His wolf stared up at her with his head lowered, his tail wagging from side to side.

Five minutes in her presence and he was already under her spell. Amber Graves was an amazing woman.

"Never do that again," she snapped as she rose to her feet. "And no more disappearing acts. You weakened Richard, and he could have been killed a number of times. And what's with following me around? In the bathroom, in the bedroom... that shit will stop right now."

"Yes, mate." His wolf inched closer to her, nudging her hand.

"No biting." She finally sucked in her fear and touched him.

Richard purred. He could feel her caresses as if they were on his own head.

"No," his shadow self rumbled, rubbing along her legs more like a kitten than a ferocious beast. "I could never harm that which completes us. It's our responsibility and our privilege to protect you."

"I can protect myself." Amber was realizing this more and more. "It's you two idiots who get caught in traps and chased by psychos."

"Idiots," Richard grumbled, and his wolf looked back at him and damn if it didn't stick out its tongue.

"No comment from the peanut gallery... at least not until I break this circle of ash thing so you can move."

He felt whatever was holding him to the ground dissipate as Amber used her feet to break the ash ring. He slowly rose to his feet.

He felt weak, but at the same time, he could feel his strength returning.

He turned and made to walk over toward Amber, only to be knocked onto his ass once more.

"You're stubborn," his wolf snarled in his face.

He looked over and saw Amber pale a little, but she swallowed her fear and stood there, waiting.

"So are you," Richard snarled back. "And at least I didn't run away."

"It was to teach you a lesson. You need me."

"And I hope you learned you need me too," Richard countered. "Getting caught in a witch's trap. You needed me and you brought this onto your own self."

"Hey!" They both stopped snarling as they turned to face Amber. "You need one another. You need human intelligence augmented by wolf instinct. If you two get it together, you can be an unstoppable force."

There was a tense moment of silence where wolf and man stared each other down.

"She's right," Richard sighed, holding up his splinted hand. "You protect me from much."

"You stop me from much foolishness," his wolf allowed. "We need each other." Open and honest in all things was the way of the wolf.

"I'll try to remember and to respect," Richard vowed as he opened his arms wide.

"As will I."

Then the wolf took one massive leap and slammed into Richard's chest. Instead of passing through, it seemed to encompass him for a second, a dark black aura, until it sank into his body.

Richard couldn't describe how it felt. It was like being caressed from the inside, being stroked and loved and comforted in places where human hands couldn't touch. It was like summer time and rainbows and laughter filling him once more. He only felt this way when he joined with his mate. There was only one word to describe it. Richard Strong was now complete.

"So... am I going to get indigestion?" he asked his wolf out loud as his shadow emerged, fully connected to him once more.

"*I don't know,*" it answered as his shadow-half raced toward Amber. "I never tried that before."

"Not on small animals when you were out?" He looked aghast.

"*Why eat small animals? I like fettuccini Alfredo.*"

"You both need a keeper." Amber chuckled.

She didn't look any the worse for wear, but Richard knew he had to keep an eye on her. Too many traumatic things had happened in one day for her to just walk away as if nothing had happened. There were bound to be some repercussions from this day... probably nightmares. But he would be by her side, easing her through so she would not face anything alone.

He would feel nothing. He wasn't human. The witch Mariah was trying to kill him and instead she'd reaped what she sowed. There was balance in the universe once more.

"*You mated.*" His shadow danced around her. "*I can smell it and -- yip!*"

"Get your nose out of my crotch, wolf," Amber growled. Richard's shadow-self hunkered down whimpering, before he lifted his tail in the air playfully, twirling around their mate in a show of air and darkness.

"How did you know her name?" Amber asked, and Richard listened in. It was something he really wanted to know.

"*Witch was insane, smelled wrong, like she needed to be put down. She mumbled her name a lot. I listen.*"

"This is going to take some getting used to," Amber decided.

"But are we worth it?"

"Will your stamina increase?" she asked, a wicked smile on her face. "I mean you're amazing in bed... but if it gets better..." He could smell her sudden arousal. Okay. Sex was a good coping mechanism.

"It will," he promised. "Tenfold. I still missed some spots when I was licking you down. I wanna find all of those tonight."

"Good," she breathed. "You know, of course, you're going to have to carry me to the bathroom to clean up, right?"

"Just wait until you see my shower," he promised. "It's orgasmic."

He could feel his strength returning as she grabbed his arms and started pulling him toward the car.

"Then get a move on, Sheriff. Time for you to protect and serve."

Their laughter echoed around the forest, carrying toward the gently bubbling falls... getting lost in the low babbling of the waves as they fell into a deep blue pool.

Epilogue

"I can't believe this," Richard grumbled, staring at his cell phone as if it had personally affronted him. "I got to put an APB out on someone. This is a first."

"Who?" Winston asked as he paused in hefting a box to his shoulders. "I didn't think you had enough criminals in this podunk town --"

"Hey!" Richard protested his town being called something as mundane and insulting as podunk. "My town is awesome."

"Nowhere else in the world is like it," Klint agreed, his wings out and free as he moved past them both. He was openly sporting his wings around town now, drumming up more business for the Fae movie now in active production. Whenever anyone saw them, they demanded to know where he got them and if they could get a set for themselves. Somehow Grame had used some special effects magic and created a set that almost mimicked Klint's colorful limbs. He was marketing them to movie companies. He promised to have a cheaper set commissioned and created for the general public for the Fae movie, so long as he got a cut of the sales.

"And I had one criminal who was supposed to come back here and face justice," he grumbled. "But someone had to go and be all altruistic and post bail for him." He glared at Amber as she carried her most prized possession into his house.

It took some doing to convince the skittish Amber to move in with him, but the practical benefits of not having to race home, allowing them to lie in and enjoy the afterglow of their awesome sex life was a major convincer. Lila approved of their relationship and would only be needing her room for a few months until she went off to school. Besides, the apartment was still the scene of Toddy's break-in, and because he had invaded her safe zone, Amber found herself uncomfortable when home alone. The bastard had stolen so much from her and had still managed to take a bit more before blowing town.

"I just wanted him gone."

He followed her into the house and into the living room where her entertainment center now held the place of honor. His glass-and-brass TV stand had gone to Lila's room and would follow her to college, along with his barely used pots and pans, his old writing desk, and about three cases of pepper spray. He wasn't Lila's father -- she was far too old to be babied by her mother's lover. But he wanted to do everything he could to make the young woman, who he saw as more of a bratty little sister than a daughter, safe when she was far from home. The pepper spray and the knowledge that a few of his "network's" offspring would be attending the same school, reassured him when she was out of his sight.

"Really," he drawled, walking up behind her and wrapping her in his arms. He relaxed as she leaned back into his embrace for a moment before leaning forward to place the dented space ship in its case dead center on the top shelf, which was so high she had to rise up on tiptoe to get it in place. Richard, never letting an opportunity slide by, ran his hands over her sides where her shirt had risen up, delighting in the soft feel of her skin.

"Really, Richard. I just wanted that asshole gone. I didn't need him in my town, polluting the air I breathe. So posting his bail was a small price to pay to be rid of him once and for all."

"Well, you're going to have to deal with him

some more when we catch him. He failed to show up at court. Deputy Markus reported in and waited until the judge issued a bench warrant. I had to put out an APB on the son of a bitch because he's that dangerous. I'm afraid you lost your bail money on this one."

"I'm not worried." She shrugged as she turned in his arms. "Not when I have such big strong men to protect me."

"Damn right," Bryan called as he walked in, placing a box labeled "kitchen" on the breakfast bar. "We got you covered."

"And I already sent the bail money back to you," Angel added, walking out of the bedroom holding a bright captain's-red colored thong on one finger. "I didn't take you for the type, Amber."

"Klint! Control your man!" Amber squealed as she lurched from Richard's embrace, leaping to tear the thin underwear away from the man as he held them above his head, high out of her reach.

"Yeah, Richard," Angel teased. "Especially since this banana hammock is for men," he teased, holding up the price tag on the new pair of undergarments. "When you asked me to put the bedroom boxes in the bedroom, I didn't think this would be hanging from the ceiling fan…"

"I never got to model them, either." Richard laughed as Amber's cheeks flamed red. "I pulled them out of the bag and she pounced like the wild animal she is."

"Richard," Amber wailed, finally jumping up and jerking the undies away from a laughing Angel.

"Oh." Klint smiled, fluttering his wings as he watched his mate and his heart-sister play. "We have those in every color spectrum. It appears Angel can't stop ripping them off of me when he feels the need for an oral fix --"

"Enough about your creepy X-rated sex lives," Lila screeched, diving into Bryan's arms and hiding her head in his shoulder. "The last thing I want to picture is mom and Dick Strong having sex."

"Don't call me Dick," Richard grumbled, pulling a giggling Amber back into his arms. "You'll scar my delicate ego." Only he and Amber actually heard his wolf snort in laughter, though it seemed that everyone in the room, besides Amber, saw his shadow grow into a menacing form on the far wall before he began wagging his tail.

"No, scarring is seeing you take down my sperm donor buck naked." Lila shuddered. "I'll never forget that as long as I live... But I have to admit, I understand why Mom fell for you."

"You won't have to worry about that abusive asshole again," Richard promised, hugging Amber tighter. "In fact, as far as I'm concerned, you never have to lay eyes on him again as long as you live."

"*Got that right*," his wolf chortled, and Richard jerked back a little as Amber flashed his wolf a conspiring glance and a wicked smile.

"What --"

"I have you to protect me." Amber turned to face him, cupping his face in both hands and pulling him down for a kiss.

All thoughts of conspiracies disappeared as he touched her, as he wrapped his arms around her, pulling her body flush to his, and he lost himself in the flavor of her.

He lost his train of thought and never noticed his wolf give a self-satisfied belch as he licked his chops and settled in, with his full belly, against the wall, watching his human with a smirk.

Rare as a Unicorn
Stephanie Burke

Baylin and Torin are not totally complete. The pair of veterinarians in Angel Falls have a lot going for them -- talent, exciting careers, the love of each other, and a strong relationship... so why can't they get a third to commit to being with them?

Jova is a warrior, a savior, and a martyr of his people, giving up his life to ensure their protection. He never expected Magic to have its way with him and send him to this new place of sanctuary. The only problem is what to do with these damn hands? He was once a unicorn, masterful and proud... now he can't fathom human bathroom practices. People are strange, and none more strange and desirable than the pair who rescues him one snowy morning.

The attraction is immediate, but how can they make this work?

Prologue

"They are coming!" Jova's second nickered as he drove the rest of the herd toward the designated spot.

"I know," the stallion muttered, his pale coat glowing in the dark gold of the night sky.

Would he ever see the night glisten so prettily above? How could he be so selfish? Would any of them ever...

"I will create the vortex," Jova decided.

"But --" his second protested.

"I am the only one powerful enough to do this!" the head stallion snapped, turning white eyes to his subordinate. "It is up to you to lead them after I get them to safety."

"But --"

"Are my words not heard?" The bellow almost drowned out the sounds of the screaming winds and the snapping of trees, the signature ploy of the hunters to confuse and frighten their prey.

"Yes, Lead." The second bowed his head for a moment before turning and racing off toward the milling herd, instructing them to make ready to depart this planet and maybe, if what the Lead had been discussing with the elders was true, this dimension.

The Lead bowed his head, his slick body buffeted by the winds, his long mane whipping about him almost as wildly as the emotions that flowed through him. But he was a strong male, a powerful male, the only one capable of harnessing the powers in this storm and using them to boost his own magic to the herd's advantage.

With his powerful neck bent low to the ground, snorting in determination, anyone watching could see why this male was chosen to lead.

He was all muscle, with large, rippling flanks that defied the attempts of the gale-force winds to knock him from his hooves. His withers were wide and solid, and broad, showing his strength. His whole body rippled, straining, as he refused to give into the artificial elements designed to startle, frighten, and confuse his herd.

He refused to move, planting his feet solidly, in defiance of the conjured storm. His upper lip was drawn back, his fangs gritted and bared, as if daring the magic that flowed within him to defy his order.

He snorted once, stomping his rear hooves as the magic began to build and his horn, a long spiral of flesh and magic, began to glow.

"Behind me!" he bellowed as he closed his eyes. With a wet, tearing sound, the air behind him blackened and spun. He could feel his heart racing as he fought to keep the storm raging around them from forcing the air from his lungs.

He could feel his magic, feel himself gathering the power of the storm that surrounded them, feel his dying planet offer up the last of its energy as if it understood he was to protect the beings it had sheltered within its earthen arms since the dawn of time.

Fire flashed throughout his blood, making his body hum as he struggled to hold himself together against the enormous influx of wild magic, of energy that would have torn apart a lesser being. The burn was… It was beyond anything he had ever felt. It was a sweet benediction; a selfless offering of love at the same time it was a torturous rite that no one else could endure, that no one would want to endure. Yet… he had to endure. There was no other option. If he failed, then his herd, the last of their kind, would diminish and fade into stardust, a shining memory to those who were enslaved and those who still fought to be free.

When the pain was nearly enough to drop him to his knees, he tilted his head up and began to shout the spell. The wind tore the words from his mouth; his long mane seemed to transform into a silken net that lashed painfully at his face and eyes. He screamed the spell, pronouncing each word, clicking and nickering where such emphasis was needed until a vortex of swirling blues and grays slowly formed and grew behind him. Once the vortex was stable, pulsing with the combined magic from his soul and the offering from Mother Earth, he lowered his head, his sides heaving with the effort of holding the magical gateway steady, and lifted his eyes enough to stare at his second.

"Move!" His second repeated his order, beginning to drive the frightened mares, fillies, and colts before him.

This herd was small, numbering no more than eighty; a group of foundlings that the Lead had discovered and brought to a place of safety after the culling had begun. He had risked more than his life to bring them all here and unite them as one herd. And he would be doing more than risking his life once again to see them safe.

Clods of grass were sent flying, swirling in the cold and bitter wind as the first of the unicorns, frightened and confused, raced into the magical pocket.

And through it all, with head bent and teeth gritted, the Lead held his stance, pulling power from the air, grounding it throughout his body, and bending it to his will.

Soon after the mares and their young were

through, the older males and the elders galloped past, each nodding to their great leader, sadness in their gazes. They knew he would not survive to make it to the safe lands he had sought and found for them after many turnings of the seasons.

The wind was whipping harder now, screaming and whining as if someone had given it a voice. The force of it increased until trees were uprooted and branches whizzed dangerously through the air.

"They are through," the Second called out, racing to his leader's side.

"Then -- why are -- you -- still here?" The strain on his body and voice was evident. "You need to get through."

"They need you!" the Second screamed, his voice strained, terror and regret vying in his heart for dominance. The Lead could almost read his mind, could almost see the questions flowing though his head. He was too young... he had not been Second long enough... and the most scary question... what if he failed and his people died?

"They need a leader!" The Lead blinked his eyes and slowly, still fighting against the wind, turned his head to stare at the smaller male. "We are the gatherers of dreams made whole. We are the keepers of fantasy and purity. But we will not survive unless you are strong enough to take command of the herd."

"But -- but --" the Second's wide black eyes watered as he snorted in frustration. "The vortex will last for a few moments after you release the power. You can race after us! You can make it!"

"Not if -- I cut -- the magic."

The Second's eyes widened as he stared at his leader in disbelief. "That will create a backlash!" he screamed, his own powerful body quivering with the force of the storm and with his shock. "You will not survive that!"

"I -- know!"

"But --"

"I chose you --" The Lead's body shuddered as he fought to hold the vortex true and direct its course throughout time and space. "I chose you because out of all the males I reared, your soul -- it shines the brightest." He looked at the large white body, and he felt a sense of pride that momentarily blotted out all fear. "Your soul is the brightest of them all, my son. You need -- to go!"

"Damn you!" the Second roared, tears openly running down his cheeks as his black hair swirled around them, mingling with the silver white of the Lead's -- of his sire -- encircling them both. The glow in his Lead stallion's horn began to flicker. "Damn you for doing this, for being their hope! And damn them!" The Lead's son turned toward the approaching hunters, his whole body quaking. "Damn them all!"

"Go!" the Lead snapped, turning his head back toward the newly torn path in the earth that his people had blazed to get to this clearing. "They are close, my son! I cannot hold this for much longer!"

"Jova!" his Second screamed the name, before the powerful head lowered to nuzzle his Lead's sweat-soaked shoulder. "We will never forget you." Then, in a swirl of black mane and golden hooves, the Second disappeared into the vortex, bellowing for the people, now his responsibility, to move back and brace themselves.

"You are my successor!" the Lead stallion called out, knowing his voice would carry through. "In all things that I protect with my life and my soul, I charge you to defend --"

Before he could finish the ceremonial words, the first of the hunters burst into the clearing.

"Go with the creator," the Lead muttered before turning to face the approaching horde of gray-skinned hunters, tossing his head in defiance.

"Get them!" one of the leather-clad monsters bellowed, his huge mouth open as he charged forward, battle ax held at the ready.

But with a sneer, the Lead snapped the energy lines that held the vortex in this dimension.

There was a whoosh of sound, a shriek louder than the wind, and the deafening sound of a booming explosion as time and space were displaced. The vortex, once a blue and gold swirl of energy, collapsed into itself, creating a small pocket of black before it winked out of existence.

His people were now safe.

The Lead stallion's whole body shook at the sudden break in magic; his legs wobbled as his body sought to compensate for the loss of his own personal magic. His vision swirled as he fought to remain conscious. Using his own personal energy as a stabilizer for the storm had taken a powerful toll, and yet he was the only unicorn strong enough to hold the vortex and send it spiraling among the stars, directed by will and magic to a place of safety where the hunters could never track them.

The energy depleted, leaving him weak and drained, barely able to hold control of his powerful equine form. It was sheer anger and sadistic delight that kept him standing, as shaky as he was. But it was more than worth it to watch the pitiful creatures who hunted them lose out on the prize that had so eluded them once again.

"They are gone!" he roared as the first of the

hunters drew close enough to hear him over the storm. He drew his lips up in a sneer as he watched understanding blossom in the hunter's many sets of orange eyes.

Rotund, leather-clad demons they were, he thought, his breathing ravaged as the storm came to an abrupt end. There was no reason for the beasts to maintain it now that their quarry had gone to ground.

He could not understand their language of squeaks and clicks, but he understood the anger in their faces and in their stances. He could smell the rancid scent of it perfuming the now still air.

He took a step, his hooves helping him take a stance as he faced the creatures he knew would take their anger out on his body before they gave him the sweet release of death.

They clicked at him, pointing and growling in their anger, and he tossed his head defiantly.

"Come and get me, then!" he roared.

The beasts moved forward, and he stared them down, head held high as he cast his thanks to his dying planet, thanks for offering up all that was left of her and allowing those who loved her like good sons and daughters to live somewhere far off where not even he could find them.

As he watched death approach slowly -- they knew he had nothing left in him so there was no need to rush -- he prayed to the magic that had sustained them this far, that he would pass before they began to feast on his body. The hunters had been known to eat their prey alive.

He watched them, and they sneered as they approached, axes at the ready. He watched as a pair of muscular arms swung the ax high and then... then there was a cracking sound as the earth pulsed beneath his hooves.

The world heaved, splitting itself in two as a wave of energy passed over him. He was unprepared when the energy took on sentient overtones and snatched control of what was left of his magic. He felt his whole body hum as the hunters were knocked off their short, muscular legs. His whole body began to glow, his blood to pulse as he was infused with feelings of… of love and regret.

"Safe." The word seemed to float through his frantic thoughts as his hooves left the ground.

There was a roaring in his ears and a beautiful, agonizing pain filled his body. One part of his brain was focused on the hunters, watching as they scrambled, fear in their glowing orange eyes for once, while the other part was struck numb by the beauty of the magic now filling him.

He felt as if he were being balled up, twisted, and shrunk by harsh but loving hands.

"Safe." The word floated through him once more, calming him as his eyes fell closed and he found himself floating in a sea of black.

There was a pop, more felt than heard, and suddenly he was hurtling through the dark of night. He felt those hands, those awful, wonderful hands caress him once more, a full-body embrace, and then he was flung far away. Clouds enveloped him, making him shiver as his lungs struggled to take in air.

What… how… The planet, he realized. Mother Earth had once again reached out for him, saving him, giving up the last of herself to see him -- her last child -- safe.

Before he could dwell on the enormity of their planet sacrificing what was left of herself to save him, there was an explosion of sound, and he was hurtled through something warm and wet before the ground reached up to him, slamming him into unconsciousness.

Chapter 1

"What the fuck?"

Without meaning to, Torin bucked so hard that Baylin went flying off the bed and landed on the carpet with a painful-sounding thump. But just as quickly, she was on her feet, racing to the large picture window that overlooked the forest.

"Poachers," she hissed as she tossed her hair over her shoulders and ran for the en suite bathroom to give herself a quick high-low sink bath.

"You just going to sit there with a wet dick?" she asked as she began to scramble into her clothing.

The "yes" was on the tip of his tongue -- the devil on his shoulder was just urging him to say it -- but he was sure she would hurt him if he laughed. His fiery Italian babe was unpredictable like that.

"Coming," he said softly as he pulled his body from the tangle of blankets and sheets and gained his feet.

His dick was still hard... and as she'd said, wet. His whole damn groin was wet because his wife was just so... She was hot. They had started the evening with a glass of wine and oral sex, a wonderful combination on a cold winter night.

He licked his lips and could still taste the musky sweet flavor of her pussy. His face had been slick and shiny with her, and she had been choking, slobbering, and gagging on his dick like she would die if she didn't get it into her soon. She had one hand rolling his balls as she managed to deep throat him and lick his balls at the same time. She had shoved him down onto their bed and mounted him like Annie Oakley when he was startled out of his zone and tossed her on her pretty shapely ass. Once Baylin got her engine running, nothing short of an act of God or what sounded like shotgun blasts would stop her.

Once on his feet, he shook off thoughts of what could have been and began to dress in his discarded clothing.

He paused with his boxers in his hands and shrugged. Why not? It would not do to maybe run into some criminals smelling like stale sex -- not that poachers deserved their courtesy. He respected his wife too much, though, to allow that to happen. So he moved in behind her, gripping the full cheeks of her ass to give them a squeeze -- he couldn't help himself. There was a magnetic attraction between his hand and her ass, and he smiled as she tossed her hair in his face. Baylin was such a tease.

As fast as humanly possible, they each did a preliminary wash-up and donned their winter gear. As the only vets in about a ninety-mile radius, they had to be prepared for anything no matter the season. They were wearing thick snow pants and matching parkas. They had convertible gloves that allowed them the use of their fingers when needed and wore skullcaps on their heads. Winter in the mountains of Angel Falls was nothing to play with. Several tourists had gotten lost in the forests surrounding the falls in the past, and more than a few of them had succumbed to frostbite.

"Only one shot," Baylin muttered, as they stood outside on the front porch of their office/home. "Maybe it was poachers. You know there are some wolves and bobcats roaming the woods."

"If they are stupid enough to go hunting in the woods where nocturnal apex predators hunt, then they deserve what they get."

Torin inhaled deeply of the cold air, letting it fill his lungs, the sting of it shaking away any lingering sexual thoughts.

The forests at night, even in winter, were beautiful. The dark purple sky reflected off the snow, casting everything in an ethereal, glowing light. The dark, tall shapes of the trees, denuded of their cheerful fall foliage, cast long shadows along the freshly fallen snow. The full moon was a glowing yellow disk that brought up memories of his Obasan's tales of Yoko Ono and other supernatural beings that went bump in the night. Japanese mythology was filled with them.

He looked over at his wife and noted the intense look on her face. She could have been an avenging spirit, out to punish humans for messing with the animal messengers of the gods.

She was very protective of the things that she loved, and thankfully one of those things was him. Her animals came a close second, but Baylin looked like she was gearing up for a rescue mission.

"I'm going to go south." She pointed toward the area where they had seen a den of wolves that fall. Wolves were near and dear to her heart ever since she was a child and saw them on a nature program, protecting their young. Watching their society and their civility inspired her to become a vet herself.

The animals treated their own more kindly than humans treated theirs.

"I got my radio. I think I just want to check on some things. There was only one shot, so either they were poachers and they got what they were hunting for, they were just defending themselves, or they are still out there looking."

"They could be lost tourists?"

She shot him a telling look that called him a cute adorable idiot.

"This time of year? There aren't many tourists

here in the winter, Torin. It's one of the main reasons we can't get a third partner to stay. And if there were tourists in the area, the sheriff would have let us know so we could look out for them."

She had a point -- not that he would ever tell her. Her smugness would have been unbearable. The last two temporary partners had loved the crazy town where something unusual was always happening, but no one could really take the harsh mountain winters. He and Baylin had just about given up hope on getting someone from outside the mountain to become a permanent partner and were considering looking for the willing in town. It was not the most ideal solution to their wants, knowing the history of the town and its denizens as well as they did from interaction and gossip, but it was that or giving up on finding a third for their relationship.

"I concede your point," he nodded. "I'm going north. I want a check-in from you every fifteen minutes. If you come across anything -- anything at all -- signal me. Don't go charging in ready to give your life to the greater good."

"Like I would do that." She snorted, rolling her eyes before rising on her toes to kiss him on the cheek. "And you'd better hurry, lover. Once we get done with this job, I have another one for you to complete."

"Well now, that is a little bit of all right," he purred, his hands going to her rounded hips to pull her in close as he pressed a small kiss on her lips.

If time permitted, he would unzip the front of her snow pants, bend her over, and plow her into the nearest tree trunk or snow bank. He loved Baylin, but he also loved the hell out of Baylin's body. She had enough ass to cushion his somewhat bony hips, and her pussy... He would love to sit down and have a five-course meal there.

He ground his hard dick into her stomach, just so she would know how much he was turned on by her very presence, before he let her go.

"Be safe, lover," she chuckled against his lips before she pulled away and took off into the snow, fearless, as if nothing in the world could harm her.

He wanted to protect her, to coddle her because it was dangerous out there. But telling her that would probably result in her slapping his head into next week... then demanding that he go and pick it up. Torin's mother had reared no fools so he kept his damn mouth shut and spent a moment appreciating her walking away from him -- damn, that ass was fine -- then he turned and headed out into the cold, dark woods.

* * *

"Men are so easily led by their dicks," Baylin snorted as she tramped through the fallen snow, grateful that more hadn't come down while they were at home.

Her evening had been going great. She made dinner and Torin got off his butt to help, which was an amazing thing when one realized how rarely it happened. Torin was a product of his Japanese father and his Southern Belle of a mother and had some interesting views about what was men's work and what was set aside for women. That and the man could burn water. She had watched him do it once and stood there in amazement as he ruined her pot. He was not allowed to cook without adult supervision, but he could be a decent sous chef when she prodded him into it.

He didn't complain about the scarcity of her home cooking, but when she was bogged down with work and didn't have time to make dinner, there was that disappointment in his eyes. He would not help her do dishes if she was in the kitchen -- said she criticized his technique -- but if she wasn't watching over him, he would break dishes and create more work.

Her workload was almost identical to his, yet she was the one cooking hot meals almost every night and doing most of the prep and clean-up too. It wasn't like the man didn't support her. He was always there to help out with the animals she brought in or with any number of research papers she had to write, edit, and get ready for publication. But getting that man to do housework was like pulling hen's teeth.

Which meant that most of her evenings were spent racing to the kitchen at the end of the day to at least put in a frozen pizza for them to share, but sometimes the whole situation was just tedious.

But today? Today was one of the good days.

She had tracked her wolves earlier in the morning and found the pack settling in nicely for the upcoming winter. The injured eagle she was caring for had begun to take meals and that meant his depression over having a broken wing was ending. She didn't spend too much time coddling the huge raptor, but he and his surly ways were beginning to grow on her.

She and Torin shared clinical hours, and that meant there were a few constipated cats to deal with as well as the usual spaying and neutering. There was a sick bunny with a cold and a hamster with wet tail, but all in all, no losses, and everyone went home happy.

Torin cleaned the pens for the adoptable animals while she put together specialized meals for both the patients and the animals looking for a good home. Then in a surprising twist, Torin came in after dinner and helped her with the dishes. After that he produced a very good dessert wine, and they sipped while warming their toes by the fire.

There wasn't much to do in winter in Angel Falls, so enjoying enforced time together sometimes became a bit of a challenge. Before they moved here from Baltimore, there were scenes to explore, couples who were in the same alternative lifestyle they enjoyed bonding and spending time with -- even just taking a walk or going to a movie house was an easy thing to do. Life in Angel Falls was challenging and was great for their work ethic, but so damaging to their social life. The most excitement they'd had in years was when the ex-football player/writer guy had his home assaulted by some religious nut jobs and the town was overrun with reporters, and then again this past summer with a rash of looters at some of the area's numerous campsites. No wonder they couldn't find a third who wanted to trade in the excitement of the city. Dull was not exactly the word to describe the place, but it did almost fit.

Anyhow… wine led to a hot oil massage, and that led to her being so grateful that her aching back and shoulders were seen to that she damn near choked herself on his cock showing him how much she appreciated his help.

No, there could be no complaints about their sex life. Torin was a master when it came to sex.

In oral, that man developed a vibrating tongue that had some kind of radar that sought out all other hot spots. His fingers were long and fine, but thick enough to stretch her walls perfectly. He never forgot to stimulate her labia and her clit, and he sincerely enjoyed going down on her. In fact, she had to grip him by the hair and pull him up after her third orgasm of the night.

She threw his ass down on the bed and had mounted, ready to ride for a gold medal and at least a rose wreath when the shot had been fired, and she had been summarily dumped onto her ass.

She was sure her ass had carpet burn as well as an imprint of the wood floor underneath it, but she ignored the slight pain in a rush to get dressed. Her wolves could be in danger.

She had never gotten dressed so fast. She cleaned up a bit and threw on the clothes she had earlier discarded in her haste to fuck, and was ready to go, her concerned husband right behind her.

And now she was tramping through the snow, praying her wolves weren't the victims of a poacher. She would skin those bastards alive if they hurt one hair on her babies' furry little heads.

There was the alpha male she called Sundance and the alpha bitch that was named Butch. There were four pups, all born a bit late in the season, but healthy. Mamma and Daddy were attentive, and they appeared healthy, and all six of them had better still be in their den or so help her God…

Heaven have pity on anyone who would disturb them, because she had none. She knew where to dispose of the bodies if it came down to that.

With thoughts of protecting her pack in mind, she moved a little faster, heading toward the direction she thought the shot had come from. Then she saw him… her… them.

Tossed at the base of a tree like so much garbage was a pale body that glowed even in the purple twilight and the growing shadows of the denuded forest. She stepped closer to the figure, concerned when it didn't move, before racing over and dropping to her knees beside it.

It was a human being! Someone had tossed a naked woman -- man? God, she didn't know -- out into the snow.

She ripped her gloves off with her teeth, stuffing them in her pocket with one hand as she reached for the figure's neck, but pulling back at the last second. She didn't know what to do! If it had been a wolf...

There was a lot of silver-blond hair and long, slim limbs and not much else there.

She pressed her comm and called for her husband.

"Torin, I got a body --"

"Your wolves?" She could hear him turning around as the mic picked up the crunch of snow under his feet. He began to move in her direction at a rapid clip. "Was it --?"

"Human," she corrected as she began to pull off her jacket. "There's a young lady... man... person here, Torin. Someone dumped them naked in the woods."

"Are they alive?"

"I -- I don't know!"

"I'm calling the sheriff --"

"Get over here and help me get them back to the house," she insisted. "Make a note of the time and call later. They are naked, Torin... I don't -- I don't know what or who did this to them."

As she spoke, she began to tuck her coat around the figure on the ground, ignoring the cold that seemed to wrap around her and squeeze her lungs into silence. It hurt so much to breathe. Or maybe that was the shock. Even under her layers her flesh pebbled up with goose bumps. It had to be so much worse for the poor thing lying in the snow.

And she didn't even know if they were alive.

Casting aside her fear, Baylin reached out and

pressed her fingers against the long, slim neck.

"Thank God," she breathed, unaware that her radio was still receiving. She pressed her fingers deeper into the cool flesh, feeling the faint thrum of a pulse when light flashed, pain shot up her hand, and she found herself screaming as she was thrown across the clearing.

Her back impacted harshly with the snow a few feet away from the person as she struggled to sit up and try to figure out what had happened.

"Baylin!" Torin was screaming into her earpiece as she sat there dazed. "Damn it. Answer me, Baylin!"

He was huffing -- running faster, she realized -- and managed to sit up just as he raced into the clearing.

"Baylin!" He tripped across the snow, sliding on his knees, kicking up tufts of snow as he came to rest at her side.

Her fingers were still tingling as she stared wide-eyed at her husband. "I -- uh --"

The moaning of the person had her pushing away from her husband and moving back to their side.

"What happened? I heard you scream --"

"I -- I don't know... lightning?" she tried to joke, but the tingling was giving way to a scary numbness, and she couldn't maintain her position on her feet.

Torin helped ease her back into a seated position before removing his jacket and wrapping it around her. Baylin snuggled into the comfy warmth of her husband's coat, breathing in his musky scent.

She didn't know what to tell him. One moment she was getting proof of life and then she was lying in the snow feet away with burning fingertips and numb arm.

But the person moaned again, and her husband

was moving toward them, reaching out to touch him...

Touch them... Touch...

"Torin!" she called out in warning, but too late. There was a flash of light, and her husband was on his ass beside her in the snow, looking just as dazed and confused as she must have looked. "Uh... I touched them last."

"I gathered," he muttered, seemingly not as affected as she was. He struggled to his knees and moved cautiously toward the moaning body.

"Static?" She hazarded a guess, knowing how stupid it sounded.

"Only if they came hurtling in from space," he grumbled. "Protection device?" he asked as he reached out one hand, touching the head. "Maybe a TASER?" Baylin winced, waiting for a repeat of the static blast, but let out a breath she wasn't even sure she was holding as nothing happened.

Torin looked back at her and nodded as she managed to get to her feet and stagger closer. The numbness was leaving her body at a rapid pace.

"The electricity has dissipated," he explained, pushing hair out of the person's face until he encountered a...

Baylin leaned closer. Was that a horn?

Dammed if it wasn't a tiny horn embedded in the middle of his -- her -- even with the face exposed she couldn't tell.

It was a fine face, though, very feminine with no masculine undertones. The skin was nearly as pale as the snow, as pale as the frosty white hair. *It* had nearly invisible eyebrows that framed almond-shaped eyes and an aquiline, narrow nose. The lips were full and a tiny, pointed chin gave the face an elfin look that the slightly pointed ears completed.

"Does electricity dissipate?" she asked, still confused by the whole affair. "I swear if felt like I was struck by lightning."

"M-magic b-back-backlash."

The words caused both Baylin and her husband to stare down at the form in the snow. The voice was strange, low and deep but light and lilting. There was an accent there, but she couldn't place it with just two words.

"Magic…" As she began the person moaned and its eyelids fluttered. Its eyelashes were black and framed the most beautiful, eerie set of black eyes she had ever seen. Really, they were black. There were no whites in the eye to be seen at all, and they seemed to be sprinkled with stardust as the lashes fluttered and the person licked their lips.

"Where --"

They tried to lift their head, but Torin stopped them.

"Don't move," he said softly.

Those black eyes turned to him before they widened in shock, the nostrils flaring in very real fear. It was a reaction they saw in wounded animals all the time, and it translated well to the unguarded human face.

The creature's head tilted as it looked around the area wildly before it's gaze settling back on her husband who was reaching for the person.

The person tried to scramble back, nostrils flaring as they began breathing harshly, the panicked look increasing. Their whole body seemed to freeze before their eyes rolled back, and they passed out as her husband jerked back.

"What the fuck was that?" Torin was looking both hurt and confused as he stared down at the figure in the snow. He was a healer, and he was not used to people -- to any being -- staring at him like he was a monster.

"Naked, scared enough to pass out... Torin, you think they were sexually assaulted?"

"Fuck," he sighed. "He or she was afraid of me."

He hung his head for a moment, as if the weight of the world had suddenly settled on his shoulders, before he shook his head and reached for the now still body.

"Torin..." she protested, but he waved her off.

'They are already passed out, Baylin, and we can't leave them out here. We have to get her or him warm and dry and then figure out what to do."

As he spoke, a heavy snowfall began to coat them both in a fresh, innocent blanket of white.

Nodding, she rose to her feet, her arm finally cooperating, helping by keeping the long, slim body covered as much as she could in her coat.

Their hair was like a blanket, totally covering any identifying body parts, and Baylin didn't feel right trying to push the hair aside to see if the person had small boobs. If she and Torin were right in their assumptions, the person had been violated enough.

Silently, they moved toward home, bearing their silent burden, their hearts heavy as the snowfall obliterated any traces of their passing.

Chapter 2

"I don't know, Sheriff."

The words were so odd, yet made a strange kind of sense to Jova as he struggled back to consciousness.

He wasn't being roasted over a spit or having his limbs ripped off and eaten while he was awake, that was for sure. But he had never been so cold in his life. His legs… legs… His body didn't feel right.

What had the invaders done to him? He was cold and his limbs… They felt odd, awkward… not like his own. And he was wrapped in something cocooning, something soft and warm, but that strange warmth only scared him more. Had they broken his legs? Were they encasing him in some cocoon for later consumption? And that voice speaking the strange words that he could almost understand…

Where was he?

Even as these thoughts passed through his mind, he was almost overcome with the urge to scream for help or to at least cry. Yes, he wanted to cry. He wanted to cover what remained of his body and hide so no one could ever find him and the evil that was happening to him would just go away.

But -- but that was not in keeping with his warrior's code. As a warrior he was to meet every enemy head on, every situation with a confidence that would have him laughing at death, pissing in its eye… and maybe hiding under a bush.

No. He was a warrior. Warriors did not hide or cry but… but he couldn't help it. He wanted out. He wanted to know where he was. He wanted to know what had been done to his body.

He had to open his eyes.

"Sheriff," the voice growled, and curiosity took

over the overwhelming fear that was doing its best to paralyze him.

Jova opened his eyes and... promptly slammed them shut.

What he was seeing was not real.

He opened them again, just a crack, and though his vision was impaired a bit by the fall of a silky long mane -- hair, his magic seemed to whisper to him -- he saw the strangest creature he had ever beheld.

It had two legs like the invaders, and two appendages -- arms, his magic supplied -- and a rather small, rounded head, but that was where the similarity ended.

This being was not an immoveable wall of thick skin and muscle. It was slimmer, shorter, and had the most unusually colored fur -- or, rather, skin.

It was walking -- pacing really -- as it spoke into a small device, its tones and movement suggesting distress.

It paid little to no attention to him at all as it moved, running its hands through its interesting mane of hair and running a... a hand over its face.

It had two eyes and a nose and a pair of smallish lips that he somehow was finding very attractive, which he decided was odd because there was nothing equine about him.

Where was the huge barrel of a body, the slim muscular legs, the soft covering of fur, the dainty hooves and most importantly, the bright single horn that should crown his forehead? This thing was an aberration... an aberration he was finding rather pleasant to look at. It was all so confusing.

As it turned its back to him, he noted it didn't even have a tail, though its buttocks were well rounded under some kind of covering -- pants, his magic supplied -- and it was a shame it was covered like that. The being seemed to have no fur, well, at least not any like the long black mane on its head. He squinted to peer closer at this intriguing being. It appeared to be very hairless. Its bare skin would have frightened or at least concerned him before but now it only made him curious to see how it would feel under his muzzle or his tongue.

Tearing his eyes away from the strange thing and its screaming into its small box, he turned his attention to the place where he was being kept.

It was unlike anything he had ever seen. There were walls -- he recognized them from his dealings with the elves who once populated his planet before they warned of the coming danger and fled. There were walls and a roof and a lot of things he could not fathom the use of.

There were platforms and things stuck on the walls. There were objects on the floor and even more boxes of unidentifiable things. In fact, the place was like one huge, confusing box. In the center of the roof was a light source that his magic could not figure out. Electricity? What sorcery was that?

As he was puzzling over something called a hertz, another of the creatures rushed in. This one was different form the first, but just as strange.

It had the long hair and the limb arrangement, but it had some strange bumps -- breasts -- in the center of its chest. Breasts… tits! It had tits but only two of them. Its skin was a different color than the first, darker in a way, but appeared just as hairless. Its mane was of a rich dark color, like the first, but was left to hang wildly about the face. It moved differently, walking with a soft swaying motion that drew the eyes to its rounded flanks… hips. It had wide hips that something in him approved of though he had no idea why.

He would not be able to mount either of them. He would crush them with his weight, as they looked very delicate and small to his eyes. And why was he considering mounting them at all? They were not Unicorn. They were... they were something called... human.

The urge to cry came back, and this time he could not stop a tear from rolling down his face.

"Torin!" the second human, the one with the two tits, called out as she rushed to his side. "They are awake." Then his personal space was being violated as one of them pushed the mane -- the hair -- from his face and then was almost nose to muzzle with him.

He blinked as the urge to bite and maybe to preen a bit at the same time nearly overcame him. What the hell was going on? What was hell?

"Oh, you poor dear." The voice was higher pitched than the titless one. "What have they done to you?"

That was indeed a very good question. What had been done to him?

As his magic raced to fill his mind in on the facts, he watched as the one not named Torin seemed to dance in place, one hand reaching out for him and then pulling back.

He blinked at her as the answers became clear in his head.

"Th-they?" He blinked at the rather vocal response. Unicorns did not speak with their mouths. Mouths were for eating and drinking, and tasting a mate. Unicorns did not speak, nor did they have the vocal cords to do so.

Well, you just did, a rather droll mental voice

whispered in his mind, and Jova realized with a stomach-twisting jolt that not only was he communicating verbally, his mind seemed split into two distinct parts. The voice whispering at him was amused and still seemed to be an aspect of himself that he'd never noticed before. How had this come to pass?

"I knew it!" the not-Torin wailed. "He... she... they have been attacked!"

And that would be the first thing she would think, a second voice grumbled.

Jova frowned as he realized there were three distinct voices in his head with him, not just two. And the two new voices were him, but changed... just different.

Integration, the first voice provided. *If you paid more attention to yourself instead of your surroundings you would know that.* Jova was being rather stern with himself, but he listened and closed his eyes, now seeking internally for answers magic could not provide.

Since this was happening within his head, he had to seek answers from his own consciousness... and suddenly there were three. If he had been anything other than a practitioner of magic and an alpha in his own right, he was sure he would be going mad under these circumstances.

So instead of getting lost in the contemplation of things he could not change, he closed his eyes and decided to deal with what he could. He needed to know about these new aspects of himself.

One voice, the first one that seemed to be bent on observing everything around him, seemed the most vocal. It was gathering information at a rapid pace on the beings who occupied the box-like room, the material he was lying on, the fact he no longer seemed to have four strong legs…

Don't panic, the second voice whispered, sending out protective thoughts that were more similar to his usual thought patterns. This voice, this mindset seemed more interested in finding ways to get away from these beings and in protecting himself with direct confrontation if they became dangerous.

His eyes snapped open. The not-Torin being had drawn closer and was looking more and more worried. Something in him wanted to push her aside, to confront the Torin, and then pound hooves away until he was clear of them all and could regroup and discover exactly what kind of situation he was now in.

The one thing that kept him in place was the fact that both new voices in his head were tempered with the flavor of his usual calm thinking. There were no outside minds invading his or trying to control him, so he tried to relax as magic raced to provide answers only it could.

Slowly, he began to realize he was acclimating to this place, to this… Earth.

Earth, he somehow knew, and the answers were not all coming from his magic. There was another… an almost sentient whisper in the back of his mind that was augmenting what knowledge his own magic could gather.

This place was called Earth, and his own brand of magic was being used to assure his survival. Even now, he could feel this new magic mingling and altering the sacrificial gift his dying planet had bestowed upon him.

He was being changed to fit in with the beings who resided here, but the planetary magic had played out, most of it consumed in transporting him from his place of birth to this place of safety where none of the hunters would be able to find him.

Because the magic had been nearly spent, this outside force seemed to have taken pity on him and stepped in, to assure his survival.

His own augmented magic had altered his body greatly, but the process had been halted in the middle of his transformation. This new magic had stepped in and assisted as much as it could, but the majority of the alteration had been done by sacrificial magic and could not be changed or forced to complete what it had started. This new magic could only shore up what was already done and ensure that his life force would not drift away.

The end result was that he was very similar to these beings, these humans, but there were telling differences that he would not be able to hide. He felt remorse from this sentient magic and rushed to send out the emotion of thanks and relief. He was alive because it decided he was worth the effort and no matter how changed he may be, he could only be grateful to it for his life.

One of the major differences was the alteration of his mind. That was the only reason he wasn't racing about in a psychotic haze destroying this box-like dwelling in an attempt to flee. His mind was being altered to accept this new circumstance without him going mad. Although he was not fond of this mental tampering, he understood the magic was doing all it could to see to his continued existence.

The two new voices, he realized, were the work of the new magic source. His body was being slowly adapted to this planet and in the midst of that, the not-Torin had touched him, pulling in information and experiences from that first human mind.

His magic had been struggling to accept this new

point of view when the second being, the Torin, touched him, and the magic began to absorb his experiences as well.

Jova's own mind was still there, that was apparent, but it was very slowly subsuming the other two personalities that dwelled with it. No, subsuming was not the proper term. Maybe… merging. Yes. His mind was merging with the two fresh minds, creating an augmented mind that would ensure his survival on this Earth.

He winced as he realized the personalities of both the not-Torin and the Torin were merging with his own mind, turning him into something completely new.

Male and female, his magic supplied, and he opened his eyes again, this time trying his best to determine which was which.

"Female?" he asked, because something in him led him to believe that this not-Torin was very much like the first voice in his head. That and tits…

"Female? Women did this to you?" The Not-Torin seemed very excitable. "Torin, tell the Sheriff --"

"You are female?" he asked again, understanding the words she was speaking to him, though it took a moment to absorb the context.

"Oh, my God, brain damage."

"Multiple lines of thought proceeding at the same time," he muttered, his voice scratchy and sounding almost painful to his own ears. Mental projection was much neater, cleaner, but it seemed that the humanity on this planet were not capable of such things. Actual speaking took a lot out of a unicorn. "Female point of view."

"Huh?"

"Can you tell me your name?" the Torin asked,

moving to the side of the not-Torin, staring down at him intently.

"Male." He nodded, singular in thoughts and deeds.

"Your name?" he asked again, his magic providing the proper pronoun. Pronoun... they had names for their name words.

He closed his eyes as he realized these beings had names for everything, names and rules and exceptions. Everything was labeled, categorized, and pushed into its proper slot. It was interesting to the point of being horrifying, to say the least.

"Torin." He spoke softly as he struggled to sit up, something he'd never had to do before. Unicorns didn't sit. They knelt, they lay, and they stood majestically towering over their territories, but they never sat.

Slim hands and arms reached around his back -- oh, magic, his spine was vertical -- and eased him into a more or less upright position.

He turned his head to see the female staring at him, concern and her desire to help bleeding all over him.

"The not-Torin." He nodded. "Female."

He turned his head again. How he managed to hold his heavy head upright with such a skinny neck he would never know, but he looked between the two of them and watched as they stared back at him in shock.

"You have a horn," the female pointed out, a fact he already knew. She had a knack for stating the obvious.

"Yes," he said softly. "And you don't."

He frowned at that before he raised his hooves -- hands -- and stared at them.

The two forelegs were called arms, and arms had hands at the end. His two hind legs were just considered legs and at the ends, they had feet.

He lifted his hand to his face and frowned. There was a gasp, and he looked over at the not-Torin and noticed she was staring at his hands too.

He observed hers and then his and noticed the difference.

"I only have three phalanges and a thumb." He frowned as he wiggled his fingers. "An opposable thumb. What am I supposed to do with that?"

"Open doors?" the Torin said, his eyes going from Jova's hands to his horn and back again. He jerked as a voice coming from the device he held, the phone, called his attention. "So... we'll keep the victim here until the snow stops... Blizzard... three days." He nodded. "Well, Sheriff Strong, you know where we'll be. Any medical needs we can see to and we'll document everything." He hummed in response before he spoke again. "Understood, Sheriff. This is not life and death, and we'll see you when they get the pass dug out in a few days. Goodbye."

He pressed something on the face of the phone, and Jova was slightly unnerved that his eyes never left Jova while he spoke. It was a rather Alpha move ,and he resisted the urge to rear up in challenge -- as if he could rear up with legs -- but it went against all the rules of propriety to assault someone who was doing their level best to assist him while in their territory.

Thinking with this new knowledge was becoming easier with each passing moment.

"Open doors," he muttered, his eyes narrowing. These creatures, these human beings, were watching him. He could smell the confusion, the slight taint of fear, and it was making him nervous.

He lifted his hands again and brushed his hair from his face and took his first clear look at humanity.

He remained unimpressed.

The female -- he recognized her for what she was now, his brain sorting out the pronouns -- was looking at him like he was some rare beast she could not wait to study.

The male looked ready to put him down at a moment's notice, and that was something he respected. After all, he was an incursion into their lives and their dwelling.

"What are you?"

Jova didn't really have an answer for that question. What was he? He looked up at the male, his head tilting to the side as he contemplated his answer.

He was not human. He was no longer a unicorn. From what he could see of his body, he was some strange amalgamation of both.

He looked down at his hind legs and noticed the knee was lower, that it still bent in the correct direction, but his ankles were much lower, his calves were bigger, and his thighs were much smaller. His legs were like those of the elves that used to share his planet. His new long feet had three shorter fingers -- toes and a thumb too, but it was called a big toe. There were no hooves, but he had fingernails and toenails and for a moment he contemplated how he was supposed to walk on those before he realized he would have to use the whole foot.

He snorted, tossing his hair, and watched as his humans jerked in reaction.

His humans. He liked the sound of that.

He turned his attention to the female again, noting how tense the male became, but at this point he was strictly observing. He could smell her anxiety as she stumbled backwards to stand beside the male. The male, the Torin, pushed her back as he continued to stare.

She was... pretty, he decided.

If she had been a unicorn, her fur would have been a rich beige color with hints of rose and cream. Her mane and tail would have been long, black and wavy. As a human, he was finding her rather pretty. As a unicorn, she would have been devastating.

He turned his attention to the male and noted that his fur would have been similar to hers, but paler with less rose and more ochre highlights. His mane would have been long, straight and black, if the hair on his head was any indication. As he stared, he noticed a softening in his own chest as his nostrils flared and he inhaled their scent. His heartbeat increased as did his breathing. It made scenting them easier, but their mingled scents were causing the strangest reaction in his body.

He looked down at his... groin. Mother Planet, he could see his groin.

His rump was being used for sitting, and his body was arranged in such a way that if he removed the covering they put over him he could see his groin.

How unnatural was that?

And he could feel it, feel the blood rushing to his cock. Well, that sensation was familiar, but the actual ability to see it... He had never seen it before, and he was curious even as he was horrified. But with his human hands, he could not only see it -- he could touch it too, if he wanted. That was something he had never been able to do before.

It was not the way things worked.

He was supposed to be able to scent heat in his partner; his cock would swell and his balls tingle, signaling readiness. He would display his eagerness and if his partner were receptive then they would lower their heads and brace themselves.

He had never had any complaints about the length or the thickness of his cock. In fact, his partners both male and female had raved at his performance even before he became herd alpha. And the fact he had borne his son at an early date made him all the more appealing, for it proved he had expertise dominating and being dominated.

Thinking about his many past conquests was starting to have a troubling effect on his new body.

He stared down at his groin. Instead of dragging toward the ground hot and heavy, his cock was staring to point up into the air.

Mother Planet, human beings were strange. How would he ever cope with this? If he bent his cock would it break? How was he supposed to mount? He just didn't know.

"Okay, who are you?"

The male Torin's voice brought him out of his musings, and he absently pushed the long hair that had fallen forward back behind his ears -- such tiny, pointy ears -- and looked up at him again.

His was not the only attention on his crotch. They both were staring at his lap in fascinated horror. It was a good thing the material over him was still covering it, if a bit raised -- tented -- over his upward-thrusting penis.

"Who are you?" he asked, tilting his head to the side, raising his hand to paw... no, he had no hooves, and they were not on the ground. He glared at the useless thing before turning to stare the male in the eyes.

The Torin blinked at that and nodded slowly. It

was almost a respectful gesture to an alpha, and it relaxed him a little. He hadn't even realized his muscles were growing tense until that moment.

"Fair question," he allowed. "You know my name is Torin."

"Not-Torin." He pointed to the female, and they both stared at him silently.

"Torin." He pointed to the male. "Not Torin." He pointed to the female. This naming thing was easy. He pointed to himself. "Not human. Jova."

"Not human." The female was sounding more excited. She moved closer, though the male pulled her back a bit.

That was good. He was protective of her, though Jova could see no real alpha in this group. How did that work?

"Not human?" the male asked, and Jova snorted, causing them both to jump. For some reason that amused him greatly so he did it again, adding a headshake. He felt his lips pulling to the side, baring his teeth, yet he was not ready to attack.

"Oh," the not-Torin gasped. "He's smiling, Torin," she muttered. Her gaze dropped to his crotch for a moment before a red flush softly covered her face. "And it is a he."

"Jova." The Torin pointed to him. "Not human?"

"Not human," he returned. The more he spoke, the easier this talking thing became. Perfection and ease came with practice, both new voices in his brain concurred.

Now he had to establish his dominance.

He made to rise to his feet, slipping his legs around until they hung off the platform he was sitting upon. Both minds agreed with this action, and his brain supplied the motions for standing.

Easy, he decided as his feet touched the ground. He winced at the coolness of the hard not-ground -- floor -- and now all he had to do was rise.

He allowed more weight to rest on his feet, lifted his rump... and fell flat on his face in a tangle of long, pale, thin limbs and hair.

"Ouch," he muttered, though he didn't know why, and felt his face and body heat as some strange sound erupted from his humans.

His brain classified the noise as laughter.

No parts of his brain were amused.

Chapter 3

"Maybe he's an alien."

Torin turned from the mass of hair and limbs -- and erection, let's not forget the erection -- that had tumbled to the floor to stare at his wife.

"What?" She almost sounded indignant. "He has three fingers and a horn, Torin."

"Baylin --"

"Horn!" she insisted, pointing to the heap on the floor.

"Maybe he was drugged --"

"And his body scientifically altered to look like something out of a Tolkien novel?"

"Tolkien --"

"Ears, Torin! He has pointy ears!"

"And opposable thumbs." The deceptively deep voice came from the horned heap, and Torin didn't know whether to weep, laugh, or pull a tranq gun.

"And opposable thumbs," Baylin agreed, almost cooing at him... and from the size of the erection pushing the coat and blanket aside, it was a him.

"For opening doors." The man adjusted his body and struggled to sit up -- struggled and failed, Torin noted as he flopped back prone in an even worse tangle of hair.

"Oh, he is so cute," Baylin purred, and Torin stared at her as if she had lost her mind.

This creature was not cute. This creature had a hard-on and what appeared to be basic use of the English language.

"Torin, help him up." She was trying to get closer, he was trying to pull her back, and the whole situation was beginning to take on Keystone Cop-esque overtones.

"He could be dangerous --"

"He can't even lift his head!"

"Not-Torin is correct. I am a dangerous unicorn, human."

"You are not," Torin scoffed, his fear lessening as he stared at the talking hairball.

"I am," it insisted, turning its head to the side, the small horn peaking through as large black eyes glared balefully up at him. "I am alpha. Respect me."

Torin snorted at that, trying not to chuckle in the face of such a strong and superior alpha.

"Unicorn." He lost the battle to hold his amusement in when the creature on the floor snorted at him. It was all very horse-like. He even attempted to toss his hair, which only made the platinum and silver mass again tumble into his face.

"Humanish unicorn," the man agreed. "Why are you laughing? Do I look funny? You think I look funny. It's not right to laugh at people. It's... I used a contraction. And you are laughing at me."

Torin lost it, laughing so hard he had to bend over at the waist and brace his hands against his knees. "Oh, my God," he roared. "He used a contraction."

"Not funny," his wife hissed, moving around him to kneel at the great alpha's side. From what he could tell, the man barely reached Torin's shoulder. Torin was shorter than Baylin, yet he tried to pull off the master-of-all-he-surveys routine.[KK1]

"There, there," she soothed, brushing the hair back from his face. Torin went through a mental list of what could be wrong with this guy. Obvious physical deformity, he noted. Maybe some mental problems too. After all, he'd been running around butt naked in the dead of winter.

But there were the gunshots. Maybe he'd been

kidnapped. Sideshows would pay a lot for a mentally disturbed individual who had a horn and three fingers on each hand. They would bill him as a human unicorn.

"Your name?" he asked, his amusement drying up rapidly.

"Jova," the man repeated, and with Baylin's help was able to stare up at Torin sans hair in his face.

"Jova. What happened? Is there anyone we can call for --"

"They were going to kill us all."

The seriousness of that statement sapped any good humor that might have hung around after his realizations. His wife gaped at him, her hands stilling on Jova's hair, a look of horror dawning on her face. He stared down into those non-human black eyes and took a deep breath.

"You need to get off the floor, and I need to check you over."

That said, he reached down and picked up the young man. Maybe he was still a teenager from the size of him. He weighed practically nothing.

The swat to the chest caught him off guard and almost made him drop the load he had bent to pick up.

"Who gave you the right to touch me?" Indignation was in every line of Jova's stiff body. "You just don't go and take liberties... another contraction. You should always ask before invading personal body space."

Torin looked down in shock as Jova gripped the coat tightly over his chest.

"Yeah, Torin," Baylin agreed, staring at Torin with fresh anger. "You don't treat a patient that way. You ask for permission, and then you explain what you are doing. You don't know what they did to him."

Torin realized he was at fault, but the realization didn't make the anger fade. Embarrassment was a hard thing for a man like him to accept.

"And I can speak for myself." Jova turned to glare at Baylin, though the look that crossed his face was more surprise than actual upset. "I can, can't I?"

He looked up at Torin for assurance.

Now Torin was getting a weird mix of male/female/victim/victor vibe from Jova. It was confusing to say the least.

He tossed the man onto the examination table and threw his hands up in the air.

Baylin looked shocked, but was slowly nodding in agreement. "It's about time you made some choices in your life."

"I've always made my life choices, not-Torin," Jova protested weakly, running his hands through his hair, wincing as they tangled together, almost as if he had never used his hands before. He frowned at them and then tossed his head in such a way that his hair cascaded behind him.

He bared his teeth -- it wasn't quite a smile -- at them before staring down at his hands once more.

He kicked out his feet and stared down at them, nearly tipping over, before he gained control of his midsection and managed to stay upright. It would have been comical if it wasn't so sad. What had those people done to him? Had there been people at all? What had happened to Jova to turn him into this mix of contradictions that barely even marked him as human?

"These things are strange," he muttered, still staring down at his feet. He flexed his toes and tilted his head to the side, snorting a bit. It was all very horse-like. Maybe the people who had him wanted him to behave like a horse so they could cash in on the Unicorn thing.

It was no use speculating, he decided, not when he could get some answers straight from the horse's mouth, so to speak.

"So, these people who tried to kill you," Torin began, ignoring his wife's glare. Baylin would mother the whole world if she could. "Where are they?"

"I don't know." Jova finally looked up at Torin again. "Dead, hopefully, as my planet sacrificed the last of its magic to bring me here."

"Planet?" Okay, there had to be some kind of head trauma here or a massive delusion this poor guy was living in.

"I had enough magic to send my people away, but it created a vacuum. A vacuum is dangerous because residual magic will rush in to fill the void, and reality snapped back into place and that creates magical backlash."

"Nature abhors a vacuum," Torin spoke softly as he edged closer to the medicine cabinet. Maybe they would have to tranq the poor guy if he got violent. He knew enough human biology to estimate the dose of ketamine it would take to put him under until they could get him bound and taken someplace where he wouldn't be a danger to himself or others.

"Very true." Jova was nodding. "But instead of pulling my body apart, the planet rallied and somehow sacrificed what was left of her magic to send me here. Hopefully, the bastards who were hunting my people, who were raping her of her magic and her majesty, were destroyed when that occurred. For a planet to sacrifice itself... that is a backlash that can destroy galaxies."

Then Jova dropped his head.

He sighed deeply as one silver tear fell, landing on his lap with a tinkling sound.

Baylin gasped, moving closer, and even as Torin gripped her arm to prevent her from moving any nearer to the crazed young man, something was drawing him to Jova's side, too.

It was strange, it was frightening, and every tear that fell from Jova's eyes splashed against his lap with a tinkling sound of music. Torin had never seen or heard anything like this before.

Baylin made another noise and he looked up. Jova's eyes were swirling like rainbows even as his misery rang joyfully around him as his tears fell.

It was official. He was an alien.

* * *

"Oh my God, you *are* magic," Baylin whispered as she stared at the crying man on her exam table.

He looked like a ball of misery with his three fingers touching his face as the sound of his unhappiness tinkled merrily around him.

"What is this?" He sniffled, rubbing his fingers together as he looked imploringly up at her. "Not-Torin, what is this? How do I make it stop?"

"You are crying," she breathed, pushing away from her husband's grasp and moving to Jova's side. "You... I don't... I-uh, I cry because I am sad," she finally made it to his side and wrapped her arms around him.

He was short, but Jova was not small by any means. He was a slim but muscular man who only looked delicate because of his coloring and his confusion, she decided. Usually people were that pale when they were ill. But he didn't appear to be really ill, though his gross motor functions were out of whack. He was concussed, which was consistent with trauma, but the musical tears… and his claim to be magic… Well, with the light show his eyes were doing and his singing tears, she almost believed it.

But Baylin was a woman of science, and there had to be a logical explanation other than exploding planets.

"How do I not be sad?" he asked earnestly. "Not-Torin, how does humanity stop being sad?"

"Hugs work." She sat down beside him and winced as he shied away. "And wine…"

"Hugs and wine." He nodded, and Baylin felt her heart break a little. "May I have some, please?"

"Maybe after we examine you," she allowed and noted that, though the musical tinkling of his tears still filled the room, his eyes widened as he took in her meaning.

"You want to examine me?" He perked up a bit, and the musical soundtrack of his tears made it an interesting development.

"We have to determine if you were harmed… uh, when you landed?"

"I am not an alien." He sniffled, wiping his tears away and staring at the liquid on his fingers. "I am a unicorn."

"We want to make sure you are a healthy unicorn," she reasoned. Torin was not helping, still staring at Jova in shock.

"How would you know?" he asked, his tears easing. "You have never met a unicorn before."

He had her there. "Well, I guess I would compare you to human norms."

"You are familiar with human norms?"

"Well… horses," she admitted. "My specialty is large and exotic animal husbandry."

He closed his eyes for a moment, then the large

black orbs glared at her. "I am not a horse."

"I didn't say you were."

"You implied it. I am a human… ish," he finished weakly before tossing his hair back and sighing deeply. "I am making a mess of this."

"You are doing fine." She smiled in encouragement, and he winced before he tried to copy her actions… and failed miserably. He kept curling his upper lip in a horse-like fashion instead of the comforting glide of lips that denoted a smile.

The look he gave her called her on her bullshit, but it had the benefit of making the tears cease. The musical noise tinkled to a halt as he stared at her.

"I just want to make sure you were not hurt when you… How did you arrive, anyway?"

"I do not know, not-Torin." He wrinkled his nose in confusion, and Baylin had to bite back an *awww* at his cuteness.

"Baylin," she corrected, pointing to her chest. "My name is Baylin."

"I do not know, Baylin," he repeated, accepting his mistake without apology and correcting it. "I was there and then I was here. I have no idea how magic brought me here."

"Okay, when we found you, you were unconscious. Is it okay if we check to see if you are damaged?"

"I have two legs and two arms instead of four strong legs. I have hands and feet instead of hooves. I have this skinny neck that bends and twists too easily. How would I know if I were damaged, Baylin?"

"That is why you have us," she offered. "We would know. I want you to trust us." She looked to her husband, who was losing the shocked look on his face. She hated it when his worldview was altered. He would have to reboot his brain, and no one knew just how long that would take.

"Trust is built upon time and the slow building of communication and shared experience." He tilted his head to the side and stared at her, eyes intent. "How can I trust you when I don't know you?"

That was a good question on his part. People tended to implicitly trust doctors of all kinds, even vets. They took an oath not to harm their charges, and most people respected that and the time and education it took to hone their craft. Building trust with an alien… well…

"How do we know we can trust you?" Torin was back. He didn't look upset, just kind of dazed as he stared down at Jova, hovering a bit if truth be told. It was like his protective instincts were going all out of whack.

She kind of understood what he was feeling because her drive to mother the hell out of the odd man was in the forefront of her mind. His protective instincts had to be killing him. He probably wanted to snatch her up and run to safety; at the same time, he wanted to protect the innocent-looking alien staring up at him with the huge black eyes. That was something she couldn't explain. Even in a town as strange as Angel Falls, a real live alien should have sent her running for the handguns. Maybe he was doing something to them.

She looked over at Jova and had to snort as he nearly poked his own eye out trying to brush his hair back. He glared at his fingers as if they were independently at fault, then did that strange hair toss to get the loose strands out of his face, all the while staring at Torin.

Finally giving up, he chuffed, another horse-sounding exclamation, before he frowned at Torin. "You do not know that you can trust me. Yet I am the one at a disadvantage. You are the lead stallion, the alpha, correct? Then I find myself relying upon your good graces. Some concessions must be given, and between you and the Baylin, you can easily overpower me in the state that I find myself in. What would you do, Torin? In my situation, how would you begin to give trust?"

That was another pointed question, Baylin thought, and realized her alien might be strange when it came to all things human, but he was by no means a fool.

"Honestly, I would let you examine me," Torin answered after a moment. "If anything, you would know where you stand on this human thing. If you were a unicorn, then you were basically a horse with a horn, and now you are not. You need to learn about your new form as much as we need to assure ourselves that you aren't going to turn into some kind of monster and eat off our faces."

"You have beings that do that here?" he gasped, his eyes darting around the room before he turned back to Torin and herself. "How do you protect yourself? Great Magic!"

"No." She slapped Torin on the arm and glared at him for a moment, just until he got her point about watching what he said, then offered Jova another smile. "No, dear. There are no creatures like that. Torin was trying to make a joke."

"I don't find it funny," Jova managed, and Baylin noted again his reaction to fear stimulus was very horse-like. His eyes were wide and he was shifting, looking around him as he scented the air with flaring nostrils. His fingers were clenching and unclenching, and she was sure that if he had hooves, he would be prancing in place.

"I am sure you understand my reasoning," Torin tried again and Jova, his hand pressing against his chest, slowly nodded. "My heart is racing, my breathing is labored, and I feel as if I want to leap from this hairless skin. I will let you examine me because I am not sure this feeling is normal for a human, which I am now. I need to know for my own well-being, and if it has the added benefit of giving you peace of mind, then I would be a fool to object."

After that, it took very little time for Baylin and Torin to arrange blankets to cover him and for Baylin to excuse herself, as this was a matter between men.

She walked out of the offices and into her bedroom, looking for some of her sweat pants and T-shirts, since Jova was around her size if a bit shorter in stature.

"Alien life," she boggled to herself as she searched through drawers and pulled out socks and dug around on her dresser looking for hair bands. "There is an alien life form in our home." So used to speaking into recorders when she made notes with her wolfy friends, she happily spoke to herself as she searched and gathered appropriate clothing. "I should be scared but I am giddy. I think I am going to like Jova. He seems rather level headed and --"

"Baylin!"

Torin's bellowing her name gave her pause. He didn't sound upset, or too scared, but more resigned. Maybe they had come to another impasse because he just didn't understand the thinking of the scared alien. Goodness knows she could relate to his uncertainty in this situation as well as the tears. If it had been her who had been tossed into a new body and set adrift on a strange new planet, she would be doing more than sniffling back a few tears.

She made her way back to the office with her bundle of clothes and paused when she noted Torin standing with his hands over his eyes and Jova frowning at him.

"You mean you don't have both?" he was asking Torin, who was blushing and looking more and more uncomfortable. "Then how do you give birth to your young?"

"Huh?" she asked, looking between the two men. "Birth?"

"I am human. I don't give birth," Torin was explaining, and Jova looked horrified.

"Then how do you propagate your species? How do you pass on your genetics? How do you have sons and daughters to hold down the magics in your line and pass down your family lore?"

"Help?" he asked Baylin as he looked hopelessly down at her.

"Ah..." She placed the clothing on a nearby desk and walked over to Jova's side. "Women bear children, Jova."

"Then how do your men understand what it is to lead and be led? How do your alphas understand that war has a price that is greater than pride if they do not send their offspring to battle? How can they truly be alphas, protectors, and life-takers if they have no basic understanding of what it is to bring life into the world at all?"

"Ah." Again, those were very good questions. Impossible to answer, but good questions. "Women, the females of our species, tell them."

"Telling and having true understanding brought about by experience are two different things. The males here have the power to act like monsters if they don't understand."

She could find no fault with his argument in theory.

"What brought up this conversation?" she asked Torin, who was no longer blushing, but looked shocked.

"Well, physiology and biology..." he began, and then shook his head. He was staring at Jova in fascination and quite a bit of interest.

"Let me in on the situation."

"He has a penis -- a rather horse-like penis with a flat head and no sheath or foreskin."

"Okay." She nodded. "He said he was once a unicorn, and if that translates the same way, it means he once was a horse."

"Magic," Jova interrupted, sounding a bit disgruntled himself. "Magic has given me this form. The intent of my mother planet was to assure that I could exist on this planet alongside humans in safety, but she did not have enough magic left to complete the transformation. The magic here took pity on me and assisted as much as it could. This new form will be my new form until my life force ceases to be. It is disturbing to me, this talking and hand waving and my cock that sits straight up instead of flashing downward, but I will learn to adapt."

"Magically constructed body." Baylin wondered why she was not freaking out. "And the magic here?"

"It is very kind." He closed his eyes, tilting his head to the side. A faint glow pulsed in his tiny little horn.

"Magic," Baylin breathed, elbowing her husband. She was a believer. Musical tears, his rapid learning and control of this new body, and now a glowing horn. She should be freaking out, but she wanted to know more. Maybe it was magic. "Magic," she stated again.

"Clarke's Third Law." Torin frowned at her. "Any sufficiently advanced technology is indistinguishable from magic."

"Glowing horn," she pointed out.

"Functioning hermaphrodite," he countered, and Baylin's mouth dropped open.

"Our unicorn friend here has a penis and a vagina."

"Um..."

"Yes," Jova interrupted them, his eye glinting with silver stars as the glow slowly left his horn. "I have a functioning uterus." He almost looked insulted. "But I have already given birth to my one foal. I have passed on my genetics and my family line and now my uterus is of no use."

"You are male?" Torin was trying to understand. "And you have given birth."

"You are male," he pointed out. "And you have not."

"I --"

"You have breasts that can make milk, yet you have no means of passing on nourishment to your offspring because you cannot create offspring," he pointed out, and Torin stared down at his chest for a moment, before flushing faintly again.

"So," Baylin stepped in. "You have borne a child?"

"Foal," he corrected, with that odd lip-curling smile again. "A colt. He is strong in the ways of magic and will lead our people to safety. He is a powerful alpha stallion and..." His voice grew softer as his head lowered. "And I will never see him grow to his full maturity, though he has nearly gained his full majority."

"You… I am sorry," she offered, but the tinkle of the musical tears began and she froze.

"Sorry for what?" he snapped, leaning forward as he bared his teeth. This time it was not an imitation of a smile -- it was a show of defiance and anger. "What are you sorry for, not-Torin Baylin? It is my child who is forever lost to me. It is my people who think me to have died protecting them. It is my child who will mourn my loss, who will not have a lead stallion there to guide him when he is confused or lost, who will not have the benefit of my experience as he struggles to establish our people on another plane. What are you sorry for, not-Torin Baylin? It is I who am lost here on your plane while I don't even know if my people are safe as the magic promised. Why are you giving me this expression of grief when you don't know my mind at all?"

That the rant was given with a musical accompaniment did not lessen its impact at all.

This man had borne a child and then had lost his child while protecting his people, it seemed. Magic promised that the unicorns would be safe, and magic promised him the ability to blend in with humanity… at which it had clearly failed. From his point of view, magic had to be a fickle beast. She could try to understand his frustration and his anger and in doing so, maybe saying sorry was worse than saying nothing.

"You bore a child."

Torin's voice, still filled with disbelief, made both Jova and Baylin stare at him.

"One part of me, the feminine part, wants to scream more." Jova carefully spoke as his tears and his anger eased. "Another part wants to bend you over, mount you, and put a baby in your womb so you will know what it is like to experience this loss."

Baylin sucked in a sharp breath, wondering how her husband was going to take that.

"But you can't." Torin grinned. "Cause I don't have girl parts."

Jova narrowed his eyes for a moment before they widened in horror. "Then how can you have full penetrative sex? You have no vagina." Then his look shifted into one of pity. "Oh, you poor male."

"Feminine parts of your mind?" Baylin stopped that line of thought right there. "Your mind is in parts?"

"That would explain the excessive tears," Torin sang softly, and Jova tilted his head to the side once more, examining him.

"My magic was adapting, absorbing information with the help of this planet's magic when the Baylin touched me. Her thoughts became as mine and were added to the changing matrix of my mind. Then the Torin touched me, and his thoughts became as mine. Now my matrix struggles to combine the two to create a stronger, well-rounded mindscape where understanding of humanity is paramount. It is the only way I can survive here."

"You," Torin began, awe filling his voice. "You will be able to understand women?"

Jova nodded.

"Well, hell, man. That makes you as rare as a unicor -- Oh, yeah."

Baylin dropped her head into her hand and sighed deeply.

From childbirth to child loss and straight to sex and whatever it was Torin was thinking now. Men were such dorks.

Chapter 4

"You don't empty your bladder at a strategic spot to mark your territory?"

Jova looked shocked as he stared at Torin. Horrified might have been a better word, actually.

"No."

"But how do you keep others out of your territories, keep them from stealing your female?"

"Fences," Torin interjected before Baylin could get going on women's suffrage. "And no one steals females."

"Human trafficking…"

"Your magical connection gets Google?" he asked, dismayed while Baylin giggled. "Quiet, not-Torin," he teased as Jova looked between the two of them like they were mad.

"Google?"

"One thing at a time," Baylin explained as she moved to sit beside Jova.

The more he was up the better his muscle control became. He could almost stand and had a wonderful grasp of how hands worked.

"Truth." Torin sighed as he pinched the bridge of his nose between two shaking fingers. Alien unicorn thing… No one would ever believe this.

"Well." He dropped his hand and offered a smile up to Jova. "We use a bathroom."

"You bathe in a room and not in a spring, yet you empty your bladder inside?"

Well, that did sound kind of strange when you looked at it that way. The English language was such an odd beast.

"We bathe inside so we won't be victims of the elements. You have… had fur and resistance to the cold weather. *We* do not. *We* wear clothing."

He tugged at the coat still wrapped around their alien, and he nodded, plucking at the material himself.

"I have noticed the chill weather more in this form. The parts of me covered by this clothing seem warmer and less uncomfortable."

"We bathe indoors so we can control the temperature."

"And you relieve your bladder indoors? We don't relieve our bladders close to where we bathe. It seems rather... unsanitary.

He was getting tips on sanitation from a horse with a horn who pissed out in the grass? *Ha.*

"There are bathroom fixtures, which assure that bathing water and disposal water never meet. It's called a toilet."

Jova tilted his head to the side, a motion Torin was beginning to accept as his magic teaching Jova something, before he frowned. "I hope you keep the seat clean or I am not sitting on it. I hope you close, put down the seat too. I am not going to slide into cold water." The side-eye he was being given, and Baylin's laugh made Torin aware that Jova may have picked up something other than points of view from his wife.

"One time," he complained. "And it was when we first got together. I was not used to living with a woman who has to sit when she pees."

"You... you stand when you pee?" Jova asked, looking down at his crotch again. "How do you not splash on the floor?"

"You aim straight," he grumbled over his wife's continued laughter.

"And if you miss?"

"You wipe it up --"

"And make sure you get the base of the toilet

bowl. Urine is a liquid, and it runs down," she helpfully added and Jova snorted.

"Aim straight… with my human penis, yes?"

"Yes." Torin wanted to roll his eyes. "With your hands and not your feet, if that is what you were thinking."

"I was thinking if we stand when we pee -- that is, urinate -- what do we do if we defecate?"

"You sit down," Torin hurriedly explained. He may be a vet and used to cleaning up after animals, but he didn't have any desire to clean up after a grown man in his bathroom.

"And if you have to urinate at the same time?"

"You push your dick down… into the bowl."

"Dick…" He looked down at his crotch and then back up at Torin. "What if it touches water? I don't want my dick to touch water that has urine and feces in it."

"I've always wondered that myself," Baylin added, before Torin began to silently curse.

"Is it that big?" he asked, then blushed as Baylin crowed again and Jova looked down at his lap, considering. "It has not expanded for the purpose of urination or procreation, so I am not sure. It depends on the depth of the bowl and the length of my partially erect… dick."

He stormed off as Baylin called out to him, still way too amused than the situation called for, "Where are you going?"

"Computer pad," he called back as he made his way into his office. "I think they have some potty training videos on YouTube."

* * *

Jova gained his feet slowly, one hand in Baylin's, the other in Torin's, and winced at his jerky, ungainly movements. He had not moved with such a lack of grace since he was a colt taking his first steps. But human anatomy was strange.

He wobbled as he stood upright -- who knew a spine could do that? -- and looked around this new world with a different perspective.

He was standing in what the two called an exam room. It was cooler here, and the floor was rather barren. There were bright lights and lamps and a sharp, strange smell he attributed to the medicines they used to heal animals.

Vets. Who had ever heard the like? They were healers who worked specifically with animals. When his mind went over the differences between human and animal biology and physiology, he understood.

There was so much information coming in that his magic was having a hard time keeping everything straight.

There were voices in his head -- the two new ones and his own confused one. His head was not a pleasant place to be in the first place. With the worries about his people and his planet, it had been so long since he had time to even consider his own life. And now he was in a situation that only amplified the need for him to be in his own head.

It was maddening. He was not one to be led about. He was an Alpha; he was a herd leader. He had protected his own territory and his people for years before sacrificing to get them to a place where they would be safe for the foreseeable future. And here he was, learning about bathrooms and dicks from a pair of humans who kept calling him an alien.

Humans were such strange creatures, such a contradiction of thoughts and actions... and he was stuck among them.

It was enough to make him cry... no, not cry. He didn't want to cry. He wanted to bite something... and then maybe have a cry. Bite, cry, and then run away to safety.

Bah, he didn't know what he wanted to do other than the obvious.

He wanted to walk. Once he could master walking on these two human legs he could gather enough information to start a new life here. It was obviously what magic wanted, and he would not go against the last wishes of his planet as she sacrificed all to see him safe. But the first thing he had to do was take one step.

"Very good," not-Torin Baylin crowed, and something within wanted to slap her. Really, it was not the time to treat him like he was an imbecile. The dark look he shot her must have expressed his feelings on the matter because she took a step back.

"He is not a child," Torin pointed out, and something within Jova felt a kind of solidarity with the male.

"I was just trying to help --"

"You didn't have to yell at her." Jova felt his eyes widen as the words flowed from his mouth. Why would he defend the female? He agreed with the Torin.

But the Torin rolled his eyes, something Jova was finally familiar with, and urged Jova to take another step.

His knees shook. This was unacceptable. He pulled his hand away from Torin's and tightened his muscles as much as he could.

His next step was better -- still shaky, but he didn't feel like the ground was about to rise up and smack him in the face.

He turned to give a smug grin to Baylin,

overbalanced himself, and squeaked as he began to fall.

His arms flailed and his legs seemed to tangle with themselves and he was falling forward until his body bounced against something hard and warm and smelling definitely of male.

He peeked up and felt his skin heat for some unknown reason -- blush, his magic supplied. Torin was looking down at him, a smile tugging at his lips. The heat in his face became almost painful, and his heart started thumping.

His arms were wrapped around the male's waist and his face... So that was what a human male smelled like.

"Oh my." Not-Torin Baylin giggled, and Jova felt an odd stirring in the dick region.

He looked down at his coat and noted it was tenting again. There was a tingling in his testicles that signaled someone nearby was growing interested.

He huffed, taking in another deep breath of human male when he realized the scent was coming from the Torin.

He looked up at the male, and the blush returned to his cheeks as Torin bit his lips and looked away nervously.

Oh... Oh! The Torin found this body attractive. That was amazing considering all he had just learned from the computer device.

He was going to stand out, no matter what he did. Humanity wasn't comprised of beings that had horns unless there was some medical reason and their health was altered. The same went for the number of fingers and toes he now possessed. Most humans were not as pale as he, and most did not posses both sets of sexual organs.

Humans could also have as many foals, or children, as they desired. There was no limit like there was with Unicorns.

Unicorns could only bear one child. They all could father many, male and female alike, but they each could only bear one. It made each new life welcome and special unlike here on this planet where children could lose both parents and the ruling bodies seemed to collect them. Even worse, it allowed a few to be adopted while keeping the bulk of them in some appalling system which was not regulated based on a criteria, but seemed to be based on monetary wealth.

Maybe if humanity lost the ability to bear as many children as their bodies could, then maybe they would appreciate the ones that were born a lot more.

Nevertheless, he looked human, and he was beginning to see the subtle and not-so-subtle differences between humanity and himself, enough to begin deciding what he considered attractive.

Long hair. The long hair that some humans wore appealed to him. It reminded him of the long manes and tails of his people. A large, rounded rump was very attractive, though he would do with a well-shaped one on both males and females.

He found the lack of both sexual organs interesting, as well as how humans identified gender. With his people, it had always been what the mindset settled on. His mindset was decidedly more masculine, more protective and aggressive than his female counterparts. Here in humanity, most often gender was decided by outward appearance, though there were cases when the body grew wrong.

He really didn't have a chance to explore human sexual organs before they stumbled into something called porn. Porn seemed to make the Baylin blush and shy away even though she seemed interested, while the Torin whispered that he would show him all the best sites to explore later.

This varying view on things they both enjoyed confused him, but then again humans were confusing. The two points of view in his head were still battling, as they tried to settle within one consciousness, and often he chose to shut them both down and ignore the advice they tried to give.

"Need some help there, buddy?" the Torin asked, amused as he slid his hands under his arms and helped shift Jova's body upright.

Considering the Baylin's reaction to porn, Jova decided he would not mention the arousal he smelled, though Torin's penis did not grow fully erect.

"Stop playing, Torin," Baylin chided as she also helped to steady Jova. "Jova just needs practice."

"And a shower," Torin added. "It will help him grow accustomed to his new body."

Jova paused and went through his store of human knowledge before he nodded. "I think I would like to feel water upon my skin."

He pulled away from them both and took another shaky step. This time he gained his balance and didn't require help to remain upright. He took another step and then another, growing more confident with each one. He spun around to grin at the Torin and the Baylin and nearly landed on his rump when he tossed his hair in triumph.

They rushed forward to assist, but he waved them off and managed to stay upright on his own. He had to get used to using the whole foot to take a step, but it became easier and easier.

"Yeah!" Baylin cheered, tossing her hands up in the air in celebration.

Jova looked down at the coat that still cloaked his body and wondered if they had better-fitting clothing. The people in the computer wore clothing that wasn't so… loose.

"Follow me," the Baylin ordered. Slowly, Jova took halting steps to follow. "You can shower in the guest room, and I have some clothes for you. We can all get a good night's sleep and then deal with more tomorrow."

That was a plan, not one that his masculine voice agreed with -- it wanted to gather more intelligence -- but the female side urged him to take care of his physical form before he tried to take care of anything else.

Both were correct, but the female reasoning won out. If he was not rested, he would not be able to dig for more accurate information, and he needed facts for survival.

They passed out of the office and into a larger room with several doors. The transition from hard floor to warm carpet caught his attention and almost made him trip.

"The second door to the right is our bedroom," Baylin pointed out, and the one across from that is the guest room."

He was more interested in the carpet. It felt like thick, soft grass. It sank between his toes and he wiggled them, realizing they served a function. They helped keep him balanced. He flexed his toes again and took another, steadier step.

Being led was new to him, but he would accept it for now. It was smarter to follow those in the know than to blunder into embarrassing or harmful situations that could be easily avoided.

The Baylin led him into another boxy room, but

at least this room was more comfortable and less formal than the examination rooms.

"Bed here." She pointed to another boxy table, but this one was lower to the ground and covered in a soft material. "Bathroom is in here."

He meandered over, gaining more confidence with each step and peered into the room she indicated. It had a similar floor to the office, but that was where a lot of the similarity ended.

There was a sunken box that he recognized from the videos on the computer tablet as the tub. There were silver props and hoses that his matrix recognized as the showering system. Across from that was a tall box, which held the sink device. It too had metal workings for bringing in hot and cold water for the purpose of washing. Near that was the toilet, which was a box and a circle and would provide a means of taking bodily wastes out of the home where they would be reclaimed and treated. Treated for what he didn't know and really didn't want to. So long as it was far away from drinking and bathing water, he was fine with the human process.

"Do you remember how to turn the shower on?" the Baylin asked.

"The videos were very thorough." He tossed his head in acknowledgement. "Though I am confused why singing about doo-doos going down the drain is considered a teaching tool."

"Well," Baylin chuckled, "they are primarily used to teach children and with their short attention spans, singing a song is a mnemonic device for them to remember."

"Unicorns have no need for such a device. We merely show our foals the optimum place for evacuating one's bladder and bowels, and that is that."

"Sounds much easier than rearing children."

"It has its difficulties, like teaching them not to mount for dominance at the most inappropriate times. It can be embarrassing when an alpha from a visiting herd gets mounted in jest by a young colt. It was a good thing his actions were considered precocious, or it would have led to problems with negotiating new feeding grounds." Jova remembered the event with some pride and some embarrassment. "What of you? Do you have tales of breeding human children?"

"Well." Baylin almost seemed sad. "I don't have any children."

"Will you be having them soon? I assume that you are of a proper age and fully mature?"

"I am in my late thirties, thank you very much," she grumbled. "You are not supposed to ask a woman her age."

"Why? Thirty years is so young. I cannot even recall my thirtieth year."

"How old are you?"

"Three hundred in human terms," he nodded. "Older, but vital. I am considered to be in the prime of my life. I bore my son when I was roughly two hundred years. He is young for a leader, but that can be a good thing. His way of thinking will be not set to our old ways. This is wonderful, as they are on a new planet, and I feel the old ways will not suffice."

He felt the burning in his eyes and nose that signaled tears and quickly changed the subject. "And what of you? Children?"

"I can't have children," she mumbled. "I had to have a hysterectomy when I was young."

Jova tilted his head to the side and examined her carefully. "This distresses you, yes?"

"Not anymore." She offered him a smile. "I came

to terms with my lack of motherhood when I was a teenager. Now I baby Torin and my animals. That is enough for me."

"I see." He nodded though he really didn't understand. Magic had a way of fixing any problems with unicorn bodies so everyone was fertile when they chose to be. The new female portion of his brain was explaining how painful lack of a child could be, how the loss of unconceived children could almost be as painful as losing a child already carried, born, and loved. Yes, he could relate to her pain. "I am sorry, the Baylin."

"Just Baylin," she corrected with a smile, the momentary show of pain leaving her. "And like I said, I am comfortable with my childless state."

He nodded and turned his attention to the shower. "Water comes from here..." He trailed off as he reached out and turned the handle. Cold water poured from a spout with many holes.

"Jova!" Baylin rushed over and turned another handle, making the water warm.

"Wonderful." He nodded. "This is human magic."

"Ingenuity," she corrected, amusement in her eyes. "We like our creature comforts so we learned to pipe water into our dwellings and to make it as warm as we like."

"To shower, one must divest himself of clothing." Jova pulled down the zipper on his jacket and dropped it to the floor and got his first look at himself in all his nude glory.

"Humanity is strange," he decided before he looked up at Baylin. She was standing there, mouth agape, staring at his body. "Is something wrong?"

"Muscle," she managed, a blush heating her

cheeks. "You have some serious muscle in that slim body."

Though she spoke, her eyes were on his groin. He looked down at his penis and marveled for a moment. "So this is what my dick looks like."

That brought her eyes up to his face. "You've never seen it before?"

"I know where to stick it, if that is what you ask," he informed her archly. "But the way Unicorns are designed is not the same way that humans are designed. I never had an interest in seeing what my dick looked like, so long as it worked and my partners were satisfied."

"Were they?" This brought his eyes back to her face as she quickly averted her gaze, her cheeks turning a deep red.

"Satisfied?" He tossed his hair in a superior manner. "I had males and females flagging me day and night, Baylin. I never had a complaint, but I received several requests to teach others of the pleasures that could be had during a mating."

Her blush deepened, and the masculine part of him reveled in her reaction. The female part of his mind tried to admonish him for bragging, but he felt no shame in telling the truth.

"Oh my," she muttered, and his nostrils flared as he smelled her interest. It made his dick start to stiffen, and he looked down as he felt himself swell. It was fascinating to behold, really. His cock was about as pale as his skin, the head emerging from its sheath a pale pink. The head was different than those of the human variety, flatter and with ridges where human dicks were smooth, but it seemed to fit his new body.

He reached down and gripped himself, hissing as, for the first time, his dick was touched. Usually, it just slotted into place when he went to mount.

He gave himself a squeeze, cataloging the pleasurable stimulation, but looked up as Baylin gasped sharply.

"Um, do you want to be alone? I think you want to be alone," she stammered, her arousal growing. "I'm going… you know how to turn off the shower? Um… there are towels for drying there, and I left you clothing on the bed."

Jova nodded, half his attention on his dick and the wonderful sensations handling it could bring while the other half was on her reactions.

The male within him was crowing in delight at her want, while the female cautioned that she was not his, that she belonged to the Torin.

"I can turn off the water," he allowed. "I assume showering will be like in the bathing song with soap and shampoo?"

He ran a hand over his chest, finding it odd that he could touch himself in this manner, before he ran a hand through his hair.

She gasped again and nearly tripped over her own feet as she turned to exit the room. "Good then," she stammered. "Um, the soap and shampoo are in the shower, the towels are there" -- she pointed to a bar attached to the wall --"and I am so gone. Um… explore your new body… and stuff."

Then she was gone, leaving behind the scent of want and desire. Oddly enough, it was very similar to the scent he smelled off of the Torin, and some part of him crowed in pleasure as he realized that even in this new human form, he had the ability to affect members of both genders sexually.

Tossing his hair back, he released his dick and stepped into the shower, closing the curtain to prevent the water from splashing on the floor, though he thought it was wise to have this hard floor in a place where water might fall. The carpet might not recover from the splashing water once his body was beneath the spray.

"Mmm," he moaned to himself as his body was enveloped by warm steam and hot water. Humanity was on to something here. He relied on his matrix to understand the usage of soap and water and used both liberally to clean his new body. The fingers and hands were useful for this as he cataloged parts.

He still had teats -- nipples, rather. This body had two like his old form. His chest was rather flat. He'd never paid much attention to his chest when he was in unicorn form, only that it was broad. In human form it was still broad but not as thick.

His hair was longer than his mane and hung in wet clumps in his face. He brushed it back, noting how soft it was. His mane when he was a unicorn was never this soft, but he found that this more delicate human skin enjoyed the feel of it cascading down his back.

His buttocks, not his rump, were smaller and there was no tail, but he was not expected to hold the weight of a unicorn-sized lover so that was fine.

His legs were spindly to his view, but were strong and growing stronger. His toes and fingers were still odd things, but he realized they were necessary for grasping thing and balance. They also gave a prickly sensation when he bent over to scrub them with soap, careful to wash all the slippery cleanser away lest he fall and injure this delicate form.

He ran the shampoo through his hair, noting how the stuff made his hair feel even more like spider silk, and his fingers grazed his horn.

He'd never really thought one way or another

about his horn, if he was honest with himself. The older you were, the larger the horn became. It was a conduit for magic and a pretty amazing weapon for goring, but beyond that, he never gave it much thought. But this stub of a horn...

He chuffed in disgust before he reminded himself he was human and humans didn't have horns at all.

Poor defenseless human beings.

He ran his fingers over what he had left and wondered if it would affect his magic at all. He closed his eyes and tried to reach the magical core of himself and felt a tingling in answer. But it was weak. He had to give it time to heal and adjust. So his magic was not lost -- there was something of Unicorn within him now, he was very pleased to discover -- but until he could use it again, there were so many other strange things about this new body.

Then there was his dick.

He liked handling it. That was fun, and it felt good. It was one of the top three uses he'd found for his hands and fingers -- gripping his dick.

He gave himself a stroke as his dick swelled fully and emerged from its sheath. It was ringed, the head not rounded like the males in the computer. He thought it was odd, but then the larger surface meant more areas to pleasure. He ran his fingers over his dick, tugging at it as he never had been able to before. How did humans get anything done if they had all these wonderful toys to play with? He touched the hanging testicles, balls, below his dick and hummed softly as he rolled them around in his hand.

Then there was his vaginal opening, his pussy.

He had never paid it much attention before, preferring to be the one fucking than being mounted. It had its uses, like bearing his son, but now, since it had fascinated the humans so, he decide to explore it a bit.

As he touched it, he noted how slick and soft it was along the slit. The more he rubbed the slicker it got. Tingles flowed up from his pussy, making his new knees weak and sending fire shooting along his spine. He was going to stop right there, but something deep inside him urged him on.

He pressed hard against the slit, gasping as it opened sweetly for him. His finger sank in deeply, and he chuffed in surprise at how good that felt.

Without even thinking about it, his free hand gripped his dick and began to stroke it, to mimic the ways of mounting sex as he began to press the finger in deeper. He moaned softly, the sound of the water nearly drowning him out as the pleasurable feelings exploded. Who knew fingers were so awesome?

He tossed his heavy hair back, his eyes closing, as he pictured, not the firm rump of a wanting mare before him, but Baylin.

Oh, she would be so sweet beneath him, all caring and nurturing... with her big round human rump. Oh, yeah, she would present beautifully, her full teats -- breasts -- bobbing before him

And then there was Torin. Oh, to take the proud male down a peg or two...

The man had an obvious dick of large proportions. It kept rising beneath his clothing. Jova pumped his hand faster as he pictured the stubborn male bent before him.

Yeah, he would like to plunge his dick deep into his pussy. No, human males didn't have pussies. He would have to check out that porn later. But to have Torin filling *his* pussy. Yeah, Jova would love to feel that thick piece of meat skidding into his wet pussy as he pounded into the wailing Baylin.

Yes, with her mouth open and her hair flying around her like the finest mare in heat, Baylin would he a joy to mount while being mounted by the Torin.

Jova's moans were coming faster as his hands worked in tandem, the hunger in him rising as he fucked himself. Faster and faster he moved until something in him snapped. He threw his head back and shouted as his orgasm swamped him.

His pussy tightened around his fingers while his dick swelled, becoming unbelievably red and hot before he began to shoot creamy seed along the floor of the shower. He shivered, his body quaking in aftershocks as he slowly milked the final drops from his dick and pulled his fingers from his slick pussy with a light slurping sound.

That was really fun, he realized as he turned off the water and carefully stepped from the tub.

The things humans could do with their hands.

And the memory of the scents of both Baylin and the Torin only added to his enjoyment.

His knees shook and his muscles felt weak as he dried himself and made his way to the bed. It was odd, the way his dick kept swelling and everything in his mind returned to sex, no matter what he was thinking. And thoughts of sex seemed to naturally lead back to Baylin and the Torin.

They were both... stunning. Their smells and their scents. That he imagined them both when he drove himself to orgasm was amazing and should have disturbed him. But both his integrating male and female brain felt it was natural.

Even as he snuggled under the covers, the thought of Baylin and the Torin filled his mind. He was fixated on them, on what they felt like, how they would taste, how they would feel touching him.

His dick burned even though he just had a sexual release, and his vagina swelled, releasing more of his slick as he thought of them both.

Bah, he would consider the puzzle of his human hosts the next day. He was tired and confused, and so grateful that magic was helping him integrate. He would ponder his reaction to the humans in the morning. He was just so tired.

It struck him as he closed his eyes for the night. The swinging moods, the disjointed thoughts, the lack of control, even over this new body. He was in rut.

His eyes popped open, and he could feel the masculine part of his brain approve of his newfound use of profanity.

The female part cheered as sleep sucked him into a world of bright magic and rainbows.

Chapter 5

"We have an alien in our guest room…"

Torin glared at his wife as they began to undress. They had explained the shower to him and he had bugged out as soon as possible. There was something compelling about Jova, something Torin was afraid to put a name to.

"He can teach us so much." She was tossing her clothing into the hamper and making her way toward the bathroom to finish her toilette for the night… what was left of it. It had to be about five in the morning now; the ball had dropped and the New Year was upon them. "He has to have so much knowledge about the universe."

"He was a horse with a horn."

"It didn't stop you from noticing how cute he is," Baylin teased.

He frowned at her.

"Oh, don't give me that look, Torin. I know what you look like when you think a guy is hot. Jova is hot… in a cute kind of lost way. He making your daddy instincts rise up, lover?" She laughed.

Torin said nothing as he stripped off his cloths and tossed them into the hamper. What a fucking weird night. First *coitus interruptus* and then being blasted by an alien whose magic sucked up his life experience, if what the alien said was true. And then… Okay, he had to admit, there was something really compelling about Jova.

He did look vulnerable, but there was a stubbornness in that little man that appealed to Torin greatly. Not only that, Torin had a thing for long hair, and Jova had miles of the silky stuff.

When doing his examination, he had to remind

himself to be professional when exploring that tiny tight little body. It made him feel like a pervert to notice Jova was exceptionally built. The man was hung, nearly literally, like a horse.

He had no foreskin, but his penis was contained within a sheath. Instead of off-putting, it was rather intriguing. He had a small set of testicles that pressed closely to the thick base of his sheath, but the vagina beneath that was not expected.

He had to step back and call for his wife on that one, as Jova was the perfect mix of everything he wanted in a lover. Torin was at one time afraid to admit it to himself, but there was something arousing about a lover both he and his wife could partake of at the same time.

Oh, there were never any issues when it came to sharing -- they always found a way -- but to have both in one person... He closed his eyes and tried to tell his swelling dick to behave. Jova was not here for Torin's sexual fantasies. He was going to do his best to help the odd little man and maybe show humanity in a good light for once.

So he took his mind off sex with a dual-sexed being and steered it toward making the being happy and healthy.

Jova appeared perfectly human if you discounted the horn and the three-finger thing and would probably have no trouble at all fitting in at Angel Falls.

They had some of the strangest beings in existence already living there, like Angel Falls' lover Klint with his love of special-effect wings, and the postmaster with his cybernetic arm, or the Planet Quest Parade that happened most Fridays. A man with a horn would fit right in with this crazy little town.

"I wonder why I am not freaking out more."

Baylin's voice, nearly next to him, pulled him from his musings.

"Huh?"

"You'd think I would be freaking out over discovering aliens, Torin. I should be calling in the FBI or the X-Files for this, but instead I just want to help the poor guy. Do you think he is doing some mind control thing to us?"

Now that was a good question. Torin frowned as he stared down at his wife. "Do you?"

"Well, I don't know what to think," she admitted. "He is cute and all, but you'd think I would be more afraid."

"Are you afraid?"

"I was at first... then he fell face first into your crotch, and I decided I can't be afraid of an alien who can barely stand on his own two feet." She chuckled as she climbed into bed.

"He said he used to be a unicorn."

"That would explain his trouble walking and how fast he is picking it up," she explained as he climbed into bed beside her. "Horses are among some of the fastest walkers out there. Hours after birth, they are up and running around like their parents. It's amazing how fast they acclimate with their surroundings."

"So if you take a horse and toss him into a human body --"

"They would pick up the gross motor skills fairly rapidly."

He lay back and smiled down at his wife as she snuggled up against him, resting her head on his chest and throwing one slim leg over his.

"He said he had given birth to a colt," he reminded Baylin as he wrapped his arms around her.

"That is strange."

"Not to him or his people." She sighed. "And he said his people are all far away from him, that he didn't want to know where they were when he made a bargain with magic. Do you believe that?"

"The man has musical tears and a glowing horn," Torin grumbled. "I find myself forced to believe what he says, no matter what I want to imagine. At this point, he has no reason to lie. If he said he had to give up his child and his people to save them..." Yeah, Torin had to pause at that. "Damn."

"I know, right?" Baylin sighed, hugging her husband tightly. "I -- I don't think... I wouldn't be able... Is there such a thing as too much sacrifice?"

Torin had no answer for that. But that question was still ringing in his ears as he settled down around his wife and let sleep overcome him.

* * *

"Purple fields." Torin winced as he looked around him. "I haven't seen you guys since I tried mushrooms in my college days."

"You did mushrooms? You never told me that."

Torin looked to his left, and there was Baylin in all her naked glory. Really, she was most beautiful when she was naked and riding his dick, but lying in a field of purple flowers made her seem ethereal.

Her long dark hair flowed out around her, and her dark eyes glittered with her joy of life. She was as naked as she had been in their bed, and her scent, the smells of vanilla, flowers, and musk, surrounded her.

"There are some things I didn't tell you," he admitted, after recognizing he was having a dream. It was different than his harem dream or the one when he had five penises ready to service his willing women, but it was a nice dream nevertheless. He bent over her and pressed a chaste kiss to her mouth.

She giggled into the kiss before deepening it, thrusting her tongue into his mouth, and he let her. He enjoyed her flavor, even in their dreams tasting of her mint toothpaste. He sucked at her tongue before taking over the kiss and forcing his way inside her mouth. He traced the ridges on the roof of her mouth, moaning as she arched into his caress.

Her breasts were pressing up hard, flattening against the muscles of his chest, as her hands ran through his hair.

"Like how you get hard for our alien guest?" She had pulled away from the kiss to breathe into his mouth. Her legs winding around his waist prevented him from pulling away so he ground his hard cock into her stomach as he answered her.

"Damn subconscious," he muttered before chuckling. He could be honest with himself. "He is hot in a lost-little-boy way."

"Lost little boy?" Her nails were raking gently over his back, making gooseflesh rise and his dick jump. She ran her fingers over his sides, and he closed his eyes before answering.

"Those big black eyes…"

"Don't you think it's strange that we don't find those big black eyes scary?"

That was a good question. He pulled back to stare into his dream wife's face. She had a way of getting right to the point.

"Why would you?"

Both Torin and Baylin jumped, and Torin turned slowly. In the way of dreams, his environment was blurred and hazy, like time was folding in on itself. It made him dizzy, and he gripped his dream wife harder as his eyes began to focus and he saw standing before him a white unicorn.

It was beautiful, a sturdy body like a seventeen-hand-tall workhorse with delicate silky-looking stockings that flowed around dainty golden hooves. His majestic head was arched beautifully, and the long flowing mane covered his barrel-like body. His eyes were a gleaming black, but it was the horn that stole his breath. The horn was at least three feet long and clear, though it glittered and sparked with some internal power.

"I get the unicorn," he spoke out loud. "Because that's what our alien claimed to be, but the rainbow fields?"

He was going to go blind. This unicorn was, in fact, standing in a field of rainbows, if that made any sense at all. The colors that surrounded the horned horse -- indigo, orange, red, purple, yellow -- seemed to blaze, emphasizing the lack of color on his coat and nearly burning out his retinas with its bright display.

"Your bisexuality," Baylin in his arms explained and he had to admit, as far as a conscience went, she wasn't half bad. She was peering over his shoulder, wincing at the colors that swirled around the unicorn.

"Okay," he began to reason. "I am seeing my wife in a purple field because I think she is hot and purple is a color of lust. I have a talking unicorn because I am worried about the alien invading my guestroom, and you," he nodded to the horned visitor, "sound just like him. I am seeing him in a rainbow hell because of my openly admitted bisexuality."

"And the fact that you just like bright bubbly things," the unicorn added. He frowned. Torin frowned. "It's fine that you like fuzzy teddy bears and taking care of small helpless creatures," the unicorn added. "I know that is one of the reasons you like to help small defenseless creatures, why you became a vet. I can see it in our shared memories."

"You want to fuck small helpless creatures." Baylin laughed, and Torin glared down at her.

"That is sick, wife. I don't want to fuck small helpless creatures." He shuddered at the thought, his erection softening some as he pulled back to glare down at his dream wife. His subconscious had a sick sense of humor.

"No," the unicorn interjected, stepping forward and making the rainbow world shudder. "You just want to fuck small helpless man creatures with horns and three fingers."

"I didn't say anything about wanting to fuck him." He pouted. "I should be afraid of him. I can't believe I let him stay in the house with you right next door. I need my head examined."

"You are not worried because you know you are safe," the unicorn scoffed as much as a white unicorn with a rather impressive horn could scoff.

"But that's the thing." Torin sat up, pulling himself away from his wife's body. "I should be scared. I should not feel safe."

"Well…" The unicorn moved closer, stepping out of his rainbow world and into the field of purple flowers. "Maybe the magic has something to do with that."

As he moved closer, the rainbow swirled around him, showing his body in splashes of color as he began to meld. Torin watched, fascinated as his form twisted and shrank and then with a flash of light, the horse body was gone and in its place was the naked form of Jova.

It was Jova from his three-fingered hands and toes to the small stubby horn centered on his forehead.

His eyes were a dark starry night and his hair flowed free save for one elaborate braid that was used to hold back the waterfall of silky-looking, silvery-white hair. His cock was partially sheathed and swelling as he moved forward, his toes curling into the purple flowers as he inhaled deeply before tossing his hair over his shoulders with a flip of his head.

He blinked as he looked around the new environment, taking in the purple flowers and tentatively stepping closer. "It's so strange here."

"How is it strange?" Torin asked. "It's soothing, unlike that rainbow hell."

"It's not bright." The pale form pouted, tossing his hair as he examined both Baylin's and Torin's naked bodies. "It's cold. There is not a lot of magic… Well, there is magic, but not how I see it. I am scared."

Torin found himself reaching out a hand, offering it to the naked creature who stood before him. It appeared that pride was the only thing keeping the smaller man from running away in a panic. His gaze traveled over their bare bodies, over the field of flowers, and then back to Torin.

After a moment, Jova reached out and Torin gripped his hand, intent on leading him to sit between him and his wife. The moment their hands touched, however, Torin was sucked into something like a memory that he wasn't sure was his.

No, he was damn sure it wasn't his because there were no pictures exactly. It was impressions and emotions, the feeling of longing and desperation, of fear and frustration. Overlaying all of that was a desire to protect, to defend all that was his, to sacrifice everything if need be to see his charges safe.

Baylin moved over and patting the soft grass beside her, and Torin stared at his dream wife, wondering if she could feel the safety Jova offered with his very presence.

"You said the magic was making us not afraid?" she questioned.

"It… it makes me less afraid too," he said as he sat carefully beside her. His eyes were on her breasts and through their touch, Torin could feel the hunger-curious-need feeling that swamped over the smaller man in waves. It made his dick pulse until it was painfully erect and throbbing. He inhaled and could smell the scent of flowers mingling with musk and of all things, bubblegum. He realized the teasing scent was coming from Jova and his wife, and the desire grew. It was fighting to feel this male, pushing his hunger down and allowing rational thought to flow to the forefront of his mind. Torin carefully separated their hands.

"So it's altering our minds," Torin asked with a breathy voice and a frown. He was not going to cover up his erection -- it was his dream -- but he was going to ignore it until his mind could work out some new answers for him.

"No." Jova shook his head. "I don't think it is. I know my own thoughts, and they are still my own. I know I have your experiences from when you touched me when the magic was acclimating me to this place, and that helps make me less afraid. I believe that you also took something from me. I don't know what, but it makes you less afraid. Magic abhors a vacuum so if something is taken, something of equal value has to be given."

"In a strange sci-fi way, that makes sense." Torin nodded, relaxing. It was his dream, and he was being surrounded by beautiful people. Nice.

His dream-Baylin reached out to touch him and

gasped, her eyes widening for a moment before she nodded slowly. Then she stared at him and her husband before a wicked grin spread across her mouth.

"And because you love cute cuddly lost little things, you find him hot," Baylin crowed. "Admit it, husband. You want to fuck Jova."

"He is not little." Torin crossed his arms and glared at his amused wife and the shocked-looking Jova. His dreams were twisted and strange, but damn if they didn't judge him for being less than honest with himself. "I saw him naked when I examined him."

"I saw him naked in the shower." Baylin crowed, leering at dream-Jova, who was looking more and more interested by the moment. "He has a sheath like a horse, and his dick his big."

"The head is kind of flat --"

"Ridges," Baylin countered. "He is naturally ribbed for our pleasure."

"Our?" Torin found himself torn between excited and amused. In all their play dates, his wife was firmly on board with everything and everyone that they did. If Baylin was not interested, it wasn't happening. In his dreams, to see her so eager just made him admit to himself that he really did want the small alien.

"Oh, yeah," she purred. "I can imagine him in my pussy, Torin. All those ridges, wide and hot, pressing up against my g-spot. And you know he would beat the hell out of your prostate in a good way. You like getting fucked if the guy knows what he's doing."

"And he would know?" He arched an eyebrow at Baylin and glared at the dream-Jova, who was looking smug.

"He was a horse, man! Of course he would. He

knows about thrusting and pulling and pounding…"

"He had never touched his dick before," Torin corrected.

"I did in the shower." Jova smirked, looking amazingly like Torin's wife. "It was fun, relaxing, but ultimately not as satisfying as fucking into a hot, willing body."

Torin gulped hard and stared at the small man who was speaking big. He'd once mentioned he was a dominant, an alpha male, and in that moment, Torin could see there might be some truth to that.

"Or getting fucked." Jova's eyes traveled down, and Torin followed his gaze to see his own dick hard and throbbing, the tip leaking precum and making the plum-colored head glisten. "Love getting fucked, so long as the male is thick enough…" Jova trailed off.

"Oh, he is thick enough," Baylin said, flushed and panting. His dream-wife was getting horny. Damn, he really had nothing but sex on the brain. "And he can fuck like a demon."

"That is a good thing?" Jova questioned, and Baylin grinned.

"A very good thing."

"My subconscious is embarrassing me," Torin pointed out as his hand reached down to grip his dick tightly. It had been years since he had a wet dream, but it looked like this was working out to be a reimagining of his teen fantasies.

"Skill is skill," Baylin bragged. "But then I am your primary partner, and I am pretty damn good myself."

"Primary?" Jova questioned.

"We are poly," Baylin explained, watching as understanding blossomed in Jova's eyes.

"Many… you are many… no. You are in a sexual

relationship but with one or more other people."

"We are married and in a sexual relationship." Baylin pointed to Torin and herself. "But we are open to bringing one more in. We always feel more centered when there is another balancing us out."

"So there is a third." He nodded in understanding. "I had several lovers within my herd, though most of our relationships ended some time ago as we sought to survive. Having a third always gives another opinion and balances out responsibilities."

"And is fun to fuck," Baylin explained, leering.

"So where is your third?"

"We don't have one," Torin took over. It was his dream, after all.

"Why?"

"This place is too remote, and we haven't found anyone really compatible with our needs."

"What are your needs?"

"Well, for one thing, we don't need someone sitting around and whining about how we never spend any time with them," Baylin grumbled. "This is a slow season for us, but during the spring, summer, and fall months, we are swamped with work. We take care of pets, exotic animals, large animals, farm animals, and the occasional exotic animal that finds its way into Angel Falls."

"Then there is work with the forestry service," Torin took over. "We recently reintroduced wolves into this area, and they are settling in nicely. As a matter of fact, we thought that poachers after the wolves were out there shooting when we found you. We heard what sounded like a gunshot, and then we went looking."

"So you need a partner who understands leadership and its duties." Jova nodded. "That is important if the relationship is going to last."

"And we need someone compatible with our personalities. If you haven't noticed, we are both strong-willed."

"Not as stubborn as some." Jova absently stroked his dick. He was really enjoying the ability to touch, it seemed. "You both are willing to compromise and agree with one another about what is needed to make your mating work. It is essential for trust and understanding to flourish before you attempt to bring in another, and if you are ready, it speaks to both of your good characters. Whoever you bring in as third will have to be self-confident and assured of their place in your marriage. They have to be honorable and trustworthy in their own right."

"We want them to feel free to do what they want, to continue their careers if that is what they choose, to party and have friends, but that is kind of difficult when you are as isolated as we are here."

"Understandable," Jova concurred.

"So…" Torin had to ask. "How is the integration going? All those personalities settling in?"

"Personalities, no. Points of view, yes. They made me horny. Let's fuck."

Torin blinked at the abruptness of the request, but decided it was his dream, and if his subconscious was done untangling the mysteries of the universe, then they could get down to the sexing portion of his wet dream.

His dream-Baylin giggled and looked at him for confirmation. Even in their dreams they did all things together.

"Yes, let's fuck," he moaned and gripped his wife by the waist, dropping her on top of Jova.

The unicorn squawked, but silenced as Baylin

shoved a breast into his mouth. It was an effective pacifier because he began to suck hard, his hands going to grip her waist.

"Keep her occupied," Torin ordered as he began nibbling at her neck and running his hands down her sides.

Dream-Baylin moaned, tossing her hair back as she ran her fingers over Jova's horn.

The unicorn pulled back, hissing at her, and she grinned, leaning over to lick at the small appendage, pushing aside the braid that held it mostly hidden from view.

"Sensitive," she noted as she slid back and gripped Jova's dick.

It was a nice dick as far as horse-like dicks went. Torin was one to admit he had a passing curiosity about dildos shaped like horse penises, but as a vet never really could cultivate an interest.

But Baylin was definitely interested.

"You know how this goes, right?" she asked him, and he nodded.

"You stand and I move around behind --"

"Or this." She gripped his dick, placed it at the mouth of her sopping wet pussy, and slid down hard.

Torin laughed outright as Jova's eyes widened and he let out a strangled yelp.

"Or that," he muttered, arching up as she slid forward, working her pussy in circles.

Jova was tearing at the flowers beneath them and staring at Baylin like she'd invented rainbows. Moaning, she tossed her hair over her shoulders and called to Torin.

"You coming to join in, husband? Two holes, no waiting."

He slid up behind her, pressing his dick against

her ass, and in the way of dreams she was prepared, already wet and open and willing. He pressed in slowly, feeling the silken heat of her ass envelop the head of his cock. He growled, throwing his head back and gripping her waist as he began to sink in deeper.

But this time he could feel the ridges of the dick fucking her pussy.

Baylin screamed as he pressed deeper, her ass fluttering around him as her hands reached back to grip his hips, and instantly he halted all movement.

"I need a moment," she panted. "Overwhelming…"

"Are you hurt?" Jova demanded, his black eyes glittering as his hands gripped her waist, and Torin could feel how easily he lifted his wife, holding her so she could not sink back deeper onto the pair of cocks piercing her.

"No," she shook her head. "God, no. Too much… gonna come."

"Then come," Torin ordered as be began thrusting shallowly, moving his dick enough to stimulate the sensitive nerves in her ass.

"Not done… being… f-fucked!" she insisted.

"Like you are going to come only once." He leered and began to steadily push into her ass.

Baylin moaned, her breath coming back as Jova too began to move.

God, Torin thought his eyes were going to cross. The silky feel of his wife's ass combined with the ridges of Jova's dick… It was like getting an intimate massage on his dick while he fucked.

Jova was tossing his hair from side to side, the thin braids holding his hair back from his face coming undone as he bared his teeth, his nostrils flaring. He was so hot! Torin looked down at his wife, her head resting against his shoulder as her face flushed bright red; her mouth was open, gasping for air, her lips dry as her eyelids dropped to half mast. She looked drugged with pleasure. It was a good look for her.

Jova let go of her waist and suddenly she was in control once more. She rose up before slamming down, swirling her hips, bouncing her ass, looking for a rhythm that would work for her.

She was moaning, muttering, and crying out as her body shivered and shook. One of her hands went to the back of Torin's head, holding him fast while the other went to Jova's hand, holding on tightly.

But it was Jova who broke first. He was whimpering, his eyes wide and glittering, his horn glowing softly as his head whipped from side to side.

"Oh… Oh… Oh, magic," he was mumbling, the muscles of his stomach tightening, his pale skin flushing silver as his hips began to jerk hard.

Then he was fucking up into Baylin.

"Yes, yes, yes!" She was screaming as he lost it. His hands went to his hair, the other tearing at the purple flowers before he arced up hard and screamed…

Chapter 6

"Fuck," Torin shouted as his ass hit the floor.

It was the most unsexy way he could think of to end a wet dream, but he was sitting on the carpet, dick wet, watching as his wife scrambled to her feet.

Then he realized Jova's scream was still echoing around him. He got up and followed his wife, who was racing across the hall and into his room.

He raced in and froze when he saw Jova tangled up in the blankets, his bare flesh glinting in the light of the rising sun through the windows.

His hair was a wild tangle, and Baylin was doing her best to untangle his thrashing form and recover her breath at the same time.

Then Torin was across the room and shaking Jova's shoulder.

He winced as the smaller man whimpered, his hips arching as Baylin managed to tear the sheet away, his hard cock fully exposed and throbbing. His eyes snapped open as his hands gripped his dick and squeezed hard. His nostrils flared, and Torin found himself scenting the other male as a sweet musky sent filled the room.

"Oh, my," Baylin moaned, slowly sinking into the bed next to Jova as the sheet slithered from her hand to land on the floor.

Blindly, Jova reached for her, and Torin watched, enthralled, as his wife dropped to her knees, straddling the other man.

He watched as she threw her head back, the same posture she had taken up in his dream, and moaned loudly.

Torin was torn between staring at his wife and at Jova's cock. The man was as hung as he appeared in his dreams and was just as eager. Tentatively, he reached up and cupped Baylin's breast in his hands, shuddering at the contact.

"In the dream they felt so soft…" he breathed, his whole body shuddering as he began to sweat and that sweet musky smell grew.

"They are nice," Torin found himself responding, and Jova's eyes went to his body. He moaned as his hips thrust up as if against his will. He caught himself and stilled, his eyes trailing up to Torin's.

"I want to squeeze… in the dream…"

"You were in the dream?" Torin asked, stepping closer and taking a seat beside the pair on the bed. He was more curious than anything, and the sight of the two of them together didn't send him into mindless rage or lust.

He realized he wanted this, wanted to see this, but he had a choice.

"Magic," Jova panted, moaning as Baylin began to explore his chest. His hair was a tangle about his face, and his stubby horn had a faint glow.

"The dream," he breathed. "We were speaking…" He lifted one hand, and a handful of crumpled purple flowers fell to the bed.

"We were fucking," Torin was able to admit. "We were fucking like cats in heat."

"We were sharing the dream." Baylin nodded.

"Rut," Jova corrected. "I am in rut. I don't know why --"

"Whoa." Baylin stopped rocking her pussy against his stomach and looked over at Torin. "But how can you go into rut if no one is in heat?"

Torin looked down and chuckled to see the trail of slick she'd left on Jova's stomach. It appeared he really was fucking her; they were fucking in his dreams and in reality. Jova touched her lightly and watched.

"I do not know," Jova panted, his hands dropping down to grip her waist. "I am not human. When do humans rut?"

"Whenever we want." Torin laughed, shaking his head. He really should be going crazy, but instead he was, well, horny. "I should be freaking out right now, but I am not."

"Magic…"

"You explained in the dream. So you are saying this is happening because I really want it, and the magic is only speeding things up a bit?"

"More like showing you what you want. You can say no --"

"But that would not be fun," Baylin breathed.

"What do you want?" Torin asked his wife then had to smile at the wicked grin on her face.

"I want you to fuck me hard, and I want to suck him off."

There was rarely any hesitation when Baylin decided she wanted something. "I've wanted him since I saw him strip his clothes off to shower. I was just feeling guilty about it. But it seems he is feeling the same way. I felt it when he touched me."

"We're all on the same page?" Torin wanted to know.

"If that dream was real --" Baylin began, but Jova cut her off.

"It was. Everything you said to me, everything I told you." He picked up one of the blossoms and ran it over her golden flesh. "It was real."

"It would have to be, or we are all having shared hallucinations." Torin shook his head. "Magic… wild. It is so much easier to believe in aliens than in magic."

"But since we all believe --"

"Fuck me," Baylin chuckled. "I need to be fucked and fucked right now while I blow him."

There was nothing more to be said. Torin bent down and took his wife's mouth, forcing his tongue between her lips.

She slid backwards, finally pulling away to settle between Jova's legs.

"Blow…" His eyes widened as his hands trailed over her hair, pulling it back as Torin moved into position behind her.

This was wild. This was his dream, but it was really happening. He felt elated and happy, almost like a puzzle piece was trying to slot itself home.

"Wait," Baylin cautioned, as she dropped down to mouth at his pink nipples.

Jova hissed, his back arching as his eyes widened.

"So different than when a foal suckles…"

Baylin snorted and nipped him sharply. He hissed, his hands going to her hair, tangling in her curls as she lapped the pain away.

"Different, but I think I like it." Jova shook his head, his long hair falling around his shoulders.

In a rather horse-like move of his own, Torin tossed his hair back, and that movement caught Jova's attention. The glass-black eyes focused in on him, and he felt his already swollen dick harden further. He gripped his wife's waist, palming her ass as he smirked at Jova.

Baylin was trailing her mouth down lower over Jova's flushed skin, licking and biting. She gasped as Torin slapped her on the ass, and he grinned as he watched red bloom on her fine ass before it faded away.

"Suck his dick."

Before she could answer, he was lowering his own head and began licking at her pussy.

God, Baylin was delicious. There was something about the taste of his wife… if he was on his deathbed, just the smell and taste of her alone would revive him. Baylin whooped, spreading her thighs and giving him easy access to her pussy. He lapped at her wetness, smearing it around his face as he realized she really enjoyed teasing the man beneath her.

Jova was staring wide-eyed at them, his hands running through Baylin's hair as he stiffened more with each new sensation.

Before long the urge to complete their shared dream took over, and Torin was stroking his cock under the watchful gaze of their lover.

Lover. He liked the sound of that.

He was waiting for just the right moment, waiting for Jova's eyes to widen as Baylin sucked the flattish head into her mouth. Then he gripped her thighs and thrust himself in deep.

* * *

He tasted like bubble gum.

It was the most amazing thing ever, and that was saying something.

With this unicorn, she had shared dreams with her husband, and there was the whole magic thing… but this… bubble-gum-flavored cock.

She closed her eyes, gripped his dick hard, and sucked him down.

Jova made a strange whining sound and spread his legs wider. His balls pulled up, and Baylin grinned when she saw his tiny pink vagina all glistening and wet. She pulled back with a pop, to lap at his flat pink head as she examined him with lustful eyes.

He was so damn pretty.

His face was flushed a silvery red, his hair flowing behind him like an electric aura. His eyes were wide open and glassy. His full lips were parted and swollen from kisses and bites. Just the thought of her husband kissing him sent a thrill through her that translated into her pussy where Torin was resting his full thick length inside.

She clenched down on him, making him moan, and she ran her fingers over Jova's groin. His dick was fully extended from its sheath and such a pretty pale pink she wondered if she could get lipstick in that shade. But then that would remind her too much of sucking his dick, which would lead to embarrassing stains in her panties, so maybe it was not such a great idea after all.

His balls were small and tight, pale pink with absolutely no body hair. The only hair was his amazing eyelashes, those arched brows, and all that silvery hair on his head. His body was naturally bare, and Baylin appreciated the fact that she would not be picking pubic hair out of her teeth.

His slim legs were parted widely, leaving her space to explore, and explore she did. Her fingers ran over his flesh, watching as he shuddered and groaned, his own hands going to his sensitive nipples and plucking them as she had teased them before. He really seemed to like that.

She hissed, jumping as Torin bent over her back, gripping both her breasts and giving her nipples the same treatment. Her pussy spasmed around his cock, making him push in deeper, as his eyes closed for a moment. Her fingers tightened on Jova's inner thighs, leaving scratches in his delicate skin, but he seemed to like that from the way he pushed into the rough caress.

She pressed her nails in deeper, dragging them lightly up toward his groin as he bucked sharply underneath her.

His cock wobbled, hard and resting on his stomach, and Baylin knew that before this night was over, she was going to feel that thick length within her. She dropped her head again, inhaling the rich scent of vanilla and flowers, and her mouth watered.

She laved up his shaft, teasing the delicate skin of his engorged cock, watching as his hands fisted in the bedclothes. His balls rose to the base of his dick and exposed his tiny little pussy once more.

Baylin loved a well-cared-for pussy. She wanted to pet him and make him feel real good, but the temptation of his cock was hard to pass up.

"Do something," Torin ordered, and she looked over her shoulder at him.

He was flushed bright red and sweating. His grip on her hips was harsh, and she could feel him throb from within. He was ready to move but was giving her time to play.

Nodding, she gripped Jova's cock, pumping it lightly as she dropped her head and lapped over the thin lips of his pussy.

"Great magic!" Jova wailed, his round eyes glowing softy as a golden hue enveloped him for a moment.

Snickering, Baylin lowered her head again and licked at him, harder, and yes, he tasted like bubblegum here too.

She lowered her head and began to eat him out as hard as she could.

Jova had no clit, but his cock was leaking precum steadily as she munched on him, sliding a firm finger from her free hand deep inside. He wailed, his back arching up as his head pressed back into the pillows.

Fuck, this was fun. She could feel his slick coating her face, and she pulled back momentarily to nod at her husband. Torin pulled back and slammed deep inside her. She moaned into Jova's va-jay-jay, and his dick reacted by pulsing in her grip.

Moaning again, she gripped him tighter, stroking him harder as she lapped and licked him out. Her husband was pounding harder, pressing up against that spot deep inside her inner walls and sending fire shooting from her back to her toes. Her clit was burning as she relished the feel of his heavy balls beating against it.

She was in heaven, her face buried in a delicious pussy, her own being pounded, a cock in her hand. This was the best of both worlds.

She pushed back on her husband's dick, needing Torin to fuck her harder and faster as she pulled away from Jova's cunt to suck down his dick.

Jova wailed.

Drawing such a sound from him made her pussy tighten as she drew closer and closer to release. God, it was turning her on so much, the power, the control…

She was moaning and grinning, grunting and humming like an animal as she slammed herself backward on Torin's prick and choked Jova's cock down her throat. She tongued the ridges as she sucked him hard, her eyes looking up and staring into his as she slipped the tip of her tongue into his slit.

He grunted, almost knocking her off as she teased him, dragging him closer to orgasm by sliding another finger into his pussy.

She was working him with three fingers when her husband twisted and swirled his hips in just the right way.

"Fuck," she pulled off to say, then began pumping Jova's shaft while she concentrated on the head.

Torin was pounding her pussy, his hands pulling at her breasts before one dropped own to pluck at her clit. She jumped and squealed, nearly overwhelmed by the sensations swamping her.

She was losing her rhythm, unable to keep sucking while getting fucked, and just as she thought Jova was too polite to order her to suck him harder, his hands tangled in her hair, and he was thrusting his hips up.

God, he was fucking her face. She was getting exactly want she wanted.

She choked him down one more time as Torin slammed his thick length in deep, and then she was coming. Her pussy clenched around Torin's dick and she screamed around Jova's cock.

The vibrations of her throat seemed to be what Jova needed, for he threw back his head and screamed, as well, his body stiffening as his pussy clenched around her fingers. Then she was swallowing, drinking down the rich, sweet taste of his semen as he shot into her mouth.

She swallowed hard, gasping as Torin began to rut inside her, seeking his own release. By the time she dropped a softening Jova from her lips, Torin was slamming to a finish, wrapping his arms around her as he shuddered his release. She could feel the wet heat of him fill her as he settled back, taking a big breath and looking down at Jova.

"I think we killed him," she muttered, for the man was out cold. She patted the hair that tangled around his face, noting it felt like raw silk, and burrowed down until she could find his neck. She breathed a sigh of relief when she discovered skin cool to the touch and a faint rapid pulse.

He was alive, just passed out from the pleasure.

Torin shook his head as Baylin raised hers to grin at him. "Knocked the fuck out," she crowed and threw her hand up in a high-five.

Torin chuckled as he slapped her hand in turn.

Chapter 7

Jova was floating. He had never been so warm and content in his life. There were the two voices in his head, merging finally with his own thought matrix and the result was… stunning.

He could see Baylin cared more than she thought she did. In the dreamscape with him, she had seen a lot more than she had let on. She too had been scared about her mind being altered, but she let her husband speak for the both of them. Personally, she had wondered if they were dealing with body snatchers.

But then she touched him and suddenly, he understood. She was just as frightened, but she knew his pain and his loss. She claimed she had gotten over the loss of any potential children, but it still was an ache in her soul. She felt the loss of his planet, of his people, of his son, and it resonated within her.

She could read in his mind that he wished to do no harm, that he hadn't expected to live at all, that his life had been a gift of magic from the planet, and that he would do everything to protect that gift… even if it meant learning from two strange humans.

She found amusement in his decisions and in his realization that he was in rut. It was in fact her experiences that clued him in, comparing what she knew of her own hormonal levels to what he was feeling. He just had to pay attention to what the female side was saying. The male side was all about impressions, being first, being able to protect, but the female was all about nuances.

He could read Baylin's desire for him; she processed it quickly and didn't need any explanations as to why she wanted to mate with him. It was more complicated than that she thought he was attractive and more about understanding exactly how he was feeling.

The sex she offered was not out of pity, but out of shared experiences and want. She did find his form attractive, but she found the mind even more so, and that drew him in greatly.

To have her perform an act she though of as *blow job*... he would have never thought... he had never experienced... Magic, these humans were clever.

She had sucked and licked at his dick and his... his pussy as she called it, and he had thought he experienced several small deaths in one. The added bonus was having the possessive male eyes of Torin upon them.

Female wiles were amazing, but he wanted a taste of the masculine too.

It didn't shock him much that Baylin wanted to watch them fuck -- it was in her body language. She wanted to watch, but she wanted to be a part of it too.

That could be arranged.

Jova opened his eyes and watched the beautiful couple hovering over him.

"So, ever have an orgasm so great that you just passed the fuck out?" Baylin was giggling, but not at him. She was laughing with him, though he still flushed brightly at his passing out.

"I have never experienced anything like that."

"Unicorns don't suck dick." Baylin laughed again.

"We never thought to do such a thing, no," he agreed, sitting up a bit, but groaning when he realized his dick was swelling again. When would this rut end?

"Man, that is some recovery," Baylin went on, and Torin rolled his eyes in a human fashion at her.

"I do not know --"

"Males go into rut when they meet their true mates..." Jova began. Then lights flashed in his mind, and suddenly it all made sense. His magic had sent him to where he was safe and adapted him so he would remain safe... safe in the arms of his mates.

He was in rut because he had mates, and he wasn't sure if they would accept him or not. It wasn't magic that was making them so comfortable with each other -- it was fate.

"You blanked on the word mate." Torin was observant.

"I --" he began, but his thought matrix, nearly fully combined, was urging him to honesty. "I think I understand why we are drawn to one another."

"Yeah, magic." Torin nodded. "I get it."

"It may not be magic... not the kind I was referring to..." Jova trailed off and Baylin sat up.

She was beautiful with her full teats... breasts... and her dark gold skin. Her hair was a fuzzy mess around her head, and she smelled strongly of his rut.

He turned his attention to Torin and noted the male had moved closer to his wife. His hair was still straight and flowing down his back, but his eyes were glinting as they stared at him. His bare chest was massive, the muscles bulging in an agreeable fashion though the way he was sitting hid his full cock from view. Jova recalled how that cock felt in his hands, so similar to his own now, but still so different. He shifted to hide his own engorging dick.

"Explain," Torin said.

"I think I know why magic sent me here."

"To keep you safe. I got that in the strange magical dream world." Torin smiled.

"Safe because..." He could do this, though he had no idea why he was hesitant. Maybe it was the female voice that begged caution, but he knew he had to be honest first and foremost. Torin and Baylin respected honesty. "Safe because magic placed me in close proximity to my mates."

"Oh, boy." Baylin deflated. There was a flash of pain in her eyes before she looked up at her husband. "And I thought we were going to get to keep this one too."

"You don't understand." Jova raised his hand -- his three-fingered hand -- and they paused. He tossed his hair, snorting a little in apprehension before he continued. "I was put where my mates are. I was put... with you."

The pair of them stared at each other for a moment before they both turned to look at him.

"Us?" Torin finally asked. "We are your mates? But we are not unicorns."

"This I know, and am at a loss to explain." He offered them a smile. "But I believe that magic brought me to my mates, and now I am in rut until I am accepted or rejected."

Silence.

He made a move to get up, feeling maybe the female voice that wanted caution was correct after all. Before he could move, Baylin was reaching out and touching him. She hissed as she turned to Torin. "Despair and pain. Rejection and hurt. We are not rejecting you, Jova. It'll... It'll just take a moment to process."

"You are our mate?" he asked, shaking his head as Jova nodded. He snorted once and tossed his hair again. He was nervous, but he was getting comforting feelings from Baylin.

"Well, that would explain why we could never get a date," Torin joked, reaching out to take Jova's arm as Baylin snorted in laughter.

"Are you... but your marriage --"

"Looking for a third," Torin reminded him. "And we could never find one. I am not sure how this is going to work out, but something in me is urging me to try. So, Jova, do you want to try?"

Jova was speechless. Never had he had such acceptance before in his long life.

Now, when both of them were touching him, it all seemed to make sense. All the puzzle pieces that were his life slotted into place. He reached for Baylin and pulled her to his body, burying his face in her hair.

"Thank you," he whispered, before a beautiful high note rang out in the air and his first tear fell. "I -- I am not sad..." he muttered, pulling back and looking over at Torin, confusion written on his face as another happy tone rang out.

"Sometimes," Torin explained, reaching out to cup his face. Jova closed his eyes and settled closer, Baylin in his arms and Torin hovering protectively. "Sometimes we cry when we are happy, too."

"Fascinating." Jova looked up at the male. "You realize that the fact the fates think we are good mates for each other is by no means a guarantee of happiness?"

"I think fate or magic or just plain dumb luck put us together so we could at least try." Baylin's words were wise, and the two males nodded in agreement. "Trying is the fun part." She chuckled. "And beyond a few kisses and caresses, I haven't seen you two *try* much of anything."

Torin flushed, and Jova smirked. "I must admit, I am not at my best," he informed them archly. "Usually I am quite a bit more dominant. Once I learn the ins and outs of this new body, I assure you, my behavior won't be the same."

"I have a feeling you two are going to tear up the sheets." Baylin sounded eager. "Just so long as I get to play too."

"As if we would stop you." Torin chuckled. "I think we both want a piece of that wonderful ass, Bay. Dream sex is hot, but nothing like the real thing."

"I refuse to be a human Fleshlight…"

"What's a Fleshlight?" Jova broke in.

Torin and Baylin stared at each other for one hot second before they practically knocked one another on their asses trying to get to their bedroom and the toy chest. Jova watched, intrigued as his humans scrambled out and returned to the room with a wooden chest. Torin dropped it by the foot of the bed then Baylin nearly conked herself with the lid as she rushed to get back to the top of the mattress where he lay.

Baylin was the one to present the clear padded tube while Torin, a wicked look in his eyes, pulled the lube from the trunk.

He blinked again. Baylin's grin grew wide as she gripped his penis… No, she liked it when he used the word dick. She reached for his already hard dick and ran her fingers over the tip.

"Unlike in dream worlds, we need lube to make this slippery."

He looked between her legs and arched an eyebrow.

"More slippery," she corrected. "Lack of lube, no butt sex."

"Butt sex?"

"Like in the dream," she continued. "Because that is one place where you don't want friction burns or tears. As a matter of fact, lube everything."

That being said, she pulled the lube from her husband's hands and poured it directly over Jova's dick.

He winced, pulling back at the feel of the cool slick stuff, but Torin's hands were there, smoothing and slathering, and that felt all right. He hissed, his toes curling as an electric shock shot down his legs and back up to his dick, making it jump in Torin's grip. It was similar, yet different from when Baylin was handling him, stroking and sucking him to orgasm. Torin was surer with his grip, more knowing.

He'd probably had a lot of time to play with his own dick, Jova reasoned, and added his own hand to the other male's. "I like the spot here being stroked." There was nothing in either of their past experiences that led him to believe telling them what he wanted was wrong. His finger touched a spot below the first of the two ridges on his dick and chuffed softly as Torin ran his fingers over the spot. "Yes, like that."

He decided he really should return the action and learn a bit more about Torin's body, so he reached out and grabbed the man's swollen dick. Torin hissed, and Jova gentled his caress, easing up on his grip and stroking the smooth skin lightly.

Torin's dick was more veiny than his, and lacked a foreskin or a sheath, but it was very warm and solid in his hands. He gave it a gentle squeeze, watching the tip turn purple as he swelled further.

"Beautiful." Baylin was still holding the Fleshlight, her eyes alight with mischief as she sank one of her hands between her spread legs and began fingering herself.

"Beautiful," Jova agreed and reached out with his free hand to pet her pussy. It was so different from his. His lips didn't swell as much, and there wasn't the button at the tip of his slit that made Baylin squeak when he stroked it gently.

In fact, he loved the sound so much he stroked her again, lamenting the fact that he didn't have one of those clitorises. It looked to be great fun to manipulate.

He pushed her fingers aside and dipped them into her slit, growling a bit at the feel of her slick wetness. Oh, she was silky smooth here, almost like his own little pussy, but hers was deeper and more fun. She made the most amazing sounds when he added a second finger, spreading her legs wider so he could see.

Jova could not see his own pussy, but Baylin's was beautiful. There was a neat patch of trimmed hair that surrounded her pussy lips, the damp curls holding on to the scent of her want. She was all shades of swollen pink, with her milky pink clit poking out of its own cowl.

He added another finger and ran his thumb along the clit and grinned when he felt her inner walls clutch at his fingers. He had opened his mouth to comment when Torin gripped his balls. He gave them a tug, and Jova found himself hissing in pleasure. It was a rougher delight than when Baylin had licked at them. His eyes went back to Torin, amazed by what Torin was making his body feel.

"The Fleshlight," Baylin whimpered and handed the device over to Torin.

He took it with a grin and let go of his balls long enough to fit the head of Jova's dick into the slick opening.

Again, Jova wanted to question the validity of this device, since hands felt great stroking his dick, when Torin pushed it down over his cock.

"Great magic," he gasped, his body stilling as his

eyes widened.

This thing, this device… it was not as warm as a mount, not as hot as a willing wet body, but it was amazing in its own right.

He groaned as Torin pulled it up and then slammed it down, making Jova's hips slap up, fucking into the toy as Torin held it steady.

Jova forgot about Baylin's pussy, about Torin's dick in his hand. All his attention went straight to his cock and the sensations that were streaking through his body.

"Oh!" He didn't know what to do with his hands! They went above his head, tangled in his hair, smearing the scent of Baylin around, before he reached for Torin, gripping him by the shoulders.

"That's it," Torin urged, pumping the toy faster as Jova was slowly torn apart by the feelings flying from his groin. He threw his head back, whimpering, his legs spreading wider as he felt his pussy began to drip with slick.

Hungrily, he pulled at Torin, tugging him down until he could take Torin's mouth with his and swallow down the moans of pleasure coming from the other male. He was vaguely aware of Baylin backing off and Torin sliding between his spread thighs. Then Torin's hands were on his pussy, two fingers sliding in deep as Jova's head slammed back and he began to circle his hips, desperate for the next plunge of the toy.

"Fuck me," he moaned as Torin played his body, made him dance to his own rhythm. His head was racing, heart pounding, his breath coming in gasps… he was dying a little death, and he wanted more.

Hissing, he gripped Torin by the shoulders and slammed him back onto the bed, rising above him with his teeth bared. He noted Torin's surprise as Jova flipped him onto his stomach and bit at his shoulders.

He was an alpha. It was time he took what he wanted.

* * *

"Finally," Baylin's voice was filled with relief as she settled back to watch her two men fuck.

Jova was beautiful as he reared above Torin, his black eyes glittering as he tossed his long mane of white hair behind him. He didn't use his hands, just a quick jerk of his head and the fall of silvery white hair settled along his back.

He flexed his fingers, all three of them, against Torin's shoulders while his thumb gently caressed the base of his neck, pressing in soft circles, gentling him. He backed off, and she shifted on the bed, getting a better view as Jova dipped his head and began to nip along the golden flesh of Torin's back.

Torin hissed, his head dropping, his ass rising as he presented.

This was something Baylin had never thought to see. In all their hook-ups with other men, Torin had always played a dominant role. Seeing him now, spreading his legs, his chest low and pressing into the pillows that bolstered him, was arousing in a way that made her slip her hands between her things and press against her swollen labia. She left her clit alone. Just from watching them, she was ready to come, and she didn't want to be overly stimulated before it was her time to join in.

"Fuck," Torin gasped as Jova nipped sharply at his lower back, his hands traveling down to the rounded globes of Torin' ass, pressing deep as his thumb ran down Torin's trench.

In response, Jova snorted, his perfect upper lip curling back from his teeth in almost a smirk before he lapped his way up Torin's back. His teeth latched onto the skin of Torin's neck, and her husband bucked up hard, his muscles tense as minute shivers rushed over his body.

She watched as Jova reached for the lube, pouring it over her husband's ass before he sank a finger in deep. Torin cursed, bucking up, but Jova easily held him where he wanted him. She noted that Torin was not fighting to get away. In fact, he was acting rather eager to give himself to Jova.

That was something he had also never allowed. Torin didn't trust easily, but with Jova everything seemed to fall into place naturally. The smaller male seemed to know instinctively what her husband wanted and was more than willing to give it to him.

He pulled back from Torin's neck and again got his face right up to Torin's ass. He spread Torin's rounded cheeks and watched as his finger sank into the tiny pink orifice eagerly, hungrily.

"I see the benefit of lube in butt sex." Jova's voice was deep, dark, and sent tendrils of heat running through Baylin's body. She resumed stroking her clit as she watched. "Otherwise I would not be able to get a finger into such a tight, hot place."

Torin wailed, his hips jerking as Jova lowered his head and lapped around his finger, teasing the pink rosebud and making her husband cry out.

God, this was so hot. She sank three fingers in her pussy and began to pump them. Watching these two was better than live porn.

Soon Jova had a rhythm going, pumping her husband's hole hard while grinding his slick dick into the side of his ass. Baylin's first orgasm caught her off guard. Her toes pointed and her head went back and her hips slammed up into her hands as her pussy spasmed around her fingers. Her husband was throwing his head to the side and whimpering, his toes pointed, his hands gripping the bed sheets as he spread his legs further, submitting.

His pleasure caught her off guard, tearing through her, dropping her back to the bed as she stroked herself through the nerve-tingling spasms that signaled her release. Her eyes closed as she lost herself in the sensation, in the memory of her husband willingly giving himself over to someone else's care.

She opened her eyes to find two sets of them staring back at her, one deeply brown, the other solid, glittering black.

"Come over here," Jova ordered, and Baylin's pussy clenched, her nerves tightening as if preparing for another orgasm. But she pulled herself together and crawled over to Jova, rising to press a kiss to his mouth. His tongue invaded, tasting of bubble gum and her husband's sweet flesh as he bit and sucked at her lips.

She pulled away to drop down beside her Torin, running her fingers gently over his face, pushing his hair aside and pressing a kiss to his lips. He whimpered at her touch, and she nipped at his lips.

"He wants to fuck you while I fuck him."

That sounded like a plan.

Baylin scrambled to get in front of her husband as Jova pulled him up to his knees. It only took a moment for her to position herself before Torin was dropping low, his hard dick leaving silvery trails along her thighs as he slotted himself into place.

She was about to get fucked so good…

* * *

Torin couldn't think; he couldn't react. All he could do was feel, and he had never felt so wonderful in his life.

His asshole burned in a good way as Jova pumped him, split him open, and made a place for himself between his cheeks. Baylin was lying in front of him, her soft thighs surrounding him with her gentle heat, her scent, the years of comforting and known pleasure.

At his back, Jova was an unknown entity, a breath of fire that had suddenly flowed from the façade of a small, lost submissive.

The fact that Jova had flipped him over and took charge of this fucking was no surprise. He was the leader of his people and had several hundred years of experience on him. The fact that Torin was allowing this, was eagerly willing this to happen, was.

And now, God, his dick was pushing into its favorite place, deep inside his wife's sugared walls, and his ass...

"Oh fuck, oh fuck, oh fuck," Baylin was muttering, and Torin froze as he felt the broad head of Jova's dick split his ass wide open.

It burned so good, this helplessness of being speared, of being taken. He'd had it with toys and with an occasional man he ordered to take him, but this was something entirely different, and he loved it.

He hissed as his guardian walls finally opened enough to allow the fat head of Jova's dick to sink in to the first ridge. There the smaller male paused.

"Are you fine?" he asked, his voice sending vibrations through Torin's body.

"Oh -- fuck..." Baylin seemed to be stuck as he stared over her shoulders at the man who hovered above them.

Torin tried to look back, but a fall of silvery hair was in his way. So he lowered his head, pillowed it on

Baylin's softly rounded breasts, and pushed his ass back for more.

God, yes, he wanted more. He wanted to be taken, to be fucked, to feel the ridges of Jova's cock against his prostate, to feel those small balls hitting his own... to feel the slick of Jova's pussy sliding down and making a mess of him.

Torin was ready for some dirty, nasty sex with his wife and his new partner, for he instinctively knew Jova would be a good partner in all things.

Maybe it was fate or magic, but he knew a gift had landed in his lap, and he was going to enjoy it to the fullest.

"Fuck me!" he growled as he slid his hips forward, pushing deeper into the slick, wet heat of his wife. Jova snorted, tossing his hair, and Torin shuddered as the feel of the cool slick silk ran over his back and down his side.

Jova's hands tightened on his waist and then... "Fuck!"

There was no other word to describe it. He was being split open as Jova forged a path that few dared to tread. Torin whimpered, his hips slamming forward as Jova's ridges slid past his p-spot, battering the sensitive gland as he pulled out and slammed back inside.

Jova's actions pushed Torin deeper into his Baylin, who wailed her pleasure. Her legs came around them both, holding them together as Jova began to fuck them both in earnest.

He was fucking them both, truly. Every thrust translated into a hard pounding for the very much willing Baylin. Her head was tossed back, her curls surrounding her face as she thrust her hips upward, crafting a rhythm that left him being beautifully fucked and fucking in the middle.

His nerves were on fire. Fire zinged up and down his spine. His balls were lifting to the base of his cock as his dick swelled and his ass greedily milked Jova's amazing dick. He closed his eyes, knowing they would not be able to keep up this pace, but wanting to experience every feeling he could drag from this sex act.

Never before had it ever felt like this.

He was in heaven, he was in hell, he was going to...

"Fuck!" he shouted, his back arching as his balls churned in their sac. He could feel it ending, the tension tightening in his body, his nerves screaming as his muscles froze. He was going to --

Baylin went over first, her wet walls gripping at him as her nails dug into his shoulders.

"Torin!" she wailed, "Jova... Torin... Oh..." She was bucking beneath them, throwing her body into the pleasure, driving him along the hard edge of ecstasy until he could no longer hold back.

Jova gave one more hard thrust, those damn ridges rubbing Torin's prostate just enough to tip him over the edge. Torin whimpered like a young boy as his dick jerked inside his wife. He felt the heat of his own seed flood her passage, making it slicker and hotter as his ass tried to grab onto Jova's dick. He felt his muscles spasm, gripping down hard on Jova as the unicorn threw his head back and wailed.

Jova fucked Torin all through his orgasm, never slowing down, never softening as he panted and whimpered, before freezing deep inside as far as he could go.

"Torin." Jova groaned, and Torin felt another spurt of his seed erupt from his softening dick as the slick of Jova's bubble-gum-scented come filled his hole to overflowing.

They collapsed into a sweating heap on the bed, a tangle of limbs and long hair and exhausted joy.

Never had Torin felt like this before, like he was fully complete, like the thing he and his wife had been searching for, for so long, had finally been found.

He let himself drift as the others arranged his pleasure-drenched body and surrounded him with their adoration.

There were things that had to be worked out, discussions to be had, plans for the future to be made, but for now, Torin just let himself drift and enjoyed just being.

* * *

Jova was just sitting there unblinking as the music flowed over him. Peter Gabriel's "Solsbury Hill" was on repeat, the unique beat touching something in Torin as he stood watching his lover.

They were all sexed out. What a wonderful way to start the new year, being all sexed out and sore.

They had finally crawled out of bed and taught Jova the fundamentals of frozen pizza as they cleaned up the bedrooms and helped one another get clean... which led to more explorations in the shower.

Now sated and mellow, they moved to the living room and its huge fireplace while Torin made a few phone calls.

The sheriff understood that Jova was a traveler who had been stranded and lost, but was fine if a bit disoriented from frostbite.

Torin explained that Jova would come into town soon to introduce himself as soon as the blizzard blew over. It looked like it was going to snow for another few days at least, and the sheriff wasn't in any hurry to leave his new lady lover to risk life and limb when everyone was safe and secure.

Torin knew he would have to do something about finding an identity for Jova -- maybe another large or exotic animal vet -- but they had time to figure that out later. For now he stood in the doorway and watched his new lover and his wife, who was sprawled out across his lap.

There was something about this song, something sad and joyous all at once. It was about sacrifice, being willing to give up everything to begin anew. There was fear and longing in that song, as if the singer knew he might lose all that he had worked so hard to build, but there was an insisting, driving need for him to break out and do something different. Yes, there was fear there, but there was also a hope for the future.

It reminded him of his shorter lover; it could have been written about the lone unicorn, the only one of his kind here.

"I can't go back home," Jova said as those musical tears began to fill his eyes once more. "There is no home left for me."

"Jova --"

He raised one hand, a universal motion for Torin to hold his words.

"There is no old home left for me," he corrected as he turned his head and stared at Torin.

It was like a punch to the gut, the emotions that showed there. There was sadness, Torin was sure, for all that he had lost, and the list seemed to be endless. Jova had lost his only son, his people, his planet, his way of life, his original body...

But there was something else there in his gaze, something that was growing, making the shadows that lurked in his eyes smaller as something akin to joy filled his eyes.

"I begin to understand," he continued, "that I have been gifted with much."

The hand that was still stroking Baylin's hair paused as he smiled.

It wasn't a forced facsimile or a baring of teeth, or a wide head toss that they had come to understand was an exclamation of joy for him. No, this was a real smile, a human smile. "You and Baylin... I came here, but it is you who have brought me home... rather, I would like to try and make this my hone."

Then Torin was across the room and wrapping his unicorn in his arms, his hand burrowing though his hair to grip the back of his neck, and he pulled him in for a kiss that made his bones vibrate.

Jova's flavor flooded over his taste buds, cotton candy and bubblegum, and his mouth was so hot and wet...

He finally broke the kiss as he heard Baylin awaken and felt her sit up to stare. He released Jova as Baylin sighed contentedly.

Torin's eyes traveled from his wife's bright glittery eyes, the happiness flowing off her almost a palatable thing. He looked over at his lover, watching as those tears dried up without ever tinkling out a sound, yet his eyes remained shiny, glowing with happiness.

And he smiled.

Finally, they were all coming home.

Stephanie Burke

Stephanie is a USA Today Best Selling, multi published, multi award-winning author, Master Costumer, handicapped, wife and mother of two.

From sex-shifting, shape-shifting dragons to undersea worlds, sexually confused elemental Fey and homo-erotic mysteries, all the way to pastel-challenged urban sprites, Stephanie has done it all, and hopes to do more.

Stephanie is an orator on her favorite subjects of writing and world-building, a sometime teacher when you feed her enough tea and donuts, an anime nut, a costumer, and a frequent guest of various sci-fi and writing cons where she can be found leading panel discussions or researching varied legends and theories to improve her writing skills.

Stephanie is known for her love of the outrageous, strong female characters, believable worlds, male characters filled with depth, and multi-cultural stories that make the reader sit up and take notice.

Stephanie at Changeling: changelingpress.com/ stephanie-burke-a-30

Changeling Press E-Books

More Sci-Fi, Fantasy, Paranormal, and BDSM adventures available in e-book format for immediate download at ChangelingPress.com -- Werewolves, Vampires, Dragons, Shapeshifters and more -- Erotic Tales from the edge of your imagination.

What are E-Books?

E-books, or electronic books, are books designed to be read in digital format -- on your desktop or laptop computer, notebook, tablet, Smart Phone, or any electronic e-book reader.

Where can I get Changeling Press E-Books?

Changeling Press e-books are available at ChangelingPress.com, Amazon, Apple Books, Barnes & Noble, and Kobo/Walmart.

ChangelingPress.com